Margins and Murmurations

Otter Lieffe

Second Edition

Second edition. Published and printed in London/Zaghreb by Active Distribution, September 2017

www.otterlieffe.com
www.activedistribution.org
Cover design: Yone Liau
Editor: Liv Mammone

This is for the trans women who doubt ourselves, who internalise the lies we're force-fed every day, who once in a while need a break from the fight to be reminded just how true we really are.

This is for the femmes who are chronically reduced, called superficial and shallow and traitorous and reformist and artificial and fake and less good. We run the fucking world, never forget that.

This is for the sexual queers, the bisexuals and lesbians and gays and pansexuals and kinksters and the great swathe of society who do things differently or not at all. Our sex is beautiful and powerful, respect it and use it well.

This is for the hard-working women working five jobs or magically stretching benefits to the end of the week and spending every day trying to answer the impossible question of how much more we can give before we collapse.

This is for the forest, burned and murdered. For the sea and the sky and the herbs. This is for the clouds of starlings who might still return if we just let them.

This is for us.

I never saw *this* coming.

I've imagined all kinds of things for my life, but writing a novel? Out of the question.

Sitting and dreaming for eighteen months has brought me a world of self-questioning. I'm an activist—and the world is burning—how can I justify so much time on a single, uncertain project? I grew up working class, and still mostly just scrape by week to week—how could I allow myself to waste all this productive energy, on what? Art? I could have invested these thousands of hours into working to pay the bills and supporting myself, or into mobilising, organising, building something radical in this world so desperate for better things.

But I didn't, I wrote a novel. As I breathed life into it for a year and a half, I found myself guiltlessly enjoying the extravagant use of time—the meetings, consultations and redrafts, the eighty hour weeks of crowdfunding and learning social media and typography, the sleepless nights spent listening to my characters' voices chatting and arguing with each other in my head.

What could possibly inspire such decadence?

On the one hand, I realised I needed Margins to exist, that unless there was finally a book in the world with characters who reminded me of myself—trans women, femmes, sex workers, trauma survivors and working class activists—then I would surely suffocate and drown in this ocean of misrepresentative bullshit. On the other hand, I couldn't do anything else. A decade, and a lifetime, of activism and burnout and recovery and collapse had brought me to the point where the best thing, the only thing, I could do in this world was to tell these stories. Nothing else would have worked anyway.

I release this little novel out into the world and wish it well. At the very best, perhaps, it will become a tool to fight oppressions, double standards and hierarchies and bring some tiny piece of inspiration and new energy to our resistance movements. At the very least, it will provide a few distracting hours of escape and entertainment for my loved ones. Because we all need that sometimes.

A WORD ON (MIS) REPRESENTATION.

As a trans woman (not to mention a working class, femme, non-cis-passing, trans woman) I know all too well what oppressive portrayal can look like. As transness of any kind has been systematically and strategically erased in our culture, seeing myself reflected in the media is something so rare it almost doesn't exist. When it does happen, the cis authors, actors, and artists who portray us, win awards, fame and cold, hard millions for their brave attempts at speaking on our behalf. Tokenism in a word, co-optation in another.

This story instead, in its exploration of exclusion, intimacy and power, centres the kinds of characters who are quietly doing the real work and fighting the big fights: those who rarely get a voice, people who look a lot like me and my friends. This novel portrays a resistance movement that is strengthened by its diversity—and I use that term without shame, intentionally reclaiming it from those opportunistic, capitalist thieves who stole our word, diluted it and turned it into a commercial product.

With so many different kinds of characters, invariably I will have fallen into these same traps of erasure or utilisation along the way. There are characters in this novel who represent many real-world identities and experiences and oppressions that I simply don't have.

As a person who knows and hates erasure, who knows, and hates tokenism, I worked hardest on this part of my writing so this book could become as good as it can be. But all the consultation, research and deliberation won't hide the fact that my writing a character who is a person of colour, or lesbian, or deaf, I—as a person who isn't any of these things—will have made mistakes. And when I write a character who is trans or femme or a sex worker, I certainly don't speak for all of us who are. Only Hollywood believes in such offensive generalisations.

It's an unfortunate truth that the privileges that defines some parts of my experiences are still there in the acts I take in this world. That's simply what it looks like for a person to grow up in an industrial civilisation built on double standards and exploitation. Declaring myself an 'activist' or an 'oppressed minority' won't magically make those things go away. And saying 'but I'm x, I can't be racist/homophobic/cissexist/ableist...' has never worked for anyone. It's inconvenient and I wish things were different, but I don't believe in wishful thinking, I believe in change.

I learn, I work hard and I do what I can to deconstruct privilege and face double standards wherever I find them, but invariably I'll fuck up along the way. At least in this one epic act of dear love and hard labour, I can say that I've done my best.

THE FUTURE.

Since I started writing this novel, I've been amazed—and terrified—by how much of it is already coming true. A splintering Europe, the rise of authoritarian corporate states in the West, the backlash against us so-called minorities.

For a very long time, we trans women, were promised a great turning point in representation, visibility, rights and respect. But I never bought it. We are too convenient as scapegoats and besides intersectionality doesn't work that way. Privilege and power has never, ever, been given up without a fight.

I don't believe much in hope as a tool of change, but if the events of this novel keep manifesting themselves in reality, please let's ensure that the positive undercurrent—a powerful intergenerational resistance movement, strengthened by its diversity—also comes to pass. The world has never needed it more.

Otter Lieffe

To those who have been with me on this great adventure
with advice and help of all kinds:
Anna, Cathou, Jay, Lisa, Natalie, Nicole, Pi Jem and Torrey.
To my wonderful beta readers:
Fran, Mole, Robin and Susan.
To everyone who supported the crowdfunding and helped make
this project an economic possibility.
To Yone, for her beautiful cover design.
To Liv, for being the best editor I could have hoped for.
To Yonah, for all the amazing guidance and support.
To Anja, for getting me through it all.

Thank you, we did this.

1. Struggle

Chapter one

The old woman's body felt alive from the run. Her strong legs burned as they carried her along the uneven riverbank. At seventy-four years old, she knew she should be slowing down, should be curled up in front of the fire, but today as she left her home on the river, climbed over an ancient stile and pushed her way through a thick field of bracken, Ash felt younger than ever.

The sun was close to setting but the air was still as hot as midday. After a relentless summer, the land was bone dry—she couldn't even remember the taste of rain.

Leaning against a fence to catch her breath, she offered some water from her bottle to the land and took a sip herself. Despite the drought, there was an explosion of plant growth all around her: a thick green mat of bracken and nettles filled the valley and young birch trees pushed up towards the light, their delicate branches drooping with the lavender blooms of morning glories.

"It's so beautiful here," Ash said to no-one in particular.

A passing crow flying out from the distant forest answered her from above.

Hard to imagine that all of this was corn. Nothing but toxic monoculture as far as I could walk.

She took a deep breath of warm air, thick with pollen. The land itself seemed to buzz with the hum of bees and crickets. *Life is coming back though. Despite everything they did to us.*

Ash unzipped her backpack and crouched down to collect some nettle tips for dinner, smiling a little as they stung her. At her age, she figured she'd be riddled with arthritis by now if it wasn't for her daily cup of nettle tea and her regular brush against their stinging leaves. Soon her dark, wrinkled fingers prickled all over with the familiar burn of histamine. When she had collected enough, Ash put her hands together intending to thank the nettles for their sacrifice, but as she did so, a bang rang out from the forest.

She jumped to her feet and yelped in surprise, her heart pounding in her chest.

Gunshots. And they're getting closer every day. But Ash knew there was nothing she could do about it. *I've swallowed enough tear gas for this lifetime.*

She scratched the stubble on her chin thoughtfully, looked up and stretched her hand out in front of her. Only four finger tips separated the setting sun and the forest ahead of her. *About an hour or so until dark. I should get moving.*

She slipped her pack on again and, pushing through the abundant plant life, she continued her journey to the forest. It was normally an hour's journey from Ash's little river boat to Pinar's place, the beautiful cabin they had built together at the edge of the woods. In this heat, it would take her almost two and she'd be lucky to get there before nightfall.

Having no way to contact each other, their visits were always unplanned, always unexpected, and yet somehow Ash and Pinar had never missed each other in the five years since they came to this land. Ash knew that when she arrived, the kettle would already be boiling or a pot of soup would have just been taken off the fire in anticipation. It was as if somehow, when one of them left their home, the forest and the river themselves passed on the message and beckoned the other to stay in theirs, to leave the firewood collecting to later, to just sit and wait.

Ash disappeared into the high undergrowth, walking along a narrow path of stomped-down plants they both maintained just by hiking back and forth every few days. Her back was wet with sweat and brambles scratched her arms, but she loved this walk and hummed quietly to herself.

It was almost completely dark when the path suddenly opened out and beyond her in the forest she could hear a kettle whistling.

Not a minute too soon.

As she turned the corner, she saw Pinar, sitting outside her home surrounded by candles, her green eyes glistening in the light.

As gorgeous as ever, Ash noticed.

Pinar was only fifteen years her junior, but despite all that they had been through together, her friend seemed to radiate with youth. She wore an elegant blue dress that night and her long hair cascaded over dark, bare shoulders. She stood and smiled as Ash arrived.

"I had a feeling you might turn up today."

Pinar waved at a candlelit wooden table and chairs laid out under an old oak.

"I'll just get the kettle. Make yourself at home."

She disappeared inside the little cabin and Ash could hear her busying around in the kitchen. Within a minute, she returned with a tray full of homemade snacks, a steaming teapot and a pitcher of water.

"Here we go, I made the blackberry cookies you like." Pinar bent to put the tray down on the table, stood up and turned to give her friend a hug.

But Ash was gone.

Her body stood just where Pinar had left her moments ago, but the brown-green eyes that stared back at her were completely vacant.

"Ash?" she asked, but there was no response. Her friend's breath was shallow, her olive skin, cold and clammy to the touch. She was there, but she wasn't.

"Where are you now, darling?" asked Pinar, picking up a blanket and calmly putting it over her friend's shoulders. She wasn't worried. She was used to this.

Ash was somewhere else—in another place and another time.

More a traumatic flashback than a daydream and still much more than that, Pinar knew she was visiting, or revisiting her own life.

"Be safe and come back to me soon," she said and sat down to pour tea.

Chapter two

Ash saw herself running.

She stood in the middle of a road, soaked by a thick blanket of fog that hugged the asphalt. It was a cold, wet night and in the distance, she saw herself, younger in a long black dress, hand in hand with Pinar, running towards the open gates of the City.

Fuck, not again.

It was five years earlier and Ash remembered every painful detail.

A line of uniformed State troopers ran close behind, shouting and firing their guns into the air as they charged forward. The streets were lined with angry crowds who yelled and threw bottles and bags of rubbish at the two women as they passed.

"Get out of our city, *perverts!*" they shouted and even from that distance, Ash could see herself crying as she stumbled on a crack in the pavement. Pinar pulled her up and they ran on, towards the gate. *My god. How we ran.*

Standing unseen in the middle of the road, Ash knew there was nothing she could do here. She could barely breathe and her body was racked with shivers, from the cold or fear, she couldn't tell which. She wished desperately, with every taut muscle in her body, to escape this cycle, to stop reliving this trauma. But she had no control. She never did.

She saw that the troops had stopped running and her younger self and Pinar were nowhere to be seen. They had escaped the City, had fled into the darkness of the forest. The massive gates began to swing closed and the troops, and the people, whooped and yelled in victory.

Ash was struck with nausea and she could feel herself spinning. The shouts of men began to fade as the world itself, colours and smells and sounds, began to fade away from her.

It's always like this, she told herself. *I'm going back.*

* * *

And suddenly she was back in the arms of her beloved friend, back in the dry heat of a summer's evening. She could hear crows calling to each other somewhere in the trees above her head. She could smell mint tea. She was home.

"Are you okay, hon?" asked Pinar as she steadied her friend and helped her sit down.

"I...my god..."

"Take your time coming back," said Pinar, pouring some tea and passing her a cup. "There's no rush."

Ash stared into the darkening forest and cradled the cup with both hands. Her heart was still pounding and her shoulders ached. *How much more of this can I take?*

Her nervous system still overwhelmed, she felt sick from the stench of garbage, the smell of her own fear. Her body was dry, but she could still taste the dirty rain inside her mouth. Her muscles cried with exhaustion. Finally, Pinar's voice brought her back to the present.

"Let me take that." She gently retrieved the cup and set it down. Ash saw that her hands were shaking so much she had spilled half the tea over the table.

"Sorry..." she said weakly.

"When were you? Do you need to lie down?"

"I was in the City. We were both there. It was the night of the exile, the night we were *driven out.*" Her eyes welled with tears. "Pin, why can't I just *forget* for heaven's sake?"

Pinar held Ash's shaking hands between her own.

"I'm sorry hon."

Ash was crying.

"I fucking *hate* that place."

* * *

At some point in history, that great urban mass, lying along the storm-battered coast was known by another name, but for as long as Ash could remember, it had been called the City, or in State propaganda, "The Gem of Europe." For decades, it had become known as a centre for immigration with a strong economy built from the hard work of Syrian refugees and Spanish migrant workers, its rich culture formed by the people who lived, worked and studied within its ancient walls. It quickly became a magnet for queer, disabled and activist cultures and Ash and Pinar were among those who came to the City during that time.

But it was too good to be true, thought Ash sadly, lost again in her memories.

It had been a Sunday. She could remember because Sunday was the day Pinar went to the market down in the square to sell her herbs and, when she had the energy, Ash would come down with her and offer short massage sessions to the public. If the weather was good, they would make enough credits to get them through the next week. Or else people would exchange food for their services, or a promise to help out with work in Pinar's herb garden, or Ash's clinic. The economy was already sliding out of control and barter had become a mainstream form of survival.

The weather was perfect that day. Ash remembered the warmth of the sun on her back as both of them had worked hard in the market. She was content to be busy and just glad to have something to do—barely a day went by when she didn't feel bored or restless. Here, she could help out with people's aches and pains while also getting some food in the cupboards. She didn't need much more than that.

This was the 2020's and the global economy was already slipping into an unprecedented crisis. Food and access to medication was a problem for everyone and there were food shortages every week at the local stores. But the worst was yet to come. As a result of the crisis, the majority of countries began centralising into massive federations and the rest broke into warring city states. In the City, local government and big business had fused years before into a single entity, known simply as the State.

And their "Gem of Europe" quickly became hell on earth for the likes of us.

After years of welfare cuts, austerity and vigilance, anti-State riots became a daily sight in the City. The State was soon forced to break off trade with its more liberal neighbours and militarised itself against them.

That sunny Sunday had been a sign of things to come. Late in the afternoon, as Pinar and Ash were finishing up for the day, the square had been suddenly engulfed by a food riot quickly followed by what appeared to be all the troopers and all the tear gas the State had to spare.

Pinar had stood wide-eyed as their stall was engulfed by protesters and tear gas canisters began to rain down around them. An academic and a pacifist, she had never seen anything like it before and stood frozen, rooted in the square.

This wasn't Ash's first riot and certainly not her first taste of teargas. She got them moving, scooping up Pinar's precious herbs in one arm and within minutes they were back in their apartment watching from the window.

"Fuck," cursed Pinar as they watched another wave of troopers flooding into the square to beat the hungry rioters. "We have to do something."

"There's nothing for us to do," Ash's voice was perfectly calm.

"We didn't organise this and we don't know anyone involved, the risks are too great. We have our part to do when it's over."

An hour later and they were back in the square treating people for shock and taking some of the injured back upstairs to rest in the apartment. Their clinic was born that day and as riots and protests became ever more frequent in the City, Ash, and her restless hands, were kept busy for many years.

As the riots and social movements that grew out of them threatened the very existence of the State, its leaders soon realised that they needed to find a new enemy for the people to blame, someone to distract attention from their own oppressive governance. As it turned out, the queer communities, the trans and gender non-conforming folks, immigrants and disabled people who had formerly made the City so popular—and rich—as a cultural centre of diversity, would also make the perfect scapegoat. What happened next had destroyed Ash and Pinar's world.

"Are you with me?" asked Pinar. "Are you...here?"

Ash looked up from the knot of wood on the table she'd been staring at.

"Sorry. I was miles away."

She looked down again and started poking her spoon into the remains of soup in the bowl in front of her.

Thirty-five miles to be precise.

"Were you journeying?"

"Just remembering."

"Talk to me if you want to," said Pinar softly.

"I don't know, Pin." Ash paused and picked at a splinter of wood on the table. "I just can't help wondering what would have happened if we hadn't escaped in time. What would have happened to us if we hadn't gotten out?"

"But we *did* get out. We survived, Ash. And we're here now, we're safe."

"*Except when I'm not! Except when I'm back there again, afraid for my life again!"* She stared for a moment into Pinar's wide eyes, holding her eye contact and breathing hard. Finally the intensity of her feelings passed and she looked down and started picking at the table again. "You'll never really understand."

Pinar knew better than to respond. She stood up quietly and went inside. For a while she stared at the packed shelves of dried roots and leaves and branches and jars of seeds that filled two walls. Nothing she could say would make her friend feel better. *I'll let the herbs do their work.*

She reached for the jars of chamomile, passionflower and lavender and as calmly as she could, Pinar started measuring a dose into a teapot.

She hated conflict and she hated to be shouted at. But she forgave Ash as she had always forgiven her. It seemed that her friend was going through a special kind of hell. Much of her past had been traumatic enough the first time without having to relive it. It had taken years for Pinar to even accept the truth of her friend's 'journeying' as she called it, and now all she could do was support her the best she could. *But it's never enough.*

"I'll make some tea!" Pinar called cheerfully through the window to her friend. "Tea always helps!"

Ash didn't respond. Pinar could see she was staring at the table again.

Chapter three

D anny was so thirsty he thought he might collapse if he didn't sit down. Dripping with sweat and naked except for his squeaky rubber underwear, he ignored the applauding crowd and walked over to the bar. He perched himself on a barstool and took a long swig from the 'mineral water' in front of him. Even bottled water was getting rare these days and he could see that despite its ridiculous price tag, it was an old bottle that had been refilled, probably multiple times.

And that's as good as the State gives even its favourite workers, he thought to himself. He nearly emptied the bottle in one go.

Danny had been dancing the pole without a break for nearly two hours straight and as he sat on the stool, he could feel his traps, lats and calves twitching and burning. He ran his fingers over his buzz cut and his hand was totally wet. It wasn't usually this hot, or this busy. A new State squadron had arrived at the base down town last Sunday and since then he'd been working every night and most afternoons too.

He was used to the exercise and dancing was one of his great loves. He loved the rush of losing control, the high of being so deeply in his body that nothing else existed. Even dancing in front of this sleazy crowd didn't bother him anymore. Danny had almost learned to enjoy the attention. *I really just need more breaks.*

Fit as he was, he needed to rest between turns. But each time, as he left the stage to eat something, someone would approach the retinal scanner at the bar and buy themselves another hour. Within a minute, he was back up, spinning and grinding the stage. He had mastered the art of seeming to focus entirely on the new customer while also keeping half an eye on his uneaten food at the bar.

What can I do? It's a job. I can hardly complain.

Under the Peccatum Laws, homosexuality had become illegal again and most of the *divergents* like him, the queer folk as they'd been known in former times, had been driven away, some to their deaths. Here at least he had a place to stay and he was relatively safe as long as he kept providing his special services for the officers who, it seemed, could never get enough of him. With a body like his, he was born to be a security guard. He didn't need to work out to stay fit, he could do nothing at all and would still have perfect abs. And he was handsome; his face was rugged, masculine. His blue eyes still sparkled even through his exhaustion.

Danny blamed it on his good genes.

His bracelet lit up, meaning another account had been charged and he was up again to dance. He gulped down the last of his warm, metallic water and climbed back up onto the stage to a roar of drunken applause. One more hour and then he could rest.

One more hour.

* * *

Danny was finally finished for the night. His last dance had been by far his best of the night—the DJ had played one of his favourite tracks and the solar powered decks had made it to the end of the evening for a change. He'd received good tips and now he was tucking into one of the more expensive menus at the bar surrounded by his clients and some of his co-workers.

"Long night, eh?" asked a voice.

Danny looked up from his meal. It was one of the other dancers—a young, white kid. He was good at his job although Danny thought he might be trying too hard and found him a little over-enthusiastic.

He seemed to be barely out of his teens. *What is he nineteen? Twenty? Then again everyone seems young these days.*

Danny was only in his mid-thirties—and still looked like he was pushing twenty-nine, but he already felt like the grandpa of this bar. He was too tired to even remember this kid's name.

"Every night's a long night at this place," he grumbled and continued eating.

"Still at least we had music this time," said the kid. "My first night here, the solar panels died in the first half hour. I had to dance the whole evening to drunk people clapping. They couldn't even clap in time. Totally threw my rhythm off."

"Yeah..." Danny said without conviction. He took a long swig of warm beer. After a night like this, he'd really rather just sit by himself.

"That Major's looking at you, you know? The old one with the tiny err..."

"—Yeah, yeah," said Danny nodding. "I know him well. Not tonight though I have to get up early."

"Work?"

Actually, Danny had a resistance meeting in the morning but, like everything in the resistance, it was a closely kept secret.

"Something like that."

"Okay. Mind if I take him?"

"Knock yourself out. Make sure he tips though. His dick isn't the only thing small about him."

The young dancer laughed.

Why do I even make these jokes? Danny wondered as he played with the condensation on his glass. *Body shaming isn't funny even when it's about powerful men.*

"Have a good night...L, is it?"

"That's my work name, yeah..." said Danny. He gulped down the last of his beer and got up to leave. "Have a good night, mate."

"You too."

Danny needed to sleep. The meeting tomorrow was planned for

seven and he hated waking up early. Like all the sex workers in the resistance, he was expected to gather information from his unsuspecting customers that might prove useful to the movement. He hadn't learned anything particularly interesting this week, but he would go anyway. Being with the resistance was the one time of the week when Danny didn't feel like he was acting.

Danny stepped outside the bar and watched as some of his clients also left and disappeared into the shadows. The bar was an open secret, almost everything that happened inside was illegal.

He was feeling a bit wobbly. *Dehydrated again. And the beer doesn't help.*

His apartment was just a few blocks away from the bar so putting one foot carefully in front of the other, he set off for home.

* * *

The evening was warm and the air over the park was perfectly still and thick with humidity. Nathalie was sweating with anticipation, she loved this part of the night.

Just like every Saturday evening, the park—a massive stretch of land out in the abandoned suburbs of the City—was full. Full of women and a scattering of men. Full of night time visitors moving slowly through the shadows, picking their way through the high grass and over fallen tombstones. Each one in search of company.

Nathalie had arrived twenty minutes before, but she still stood at the park's edge adjusting her blond ponytail for the tenth time and watching as shadows moved amongst the bushes. Her muscles were tensed to run, to escape.

What am I even doing here?

But she knew she couldn't leave without exploring what the park had to offer her tonight. It was always like this. Within an hour she'd have lost herself in a spontaneous chaos of mouths and flesh and the fingers of strangers inside her, but the beginning was always the hard part.

Just push through.

Nathalie rechecked her clothes—a dark red top that complimented her pale skin perfectly and accentuated her breasts, her tightest jeans to make the most of all those hours of running after tennis balls. Nodding to one of the security women who protected the park, she took a deep breath and stepped in to the high grass.

She joined the well-worn path and headed for her favourite place, the war monument. A hollow concrete monstrosity built to celebrate some forgotten war or another, it was almost completely dark inside and was usually busy the whole night through. Nathalie shuffled carefully into the narrow passageway and leaned against a wall to wait for her eyes to adjust. She could already hear a couple a little way down the passage breathing heavily. *This is going to be a good night.*

Her chest was tight and she could barely catch her breath in the moist air, thick with the smells of sex.

This is where I should be. I need this.

Nathalie knew that as certainly as a bullet to the heart, her work placement in the State's administration centre was killing her. She worked, she slept and then she worked some more—just to afford to live. Her daily life, as it was, had stopped having any meaning and she was desperate. Even tennis, which she had played her whole life and was one of the few sports still popular since the crash, didn't really make her feel anything. She gossiped with her tennis partners and played along, but she knew she was just going through the motions. Every day when she arrived to her placement and saw the pile of papers on her desk that needed sorting she wondered if maybe she wasn't already dead.

But when she came here, to this sordid place on the edge of town, she began to feel alive again. Only here in the darkness, with a stranger's tongue in her mouth, did she know who she was. She had a purpose in the park. She had a mission.

A couple of brief minutes inside the war monument listening to the couple near her bringing each other to a subdued orgasm and Nathalie was already in the zone—her eyes were adjusting to the dark, her heart had calmed down and her sense of smell had sharpened. Like an animal on the prowl, she was ready for the hunt as she pushed off the wall and headed down the passageway into the unknown.

Chapter four

After dinner, Ash and Pinar sat outside the cabin drinking an infusion of hops and valerian and watching the darkening forest. A pair of owls were calling each other from across the valley.

"Are you feeling any better?" asked Pinar.

"A little." Ash slurped noisily from her hot tea. "I'm still a bit freaked out. I mean, I know it was five years ago, but somehow, I managed to forget that night. Or at least to dull the memory a bit."

"I wish I could do more."

"It's fine, you do plenty for me."

"I just wish I—"

Ash thumped her cup back down on the table.

"Let it *drop*, Pin. When I need help, I'll *ask* for it."

"Okay...sorry."

God, she never stops fussing, thought Ash. *There's a reason we don't live together anymore.*

"Do we have clinic tomorrow?" Pinar asked gently. She already knew the answer—their herbal clinic for the resistance had been every Tuesday for the last three years. In all that time, they had only missed one week when they both came down with the flu and neither of them could get out of bed.

"Yes," said Ash glad to change the subject. "I think Yonah might pass by in the evening to pick up another batch for the City group. She said the trans collective had run out of oestrogenics and androgen blockers again—"

"We have enough hops for sure, I think we're low on red clover

17

though. I'll go and get some in the morning."

"Perfect. There should be another hormone drop off at the river in a couple of days as well, she'll tell us when."

As Ash's boat-home was situated at the edge of the State's boundaries, she received regular medical deliveries from resistance members outside.

For years they had fought to keep the trans part of the clinic running as they were told again and again that hormones for trans women were 'non-essentials'. But Ash knew that for some people, having access to hormones, or at least the herbal replacements, was as essential as anything else: for many, it meant the difference between life and death.

"Last time there was almost nothing in the delivery," she said sadly. "It's getting harder every month to source this stuff."

"Yeah. I'm worried about that too. The herbs are great, but I'm not sure that they're as effective. Unless people take such large quantities they get liver damage."

"And the pharmaceuticals destroyed the ecosystem. And mass produced oestrogens and prozac killed the starlings..."

Pinar nodded silently. She'd heard this rant many times before.

"Guess what?" said Ash cynically. "The system's *really* fucked up."

Pinar smiled despite herself.

"We just have to keep trying," she said. "I'm a little more optimistic than you, I guess."

"How so?"

"Well, we've survived this far. Despite what they told us, it was never about consumer choices in the supermarket—or the pharmacy—or feeling guilty for social systemic evils. It's always been about wider social change, about tearing down the crap and building better alternatives."

"—Of course— "

"And although the able-bodied cis guys kept telling us that we'd be the first to die after the crash—the disabled and the pharmaceutically dependent and the trans people—you know what? We're still here."

"We sure as hell are."

"And in fact the resistance would have been nothing without us. Isn't that enough reason to be hopeful? I guess I just really *want* to be optimistic, even if it's hard sometimes."

Ash leaned over and gave her friend a peck on the cheek.

"I'll let you."

They sat quietly for a while, listening to the sounds of the forest.

"The planes stopped flying overhead," Ash commented as she looked up at the red sky. "It's been weeks since I saw one."

With no phones, no television and no internet, it was rare to get news from the outside world. Ash hadn't left the State's boundaries for the last three decades, Pinar even longer than that. They had often talked about leaving, but every time the conclusion was the same: they were still needed there, they still had work to do for the resistance.

"Maybe the oil finally ran out?"

"Maybe," said Ash. "Hopefully."

Pinar finished her tea and stood up.

"Ready for bed?"

"Go ahead, I'll be there in a minute. I just want to go do something in the forest. I'll be a while, so go ahead and sleep if you like."

"Okay, hon, good night."

"Night, Pin."

Ash stepped off the little porch of the cabin and following a route she knew like the back of her hand, she walked out into the dark.

* * *

In the shadows, amongst the trees, Nathalie was having fun. She was already on her third *rendez-vous* of the night and every one had

19

been completely different. The first was the same hot girl she'd met a few times already—a tall blonde who always wore a lot of make-up but had the softest lips Nathalie had ever kissed. She never got tired of bumping into her.

Number two was someone new, probably a soldier just passing through town. It was over very quickly at any rate.

And now after a quiet hour, she found herself happily lost in a knot of warm, damp bodies—a multitude of fingers and tongues touching her in the darkness. She looked up at the night's sky and watched the stars imperceptibly gliding by as a new mouth began tasting her nipples.

I love this. And I fucking deserve it.

Someone caught her attention. *By that bush over there.*

She was being watched, she was sure of it. And she was pretty sure this same person had been following her all night.

Whoever it was stayed just enough in the dark to keep her face hidden but just close enough to make her presence felt. Nathalie could *feel* the stranger's eyes on her, could hear her touching herself in the dark. Nathalie beckoned her over to join in, but she melted away into the bushes.

Well that's weird. Who are you?

Nathalie felt hunted, chased by a shadow, and she was loving every second of it.

It hadn't always been this way. There was a time when women couldn't even be out at night in this park without fearing for their safety.

There was a time when cruising was only for cis gay guys who despite police crackdowns, homophobic attacks, and public protest had been unable to resist the call to the parks and bathrooms of the cities. Then the Internet Years had arrived and the web did what the police were never able to. The gay guys retreated to their apps and websites and the parks were abandoned.

And now something new was being born. As the crash and the

Improvement had kicked in and queers of all kinds had been driven to the margins, somehow cruising—of all things—had come back to life out here in the forgotten edges of the City.

This open space was being declared queer territory and anyone who could make the long walk had a place to enjoy the pleasures of a night time hook-up with a stranger under the sky.

New ways of organising public space were coming into being and women led the movement, so safety was on everyone's lips and fingers. Nathalie was determined to make the most of it while it lasted.

She's there again, the stranger in the shadows.

Nathalie was leaning back against a palm tree, a dark-skinned woman going down on her. Nathalie had been close to orgasming for at least half an hour. She was certainly having a good time, but curiosity was getting the best of her. She was overcome with a thirst to know who this person was that watched silently from the trees as she played.

Anonymity was one of the many reasons people came here and Nathalie almost never shared anything more personal than sex with the people she met. But this time she felt a burning and unfamiliar sensation to know the name of this stranger, to know where she came from. *I want to wake up next to you and watch you sleeping just like you watched me.*

"Come on, join in if you like," Nathalie whispered to the shadows.

But as the fuck drew to its peak and Nathalie's orgasms started to echo through her body, and through the park, her watcher disappeared again into the bushes.

Come back, please. At least tell me your name.

But the watcher was gone.

The dark-skinned woman stood up and licked her lips.

"Good?" she asked.

"Sure, yeah it was fine," said Nathalie distantly. She pulled up her pants and went to follow.

Chapter five

Night had fallen and the forest around Ash's favourite clearing was deathly still and, with the new moon, perfectly dark. She sat amongst the ferns and nettles breathing in the smells—the dust of dry soil, the perfume of some flowering invasive, the spray of a fox who must have passed by recently. This was her nightly ritual, either at her home or at Pinar's, to just sit and connect with the living world around her. It was the moment of day that she felt the safest and the most at peace with herself. It was her time to sit and stop thinking. Tonight, though, she was distracted by her conversations with Pinar.

Why does she always smother me? No wonder I shout at her sometimes. She should know better than to push me. Anyway, it's fine, I guess. She always forgives me. Is that the owl again? It sounds like it's hunting. I wonder what's still out here for her to eat. It's so dry. I don't know if it's ever going to rain.

Ash caught her wandering thoughts and brought her attention back to her senses. She dove deeply into the sounds around her, felt their vibration in her skull—a cricket calling somewhere to the left, some small mammal squeaking way over near the cabin. She allowed herself to sense the air moving over her bald head and her clothes on her skin. To connect with her weight on the ground and the slight prickling of new stubble on her face: to inhabit her body. For some, it was such a simple thing they never even thought about it but for Ash, like so many trans folk, making friends with her body often felt like the toughest thing in the world.

I have to be better to myself. This old body won't take much more, especially if I keep journeying the way I have been. If only Pin could understand better what I go through. If I could just control it sometimes and stay in the moment. If only—

And suddenly Ash was standing.

She stood in exactly the same spot, amongst the ferns, but it was early evening. The sky above the clearing was a spectacular red and orange and she screwed up her eyes against the sudden change in light.

What the hell?

Over towards the cabin Ash could see herself with Pinar pouring steaming hot water over a naked white man, someone she had never seen before. *This must be the future then.*

Pinar was saying a name over and over again.

"Jason, Jason, Jason."

A breeze brought the thick scents of rose water and lavender to Ash's nostrils and for the second time in the last few hours she felt sick and dizzy. Her future self, still holding the pot of hot water, looked over at her and smiled. The world spun and as quickly as Ash realised what was happening she was sitting again, back in her spot.

Well that was weird. I wonder who—

Her heart skipped a beat. Over at the cabin, she could hear a voice calling her name. It was Pinar and she sounded terrified.

* * *

"What's up, are you okay?" Ash asked breathlessly as she arrive at the cabin, running.

"*There's someone out there!*" signed Pinar, standing on the porch. Like almost everyone who had lived in the City, they were both fluent in USL, a form of manually coded English. "*I heard them, maybe two hundred metres towards the east.*"

"Are you sure it wasn't a fox, in the clearing I smelt—"

"*I know the difference between a human and a bloody fox, Ash!*"

23

Pinar signed back, her dark hands flashing in the light coming through the cabin window. "*It was definitely a person, someone big, maybe a guy, and he was definitely moving towards us.*"

"*Let's listen.*"

They stood silently and listened to the forest. Ash could only hear the cricket chirping again.

"I don't thin—," she began.

"Shhh. There. Hear that?"

Ash was about to reply when suddenly they both heard the loud, unmistakable sound of twigs cracking in the forest.

They looked at each other. Pinar's eyes were full of fear as the sound came closer. They could already hear the laboured breathing of someone in pain.

"*Who could it be? Should I get the gun?*"

"Don't worry. I think I know who it is," said Ash.

Pinar gave her friend a quizzical look as Ash called out to the forest.

"Hey! Who's there?"

"I'm with the resistance!" a deep voice called back, a voice racked with pain and desperately short of breath.

"What's the passcode?" asked Pinar. Everyone in the resistance used the same identifying passcode, half in Spanish, half in English. The State surely knew the code by now, but it was a tradition, a symbol and some things don't change easily.

There was no reply, but the stranger continued moving towards them.

"What's the bloody *passcode?*" Pinar shouted.

"Las prímulas..." the stranger began. "...las primulas lucharán y the land—agh.'

The code was cut short as the person collapsed somewhere out in the darkness.

"Let's go," said Ash.

"*Be careful.*"

"It's okay," Ash replied confidently. "I saw this coming."

She took Pinar's hand and they walked out into the darkness together in the direction of the voice.

Chapter six

My god, he's bleeding everywhere."

"We have to get him to the house. We can't do anything for him out here."

"Damn, he's heavy!"

Ash and Pinar managed to half carry, half drag the unconscious stranger into the house and onto the table. Ash brought candles in and after putting her long hair up in a ponytail, Pinar put on some surgical gloves and began to look at his injuries.

"He's cut, but I think it's only in this one place," she said, pointing to a long gash down his side. "We need to stop the bleeding. Bring me some yarrow from the top shelf, hot water and towels, lots of towels."

"On it."

Together they cleaned the wound, bound some yarrow leaves to it which quickly stemmed the bleeding and then covered it in the cleanest cloth they could find. Their patient was still unconscious so Ash began to inspect his other injuries.

"He's sprained his ankle," she said, moving his left foot carefully to assess the damage. "Judging from these bruises, I reckon he's broken at least one rib. And his jaw's all swollen up—I think he was hit in the face by something—it'll probably need setting. Either way he's going to wake up with one hell of a headache."

"It's pretty bad, but he'll live," Pinar summarised as she cleaned blood off his chest with a damp cloth. "We're going to need to make up some more painkillers though. So you said you were expecting him? How? Who is this guy?"

Ash brought some more clean towels from the cupboard and

placed them next to the table.

"His name is Jason, and I guess he's resistance. That's all I know really. That's all I had time to find out."

Pinar began to understand. "You saw him in a journey."

"Yeah, just before I heard you yelling. It was very quick. I saw us outside the house and we were pouring hot water over him from a big pot. He was crying and you kept repeating what I guess was his name—Jason, Jason, Jason. Everything smelt of rose and lavender and then I was gone."

"Sounds like a cleansing," said Pinar thoughtfully.

"Yeah, that's what I thought too. Although I was surprised that we'd be doing it on someone else."

"Maybe it's necessary."

"Maybe."

They fell silent for a moment as they continued to clean Jason's wounds. Ash and Pinar had done the healing ritual they called a cleansing several times for each other in times of need, when nothing else could remove the trauma and distress that had lodged inside their minds and bodies. But a cleansing was no small deal for either of them.

Ash grew up in an army family between the US and the UK— white, working class and in her own words 'lacking in any culture except the military, microwaves and medication.' As an adult, though, she'd studied healing arts from various teachers in various parts of the world—Thailand, Argentina, Spain—and it had been an endless internal struggle for her to learn from other cultures respectfully.

As she took away another bloody towel, Ash remembered a conversation she'd had decades ago in the mountains in the north of Thailand where she'd studied and worked for a year helping out in a village clinic.

She had been preparing a herbal solution over an open fire outside her teacher's house for one of the many patients who had arrived at the clinic that day. She stirred the herbs slowly, her eyes stinging from the smoke and the pungent smell of the plants she was using. As she often did while they were working, her teacher, an older woman who had lived her entire life in the village and had founded the clinic, took the opportunity to share her wisdom with Ash. Since accepting her as an apprentice several months before, she had been incredibly generous with her knowledge. And Ash had been an eager student.

"These things we learn, they come from the land—the plants and the animals," her teacher had said. "So remember to always give something back. Even this tree we're using today to make balm for our patients, that tree is also our teacher—"

Ash nodded and continued to stir the herbal balm.

"— Now put in some more leaves or it'll never thicken up," she warned.

Ash obediently did as she was told and sure enough the balm soon began to thicken and became harder to stir.

"Good. Remember to respect all of your teachers," her teacher continued. "Not just me, but the spirits of the land too, this beautiful mountain... and Ash?"

"Yes, teacher?" she'd asked as she took the finished balm off the fire to look at her.

"Don't steal, okay?"

"Of course not."

At the time, Ash had been slightly offended at the suggestion that she would 'steal' anything from anyone. She considered herself a good, moral person. Not that stealing was necessary immoral—homeless people stealing from a supermarket, for example, had always seemed entirely ethical to her—after all 'he who steals from a thief is not a thief' - but what exactly had her teacher meant?

That evening while she was doing a laundry run for the clinic, carrying an overflowing basket of towels and sheets down to the river, Ash passed a group of noisy tourists disembarking from their bus, returning from some great adventure in the forest. They were headed to the village's only restaurant taking photos of every dog and chicken and house and villager as they went. As they passed Ash, they gave her a look of disdain. They were all in search of the same thing—exotic authenticity—and a white trans woman carrying a heavy basket of laundry wasn't what they'd come to see at all.

God, she'd thought to herself then. *They look so much like me. They are so much like me. But we don't understand each other at all.*

Suddenly Ash realised what her teacher had been telling her.

For centuries, white people had been coming to these places and taking what they wanted giving nothing back in return. The waves after waves of plastic shamans from the west making money selling *ayuhuasca* and cocoa ceremonies and Thai massage and power-ballad-sauna yoga were just the latest incarnation of a process of colonisation that had been happening for as long as anyone could remember.

Colonisation. Ash had thought to herself. *It's just another word for theft.*

Ash had always remembered that lesson and decades later when she and Pinar had been forced out of the City and come to the forest, they had begun to develop their own culture together, their own traditions, deeply rooted in this place and its living communities. Ash still gave thanks every day to her teacher—now long dead—and the plants and animals of this land that she now learned from. Traumatised, exhausted, and driven from their home, ritual cleansing with local herbs had developed for them here as naturally as their love for each other and the land.

"I have a feeling it's not just his body that will need healing," said Ash, coming back to the moment and looking down at her bruised and bloody patient. "He might be with us for a while."

Pinar put a pillow under Jason's head and carefully lay a blanket over him.

"That's all we can do for now," she said and peeked out of the window. "The sun's coming up already. Let's go to bed, hon. I'm sure he'll wake us up soon enough."

Chapter seven

Danny's alarm went off and he woke up with a jump. He was covered in sweat and his throat was sore.

I've been shouting in my sleep again.

Every morning this week he'd woken up from the same paranoid nightmare. He'd been running through the City, rain falling around him so heavily he could barely see and he was being chased by someone. Always the same person, who no matter how hard Danny tried, was always smarter, always one step ahead. Someone with a handsome face, a terrible face, and wearing a pristine State uniform.

Danny rubbed his eyes and tried to clear the memories from his mind. He pulled the blanket aside and got out of bed. The alarm clock said 06.30. For Danny, who liked to wake up at about eleven, it felt like the middle of the night.

He walked across the three metres to the other side of his tiny flat and just where he expected it to be, he found a small blank envelope pushed under the door. He carefully opened it and there was a single sheet of paper inside covered in a mess of notes and printed words. Since the crash, paper was at a premium and every sheet was used and reused as many times as possible. Danny ran his fingers over the page and felt the Braille print.

Without electricity or computers, most messages sent by the resistance were punched out on a hand-held Braille printer which covered the page in a series of tiny dots raised from the surface of the paper. As the City had been a hub of blind and deaf culture, the resistance had always had a strong representation of blind people and for a while Braille had been enough of a code to keep messages secret.

The State had soon worked out that the resistance was using Braille code itself so now the message was also encoded with a transposition cipher—the letters were changed according to a pre-set key which was changed regularly and given out at weekly meetings.

It wasn't fool-proof, and a number of messages had been hacked by the State, but since the last of their computers were dedicated to keeping the Life Accounts financial system up and running, they had to decode by hand and by the time they did, the key was usually changed.

I can never remember these damn things.

Danny dug into his dirty laundry basket and fished out a sock with a tiny piece of card covered in numbers inside it. *This week's key.*

Officially, it was never supposed to be written down and meeting members had to memorise the new key each week. Danny had tried and after the third time of forgetting and having to knock on his friend's door for the key, he'd taken to noting it down and hiding it.

Well, he reasoned, *once the State's desperate enough to be digging around my socks and sweaty jockstraps, things will already be as bad as they're going to get.*

Danny sat at his desk, picked up a pen and, letter by letter, read the message with his left index finger, noted it down and then decoded it.

THE OLD WAREHOUSE. VICTORY AVENUE.

The new meeting place.

Danny looked again at the clock. If he hurried, he'd still make it on time. He threw on some fresh clothes, screwed the message up in his pocket and opened the door.

He was too tired for all this really, but he'd been resistance for as long as he could remember. There was no other way of life for him, not anymore.

* * *

Danny arrived a few minutes late to the meeting. This was one of the inner circles, and he knew that everyone here had been through years of screening to keep out the infiltrators and informers.

He saw his friend Kit from the sex work collective already sitting down and she waved him over. As usual her perfectly straight hair was up in an elegant bun, her make-up was faultless and she was wearing something short, tight and black. To Danny, who had been wearing the same comfortable sneakers for over three years, Kit's four inch heels looked both dangerous and painful. *How can she even stand up in those things?*

He sat down and took the bottle of water his friend offered him, drank his fill, and gave her a grateful smile. He was always happy to see Kit even if it was ridiculously early in the morning.

The meeting had already started without him and a speaker from the prison group was delivering an update. Danny and Kit hadn't seen each other for a few weeks so they caught up discretely in the so called 'Universal Sign Language' that they both knew well.

USL was not a true sign language, but a kind of English encoded into sign that had developed its own grammatical features over time. It had a politically difficult history and was as commonly used by the State these days as those groups fighting it, but still, it came in useful. It was particularly good for gossiping during meetings.

"*Good to see you, Kit. How's things?*"

"*I'm good; this guy's super boring. You were late again, lazy ass.*" She always talked to Danny like a little brother, always teased him, never gave him a chance to defend himself.

There's a reason that she's a professional Domme, he thought to himself.

"*Well that's what happens when we have meetings in the middle of the—*"

"*The resistance never sleeps, you know, honey.*"

"Well, I need more—"

"Anyway, I met someone." Kit smiled and paused for dramatic effect. *"At the park. Well I kind of met her. I sort of watched her really..."*

"Really? Tell me more!"

"Well—"

The speaker saw them signing and coughed loudly into his fist looking directly at them.

"If you're *quite* ready, I'd *love* to continue with my report."

"Sorry," mumbled Danny.

Kit crossed her arms and pouted in silence. She apologised to no-one.

"Thank you for your kind attention," said the speaker pointedly. "Anyway, as I was saying..."

Careful mate, thought Danny. *Kit eats guys like you for breakfast.*

The meeting room was packed as usual. There were few spaces left to meet in the City that were central enough for everyone to get to. They'd tried meeting out in the suburbs which was safer but it took people too long to get there without transport. This week all the meetings would take place in this warehouse basement barely a kilometre from one of the State's main bases.

The meeting was known as the *mesa,* the Spanish word for table, because it used to be small enough to fit everyone around a long table. It was a central meeting point for the many collectives and groups around the city to represent themselves and their needs and to take information back to their groups. As the resistance had grown, so had the *mesa* until finally there were upwards of fifty people in each meeting and they had to sit on the floor in concentric circles just to fit everyone in.

Most of today's meeting was filled with a revision of safety protocols in light of recent raids and the sex work collective sharing intel that they had gathered since the last meeting.

"Hey, wake up." whispered Kit, with just the hint of a Thai accent as she poked Danny hard in the ribs. "You fell asleep again."

"Yeah, err, thanks, Kit. Is it over yet?"

"We finished five minutes ago. You were so cute, your head was nodding through half the meeting. Tea?"

She offered him a cup that she'd brought over from the little stove.

"Thanks." Danny sipped it. It was bitter and she always made it way too strong, but he kept his opinions to himself. Kit was well known for her fits of rage. "I should get going actually. I need to be at work at two, maybe I can get a quick nap before."

"Not so fast!" said his friend, standing up onto her heels. "I'm going dancing after work tonight. You're coming, aren't you?" It wasn't really a question.

"Dance?" Danny protested as she pulled him to his feet. "All I do is dance!"

"No. We're dancing tonight. I'll come find you at work. When do you finish?"

"Nine..."

"Perfect!"

Danny knew there was no point arguing with her.

"Sure, I guess..."

"Good boy. See you there."

Danny sneaked out of the meeting through the back door to avoid all the polite conversations he'd be obligated to have, collected his bike and cycled home for a quick siesta before work. He curled up on the uncomfortable sofa without even taking his sneakers off and within minutes he was sound asleep.

* * *

Ash woke up with a start. She heard moaning and Pinar's soft voice comforting someone. Then she remembered.

There's a man in the house.

"How is he?" she asked, pulling herself out of bed and slipping on a pair of Pinar's jeans.

"He's okay. I think he has a fever though. He's been mumbling and trying to sign, but none of it makes any sense. The only thing I understood was 'horses' and—" she signed the USL word for 'danger'.

"Well, that doesn't sound ominous at all."

"I'll make up something for his fever. Could you have a look at setting his jaw? It's totally swollen."

"Coffee first," said Ash. "Then I'll take care of our handsome freedom fighter."

Chapter eight

Immaculately dressed and increasingly drunk, the General was in charge of training today and he was loving every second of it.

"Another round!" he shouted at his men. "Go on, get moving."

Just as he ordered, his men were running laps around the square, stopping every few metres to do five military presses and ten crunches. The lieutenants under his command ran after the recruits, shouting at them and making them work harder. As General, he didn't even need to shout at his men anymore. Just if he wanted to. And sometimes he really wanted to.

I'm a king and these are my subjects.

These new soldiers, 'grunts' as they were often known, had only joined this week and the General was already getting them trained up and getting their bodies hardened for battle. They weren't the worst group he'd had, but still when they couldn't keep up with his gruelling regimen, he'd enjoyed punishing them in all the ways his creative mind could think of.

"You run like a bunch of girls!" he shouted as he leaned back in his canvas chair and ran a hand over his blond hair, the military buzz cut that he'd always found so powerful. He took the bottle of State vodka from the table and emptied it into his glass. The sun was hot on his uniform and watching the soldiers running was making him horny. *I'll need to visit the station bathrooms today—and pick up a toilet rat to use.*

It was all an act of course. Not the dominating, sadistic tendencies—that part was true enough—but his straightness, his alpha male, hyper-masculinity. No-one here could guess the secrets the General kept. No-one here even knew his real name. The new soldiers were passing by, closely followed by his corporals.

"Keep them going until I tell you to stop!" he shouted.

"Yes, General!" shouted the lieutenants, barely able to breathe.

The General stood up to get some more vodka from the kitchen, but his head spun a little standing up and he thought better of it. He headed to his private room instead.

Just a quick wank and then back to the training, he thought as he opened his door. *I fucking love my job.*

* * *

Nathalie was on her way to the State office where she worked and she felt sick to the stomach. Sometimes it felt like she was always on the way to work. Or at work, or on the way home from work. The mindless routine was making her ill, she woke up tired every morning and six days out of seven she felt numb inside. All she could think about was the next time she'd get over to the park.

And maybe meet that girl again.

Every morning, except Sundays, Nathalie took the solar train from her apartment over to the State office down town where she had her placement. The train was ancient and the solar panels, old now by anyone's standards, were showing signs of reaching the end of their life.

They stopped several times on the way, waiting for the batteries to recharge. Kids cycled by, laughing. *It would actually be faster to walk at this rate.*

But while the trains still ran and the State still gave her a free ticket, Nathalie was happy to take it slow.

God knows I'm not in any great rush to get there.

She arrived at the station, entered the building and, sweating and puffing as she went, she climbed the twelve floors to the office. *In eight years, I've never seen these bloody elevators work.*

Finally, she reached her floor, and looking in a mirror in the corridor, she vaguely brushed off her shirt and fixed her hair. She had always been called pretty, beautiful even, her pale skin was flawless and even without make-up, her sparkling blue eyes often caught people's attention. But she didn't like what she saw reflected back at her.

I look as tired as I feel, she noticed and pushed out her chest a little towards the mirror. With a sigh, Nathalie walked into the office.

"Hey guys—pretty hot today!" she announced to her workmates as cheerfully as she could, putting her bag down at her desk.

"You're late, N," grumbled her colleague, the guy from the next desk over. His name was G or B or something. Nathalie could never remember people's names even before the State reduced everyone to a single letter.

"Yeah, the trains, you know. You'd think there was enough sun to at least keep them running on time."

"I ran here and got changed in the bathroom," said the colleague. "I like sweating. Sweat is good for you."

"Err...great," said Nathalie, moving towards the office kitchen. *He's always saying weird things like that.*

Her work mates weren't too bad really. At least their oddness distracted her from her work. *And I really need the distraction.*

Her job was all just so dull. Officially her placement was 'State redactor': every day she received a list of terms to be removed from official papers and a pile of already partially redacted documents to remove them from. Most of the papers were transcripts of military and trade discussions which Nathalie would barely understand even if they weren't already covered in text blocked out by some other underpaid functionary.

Nathalie had to remind herself that this was actually considered a good placement and she had had to pull some strings and use her family's name just to get it. She wished she could do something more meaningful, but between this and working at the Nutrition factories, she'd choose the office any day.

And, thought Nathalie as she went to the kitchen and poured herself a hot coffee from the pot, *at least we get this stuff.*

"Drinking coffee again, N?" asked Nathalie's work mate. His name was B, she remembered now.

Always stating the obvious. He was probably called Boris before. Or Brian or something. Maybe Bob…

"You shouldn't drink too much you know," said B. "It's bad for your heart."

"Okay," Nathalie replied as noncommittally as she could. Coffee was incredibly rare these days and as long as the office kept giving it to her for free, she was never going to quit.

"It's extinct, you know?" said B, pointing at her cup.

"Say again?"

"Coffee. For about thirty years already," said B, puffing himself up a little at this chance to impress her. "That's why it's so hard to get. The warmer temperatures started killing the fruit and flowers on the bushes and the farmers were driven up into cooler mountains. Each year they went higher until there was nowhere else to go."

"Is that why the 'Coffee Wars' happened then?" asked Nathalie. She didn't really care about history, but everyone had heard of the Coffee Wars.

"Obviously. Suddenly one morning, caffeine-addicted Western Civilisation woke up and realised that *arabica* had gone the way of the tiger."

Bob, you sound like a documentary.

"The Coffee Wars began when global supplies ran short and *of course*, it was a useful distraction from the economic crash that was just in its early stages then. Politicians have always used wars as a distraction from the real issue. That and as a way of boosting the economy—"

"So..." interrupted Nathalie before she lost him completely in his rant. "If all the coffee died, how do we still have so much of it?"

B looked thoughtful and leaned closer to Nathalie.

"The answer is..." he said in a conspiratorial whisper. "No-one really knows."

Actually, Nathalie had heard vague rumours that the State had stockpiled mountains of coffee somewhere in the City. Or that, despite its global isolation, the State still had trade partners somewhere in the south that smuggled the beans in through the State's hostile neighbours.

Rumours, apparently, are one thing the world never runs out of.

"Well, I should get to work," said Nathalie leaving the kitchen. *Let's save the history lesson for another day.*

Nursing her drink, she sat down and stared at the pile of paperwork that had already accumulated on her desk. B sat at his desk next to her and tutted as he saw her take a sip from her coffee.

Fuck you, Bob. God I wish I was in the park right now.

Chapter nine

In the forest, it had already been a long morning for Ash and Pinar. The cabin floor was a mess of bloody towels and their patient was still in and out of consciousness.

"Is he asleep again?" asked Ash, as she opened the door and brought in a handful of sticks for the stove.

Pinar stood next to Jason adjusting a poultice she had attached to his ankle. She nodded. "Yeah, I think the aspirin's kicking in, he's a lot calmer."

Pinar was treating his injuries with infusions, poultices and oils from the herbs she had grown and collected herself. There were empty jars and packets everywhere.

"Yonah will be here in a few hours," said Pinar. "I should start getting the herb delivery together. Did you say there was red clover growing out towards the river?"

"Yeah, in the field just to the right of our little path," replied Ash, pointing vaguely to the east. "The one with all the abandoned tractors in it."

"I'll go and get some. Will you be okay alone with this guy?"

Ash looked at their patient. He was unconscious and covered in bandages. His face was swollen like a balloon on one side and his ankle was elevated on a pile of towels.

"I don't think he's much of a threat," said Ash. "Go for the clover, and if you want to, take a swim in the river too. I think you need it."

"Do I smell that bad?"

"Just, you know, take a bath is all I'm saying...".

"Okay, just for you." laughed Pinar. "See you in a bit."

Ash opened a jar of herb-infused beeswax and got to work on Jason's ankle. The scent of rosemary and ginger soon filled the cabin.

* * *

The bitter smell of cleaning products was the first thing the General always noticed here. It meant that he was back in his favourite place in the entire City. A place he knew he could never talk about at work. A place that no matter how much he tried to resist, he always ended up back in. The public bathroom of the solar train station.

He put his face close to the scanner on the wall and blinked as the laser flashed over his eye, registering him indelibly to this place and time in the records of some State computer. His Life Account was automatically charged the small fare for using the bathroom, the red light turned green and he pushed through the archaic turnstile.

No going back now.

This place had a power over him. It was too convenient that the station for the military solar-trains where he needed to change transport twice a week, was also renowned for its sordid bathroom. Renowned but somehow permitted to continue.

As long as officers like me keep using this place, they'll never shut it down. That's why they're always so happy to see me—they can't get enough of the uniform.

The General walked down the small staircase and took in the scene. This underground toilet with its cubicle partitions full of viewing holes, toilet paper strewn over the wet tiles lit only by small windows high up near the roof, was an open secret, a glass closet just like the stripper bars and the brothels.

A couple emerged from one of the cubicles grinning at each other.

Shameless fags.

The older of the two, a muscular white guy, had a tattoo on his left arm. A blue triangle with a radiation sign inside it. *The AIDS tattoo. No matter how much we clean the City, we still have this scum amongst us.*

The couple washed their hands at the sink and headed up the stairs, careful to stop touching each other once they re-entered the train station and the public eye.

Dirty, the lot of them, the General thought to himself as he walked over to the sinks and started to size up the market.

His train left for camp in two hours and he needed to get on with it or he'd be frustrated the whole journey. He scanned the room and the men lined up against the tiled walls.

Nothing too exciting.

A few local sex workers and a few off-duty soldiers who, despite their civilian clothes, were glaringly obvious from their posture.

One of the workers got the General's attention. *Built, tanned, handsome. I could do worse.*

But then he noticed the blue triangle on his arm and quickly changed his mind.

The General knew that HIV had been eradicated years ago. After the infection was controlled with antiretrovirals in the West for decades and millions were allowed to die elsewhere through patent laws, the so-called "undefeatable virus" finally disappeared in '23. But only once the cure had become more profitable to sell than the control.

The tattoos, obligatory in the State, were still there. And they were lined with an isotopic ink that showed up on State scanners.

Even if they try to cover them up, we still know who the filth are. So no, not that guy—even if he is kind of hot.

The General noticed movement behind a cubicle door left slightly open. He stepped to the right and could see one of the sex workers standing where the toilet should have been.

The rat looks good.

The General could see he had a mobile scanner hanging around his neck. *So he's a professional. Good, at least he'll be clean.*

He walked across the room, his squadron boots squeaking on the tiled floor, and pushed open the door. The sex worker smiled and got on his knees as the General closed the door behind himself and starting unfastening his belt.

* * *

Ash rubbed the warm wax into the skin and allowed it to absorb a little before she began the massage. The sprain was old and she could already feel the energy being blocked by the injury, the twisted tissues that weren't getting enough blood. She shifted her position to better use her body weight and effortlessly began to manipulate the muscles and tendons of his calf. As she worked, Ash daydreamed.

She had been a massage therapist for the vast majority of her life— five decades already. She had been an apprentice several times for healing masters and had always returned from her travels with new knowledge and a deepened respect for the people and cultures she had learned from.

Of course, it was problematic. Although she didn't know much about her family history and her olive skin had always drawn stupid comments from strangers like 'You look great! Been somewhere hot?' Ash considered herself white; considered herself to be a person who experienced white privilege. And for a white person, even a working class one, to be traveling around enjoying the great cultural supermarket of the 90's and 2000's, she had found herself mistaken more than once for the shallow, cultural appropriating hippy types who backpacked around the same places she did with too much money and too much unchecked privilege.

But fuck those people, Ash thought to herself as she applied more massage oil. *Some things may have changed but white privilege is just the same as ever.*

Ash had done the best she could in a complicated situation and she still gave respect every day to her teachers. She became well known as a healer and she had always had a waiting list of injured sportsmen and young women with infertility problems. She helped them all the best she could and became quite successful.

Or at least as successful as a trans woman can be in this world.

Jason snored a little. With Pinar gone and their patient asleep, the cabin was suddenly very quiet. Ash continued working patiently on the sprained ankle as sunlight streamed in through the windows. Outside, she could hear a blackbird calling. She felt calm now, in a place she felt safe, doing what she did best.

* * *

Not bad at all. At least he's obedient.

The General was standing with his left boot pinning the sex worker's face to the floor. *Must be filthy down there.*

Twenty minutes had already passed and without changing position, the sex worker passed the General his portable scanner again. The General passed it over his left eye and charged himself for another twenty minutes.

"Stay down, boy," he commanded and the sex worker obeyed.

I love this. I always have.

The General flashed on a time that he lived in another city with a very active fetish scene. Even there, his proclivities had been seen as somewhat exceptional, 'stomping' they called it back then. He would trample on anything he could get his boots on: people, fruit, even mice from the pet shop. That had been his favourite actually, he could never get enough of the blood.

I miss that. But this is a good close second.

The sex worker struggled a little and the General pushed down harder. He was rock hard.

* * *

The patient was moaning again. His jaw was still swollen and the handkerchief Ash had used to immobilise it had come loose. She took it off, dipped it in warm water, and tied it back on with a little comfrey root to help heal the fracture.

"Just stay still, Jason. And please stop messing up my bandages."

Even with his swollen jaw, Ash could see that he was handsome. His dark hair fell in loose curls and his face was dark, half covered in stubble. His chest was thick with black hair. *Not my type obviously, but I bet Pin likes him.*

Jason passed out again either from the pain or the painkillers and Ash sat back down on the sofa to rest. The afternoon sun was warm on her back and she felt sleepy. The cabin was wonderfully still.

* * *

The toilet cubicle was shaking and the door banged against its frame loudly as the General fucked the sex worker.

"You love it, don't you?" he growled.

The sex worker nodded and arched his back a little more. He had the General's leather glove over his mouth, he couldn't reply even if he wanted to.

The scanner beeped again and the General grabbed it and without breaking his rhythm, scanned in for another twenty minutes. *I'm not going to need it though, I'm ready to blow.*

The transaction was soon completed and the General left the remaining credit as a tip.

He left the cubicle, washed his hands, replaced his gloves and checked and rechecked his buzzed blond hair and immaculately pressed uniform in the cracked mirror. The sex worker was still in the cubicle when he went up the stairs.

Probably waiting for another Officer to come along.

The General pushed through the turnstile, left behind this sleazy parallel universe, and re-entered the busy station. He disappeared into a crowd of other soldiers.

The sex worker watched him go.

That was pretty fun, he thought to himself. *And that guy's going to find a nice surprise when he gets home.*

* * *

The blackbird was still singing his rich, song.

On the stove, Ash was heating a pot of lavender-infused beech oil to work into Pin's shoulders when she got back. She was feeling sleepy on the sofa so she stood up to put out the flame in case she fell asleep. *The oil's good and hot anyway, I'll just leave it fo—*

Suddenly, behind her, Jason sat up and grabbed Ash's dress. His eyes looked wild and his mouth was wide open. Screaming and pulling herself away with all her force, Ash knocked the oil onto the kitchen floor and tore her dress loudly at the front.

"What the *hell* are you doing?!" she shouted at him and backed away towards the knife drawer. She pulled a chopping knife out and held it in front of her.

I'll stab him if I have to.

He sat bolt upright still reaching for Ash.

"They're coming!" he cried through the wet handkerchief tied around his jaw. "The State. The horses. We have to get out of here!" He winced in pain from his injuries and shouted again. "They're going to kill us all!"

Chapter ten

Jason reached for Ash again, but she backed further away.

"Pinar!" she shouted. "Get the hell back in here."

Jason was trying to stand now and looked more aggressive and dangerous than ever.

"You!" he said pointing at the knife "You did this! You're one of them! I'll kill you!"

Ash had had enough, she stepped forward and grabbed his left ankle. She poked her finger near the sprained joint, not hard enough to damage it, but just hard enough to really hurt. He froze immediately and just stared at her in silence, his mouth closed tightly in pain.

"Now look here, whoever you are. You don't come here, into my friend's home and start shouting and tearing old ladies' dresses, Okay? I may look old and sweet, but I'll teach you a thing or two—"

Ash stopped shouting. Jason had fallen unconscious and the gash on his side was bleeding again. She approached him carefully, the knife still in her hand. He had been terrified, that much was clear, and he was probably also delusional from the fever. *But another bloody stunt like that one and I'll tie him down if I have to.*

She began rebandaging his wound, but was careful to keep the knife close by.

The things we do for the revolution.

She hoped he'd at least stay unconscious until Pinar got back from the river.

* * *

The General was settling down in an empty carriage of the Officer's section of the solar-train. He was looking forward to being back at work. Being back in control. He ran his hands over his smooth chin and kicked absently at the chair in front of him. Sometimes in these moments between work and the toilets, when he was alone, he wasn't quite sure what to do with himself. With no-one to push around and no-one telling him what he wanted to hear, the General felt uncomfortable, a bit less sure of himself.

Something in his pocket was poking into his leg. He shifted his position and took out what appeared to be a flyer made of hand-printed card. He'd never seen it before.

Where did this come from? He turned it over and inspected it. *It must have been the toilet rat. Did he slip it into my pocket while he was down on his knees?*

Angry but curious, the General unfolded the flyer and started reading:

'You are invited to a new kind of movement. A demonstration of our power in diversity...'.

"Resistance!" he cursed out loud, crumpling up the flyer in his gloved fist. "Insubordinate fucki—"

Just then, a train worker passed through his carriage pushing a trolley.

"Anything to drink, Sir?" she asked politely.

"Coffee, black, two sugars," he commanded and she served him his drink. Pushing her cart she quickly left the carriage.

The General drank his coffee too fast and burned his mouth. Furious, he looked out of the window at the passing streets.

I shouldn't be surprised, he reasoned, *half the whores in the City are probably resistance.*

He daydreamed for a while watching the City pass by the window and replaying the scene in the stall in his imagination. It was making him horny again.

Fuck it, who cares? It was fun using him and if I see him again, I wouldn't mind a repeat. Resistance or not, I have my needs.

* * *

"I'm back!" called Pinar as she came into the cabin with a basket full of clover. Her hair was wet and she looked fresh from the river. "Everything okay?"

Ash sat on the bed out of reach of Jason, watching him carefully. The knife was still in her hands.

"Ash? What happened?"

"He attacked me."

"He *what?*!"

"It was the fever. He's out again now though." Ash looked sad and said in a strange tone. "He tore my dress."

"I'll fix it for you hon. Take one of mine from the closet and I'll get my needle and thread."

"Okay, but I'll get changed outside. I don't really feel safe now, sorry."

"Whatever you need, darling. I'll watch him."

An hour later and Jason came to again. His fever had gone down and although he was still in a lot of pain and having trouble breathing, he was more lucid than before. Pinar sat next to him, Ash stood in the doorway with her arms crossed.

"Don't try to talk," said Pinar softly. "You have a broken jaw and you've been pretty badly injured. Your rib is probably fractured too and you sprained your ankle. We can sign—What's your name? How did this happen to you?"

"*Jason.*" he signed, spelling out the letters. "*My name's Jason. You're A and P right? From the Femme Riots? I'm so glad I found you.*"

"Ash and Pinar actually," corrected Ash from the doorway.

"Sorry."

"It's fine," said Pinar. "What happened to you?"

"We were attacked. I was with a resistance wing in the east of the forest securing some of the wells and a couple of nights ago, they...they came out of nowhere—maybe thirty State troopers on horseback—and we were separated. I got pretty beaten up and—"

Jason began coughing loudly and sat up. He winced in pain, his hands over his cracked rib.

"Here," said Pinar, passing him a pillow. "Hold this against your chest when you cough. And try to breathe normally."

"Thanks...I..." Jason said weakly. He lay back down and began signing again. *"My jaw really hurts."*

"I'll get you some more painkiller," said Ash, opening the medicine cabinet.

"Thanks."

"You were saying..." signed Pinar.

"So, yeah, I lost contact with the others. We scattered into the Forest and at some point, I found the river. I remembered hearing about you two, how you take care of the resistance fighters. So I walked here. It took a day or two I guess. I'm not really sure. I got sick."

"You had a fever," Ash said with an edge in her voice passing Pinar the willow bark. "You started screaming that they—the State—were coming to kill us. Do you remember that?"

"No, not at all." Jason coughed again. *"But you're so isolated out here, I think it's fine—"*

"Good."

"Try to rest," said Pinar softly. "We'll talk more later. Ash, it's hot and stuffy in here. Want to take a walk with me to get some water?"

"Let's go."

Chapter eleven

W ith no air conditioning, and no fresh air, the office was claustrophobically hot and Nathalie was beginning to feel dizzy. It was nearly lunchtime anyway so she headed back down the stairs armed with another cup of coffee and an entirely bland nutrition-meal from the kitchen.

Outside, the sky was brooding and the heat was almost as unbearable as in the office, but Nathalie liked to get away from her colleagues and have some time to herself to think.

She had a regular spot where she sat and ate her lunch looking down over what used to be the motorway out of town. It was completely overgrown and it was gradually becoming a kind of long woodland snaking through the City as each day more trees pushed up through the concrete.

She ate her meal and looked out over the woodland thoughtfully.

I remember when cars still drove here. Before the vehicle ban, before the crash. I remember driving to the seaside for family holidays.

She took a sip of her drink.

Did this stuff really go extinct? We so rarely hear anything from the outside world. I wonder if the fuel ran out everywhere and not just here. I wonder if—

A voice from behind startled her.

"I know you, don't I?"

Nathalie turned around, surprised. Before her was a beautiful woman, someone she couldn't place but who, at the same time, seemed deeply familiar. Dark eyes, full lips, perfectly straight, black hair. Nathalie knew she knew that face, but where from?

"We met the other night. You remember me, don't you?"

The other night? The girl from the park! The stranger in the shadows!

Nathalie was suddenly overcome with embarrassment and her pale cheeks blushed bright red. She'd never met anyone from the park outside before. She wasn't afraid of being caught out—anyone who even stepped foot in the park was as guilty as everyone else—but she was lost for words.

After all, they'd never actually spoken before.

This woman has seen me commit all kinds of perverted acts under the night sky and I don't even know her name. And here she is and she's waiting for an answer—

"Err.. yes, of course I remember you...we haven't really met yet, my name's N," she said, impulsively putting out her right hand.

"So formal," said the stranger smiling and shook Nathalie's hand with a tight grip.

"Oh...well I didn't mean to be formal...I'm just, you know, a bit surprised is all..." Nathalie stumbled over her words. "Do you work near here?"

"Of all the questions. Yes. What's your placement? Admin department I'm guessing?"

"Err... Admin, that's right. In that office right there, twelfth floor, quite a view, but the lift never works." Nathalie chattered nervously. "Actually, I should get back soon. I'm just... on my break, you know for coffee... would you like some actually? Coffee that is." Nathalie offered her the cup. It had barely cooled at all in the midday heat.

"I quit a few years back. No point being addicted to something so expensive."

"That makes sense..."

"But maybe just a sip."

They locked eyes as the stranger took a long, slow sip of the bitter liquid, shamelessly smiled and licked her moist lips.

"Damn, that's good."

Nathalie felt naked again under that unwavering gaze and she looked down at the ground, searching for something to say.

"I...we...have plenty at the office. I could bring you a cup tomorrow if you like."

She looked up to see the stranger—she still hadn't learned her name—giving her just the hint of a smile.

"I think that's a very good idea, N."

Chapter twelve

Y ou took a big risk leaving that flyer, boy."

The General was back at the toilet, same cubicle, same worker. He hadn't planned on coming down here. He wasn't even supposed to be in this part of town. And somehow, here he was.

Maybe this is an addiction. Maybe I should do something about it.

The General wasn't prone to self-doubt—a man with his responsibilities couldn't afford to be. But there were moments when coming to the toilets felt like a weakness, the only thing in his life that made him vulnerable. It felt dangerous. *But a man needs what he needs and I want to use the rat again, I deserve it. Once I've reminded him of his place.*

"What flyer, Sir?" the sex worker asked sweetly.

"Cute, boy, very cute. I could take you out and have you locked up right now, you dirty *verger*."

Verger was one of the General's favourite insults. For a while, 'divergent' had become an empowering term to describe people who 'diverged' from a common group. Neurodivergents for example were people with less common neurobiology such as people on the autism spectrum. Reframing it in this way was intended to put such groups on an equal level so although there were 'neurotypicals' and 'neurodivergents', neither of these groups were seen as better or worse. Within a few years, the terminology had expanded to gender divergents, sexual divergents and ability divergents amongst others.

But school children quickly corrupted the new terms and 'divergent', 'vergent' and 'verger' became the go-to insult for anyone seen as unusual. Some divergents, in turn reclaimed the insult, but these days it was still mostly heard as a pejorative.

The sex worker gave the General a coy look.

"You *could* try, Sir. But I don't think you will."

"What makes you so confident?"

"Let's just say I have some insurance, Sir. Certain photographic evidence that you wouldn't want falling into the wrong hands. All the toilet boys do it, of course, Sir. I thought you knew that."

The General was stunned but tried to hide his surprise.

"I knew about that. Of course I did. Still, don't forget your place you dirty..." the General was running out of insults "—faggot. Dirty fag...boy."

"Of course not, Sir," replied the sex worker. "Would Sir like to stand on me again today and have His boots cleaned?" Mike, the sex worker—who had a beautiful wife and two children—said as he offered up the scanner.

The General shifted from one leg to the other as he weighed his options.

This is probably a bad idea. Is he blackmailing me? What 'photographic evidence' anyway?

He looked at the cubicle door and he looked at his boots. *Well, I'm here now and it'll be nearly a week before I'm back at the station. What the hell?*

He took the scanner.

Chapter thirteen

P inar and Ash chatted as they pumped water out of the well and filled their buckets. This summer was so hot that the well was almost dry and Ash was worried that they might run out completely soon. They barely had enough today to fill the coal filter at the cabin as it was. Pinar took a turn on the pump. Above them they could hear thrushes, finches and pigeons calling each other in the forest canopy.

"What do you think?" asked Pinar over the sound of the pump. "About Jason, I mean."

"He seems pretty messed up," Ash replied, switching the bucket under the pump. "I didn't particularly appreciate being attacked, for example."

"It was the fever. And the trauma—"

"Yes, yes."

"He's post-traumatic. We could try the cleansing." Pinar thoughtfully flicked her long hair out of her face and continued pumping. "I think it might help."

Ash allowed herself a small smile.

"Well, we have to at some point, Pin, otherwise people will think I'm a *delusional* old lady instead of just a *temporally divergent* one."

Temporally divergent was Pinar's term for Ash's special trait of moving through time, but Ash had never really approved of it. She was already considered divergent in so many ways, the last thing she wanted was another marginalised category to be put in.

Pinar smiled, her face radiant in the dappled forest light.

"You're the sweetest temporally divergent old lady I know. Shall we do it tonight?"

"Okay. But let's eat first. I'm starving!"

"Just to make a change."

Ash stuck her tongue out and they both laughed and headed back to the cabin with their buckets.

* * *

"Get me that report on the wells, Lieutenant. I *said* today and I *meant* today. Not tomorrow, not next week."

"Yes Sir. Right away Sir."

"Bring the rest of the squad here and then get the hell out of my sight."

The General poured himself another glass of State vodka and drank it down in one go.

Fuck these idiots.

He was in a worse mood than usual since he got back from the toilets an hour ago. He was overseeing a military campaign in the forest to destroy the fresh water wells that the resistance depended on, but was finding it hard to concentrate.

Without the wells, the resistance fighters and villages would either die or move away. At least that was the plan.

Somehow though, even with all the power of the State behind them, these vergers haven't managed to locate a single well.

The campaign was a year old and the forest resistance was as strong as ever. *And it's always me who gets shit for it from my superiors. I shouldn't even have superiors. No-one's better at this than I am.*

The door to his office squeaked open. His squad came in and lined up in front of him.

"I think you know why you're here," said the General, leaning back in the chair and putting his boots on the table in front of him.

They nodded in silence.

"Well? *Why are you here?*" he shouted at the nearest Lieutenant.

"It was the annual review yesterday... Sir. And erm... we didn't meet the project deadline. Sir."

"You messed up, in other words."

"Yes Sir."

The General turned to one of the other men. A new grunt who had only been on the base for a month or so.

He's cute, the General noticed, *hot in a barely-out-of-his-teens way. He's also an insubordinate little shit and he's been winding me up since the day he got here.*

"And what do *you* have say about this failure, grunt?"

The General never learned the names of his inferiors. They were all 'grunt' or 'lieutenant' to him, or if he was particularly angry: 'verger'.

"Perhaps the parameters of the mission were too optimistic for the resources available," replied the soldier.

"In *English!*"

"Nothing, doesn't matter."

"Nothing, doesn't matter, *Sir!*" the General shouted despite himself. "You will show proper respect for my title or you'll be disciplined, grunt."

"Yes, Sir."

"Get out, the lot of you. Go do some work for a change." The General turned to the cute one. "Not you. You're staying with me."

When the others had left and closed the door, the General barked:

"A hundred push ups, right now!"

The soldier didn't move.

"I said *now!*"

Taking his time, the soldier got down and started doing push ups on the office carpet.

The General poured himself another glass of vodka.

That's better. He looks good down there, working up a sweat. Under my control.

Even shouting and giving out his little punishments wasn't helping the General's mood today though.

I know why. It's that toilet rat's fault that I'm feeling like this. I've been blackmailed and all the other toilet rats doing the same damn thing, apparently. Vergers—the lot of them.

I'm in no danger though; no-one's going to suspect me of being a 'sexual divergent' or whatever. I'm a General. Sure, I've been going there on and off for the last two years, and sure, I've probably already done most of the rats in there, but my record's impeccable.

The General was well-respected, and well-feared, which amounted to the same thing in the State military. *There's no way I'll get caught. No way.*

Just in case though, he'd left the sex worker an extra large tip. The General knew the dangers. His Life Account record must be full of those little suspicious transactions.

But I'll be fine. I always am.

The recruit finished the push ups and, panting heavily, he tried to stand.

"Fifty more." The General was beginning to feel better. "You're not done yet."

* * *

Pinar's arms burned as she carried the heavy pot out of the cabin and placed it down next to where Ash was clearing a circle on the ground. She was panting from the effort.

"Who needs a gym when you live in the forest!" she joked.

"Who needs gyms in general?" said Ash. "Horrible, stinky places."

As someone who, for many years, people assumed was a gay man, Ash had spent quite some time in San Francisco gyms, trying to build up, trying to look good for the guys. Cruising, protein shakes, the whole deal. It didn't take long for her to stop trying though. As she had said many times to herself at that time, if they couldn't deal with who she really was, why would she even want them? *They were all into guys after all, and I was never a man. Gays make the worst misogynists...*

The smell of rose and lavender brought her back to the present. Pinar dropped the crushed herbs carefully into the hot water and the air filled with their heady scent.

Ash looked up at the reddening sky.

That looks familiar. It must be nearly time.

"You can come out," she called to Jason, who was inside the cabin. He emerged, slowly, using a stick to keep the weight off his ankle.

"Strip, please." She saw his expression and tried to reassure him. "Don't worry, we're very, very old—well, at least I am. I promise we won't look."

Shyly and without making eye contact, Jason stripped down to his underwear. Although Ash had explained the whole process to him over dinner—the sacred cleansing to help him recover from the trauma he had experienced, the herbs to help draw out his pain— Jason looked intensely awkward as he stood in the cleared circle and waited for the ceremony to begin.

"Ready, Ash?"

"Ready."

As she always did, Ash called upon the memory of her teachers to guide her.

This man needs our help. This land is distant, this forest would be foreign to you, but if you can, please help us to heal Jason. To help undo the damage the State has done to him. Spirits of this place, we ask you for help tonight...

Pinar was burning the wood of an old tree which had been struck by lightning years before. As the smoke enveloped him, Jason's eyes began to burn and water. Ash coughed and together with Pinar, she lifted the pot over Jason's body.

∗ ∗ ∗

It was already getting dark outside when the recruit finished his push ups.

"Done," he announced as he stood up and grinned smugly at the General.

Ever since he arrived on base, he'd been distracting the General from his work. The way the uniform hung off his torso when he was doing the morning exercises. The shine of his boots after inspection. The sweat on his back when he was running in the yard. This soldier had something about him that intrigued the General and it was just making him more frustrated and more horny.

"Done, *Sir!*" shouted the General, immediately angry again. He was losing control, he could feel it. This guy knew just how to get under his skin.

"Shall I do another hundred?"

"ANOTHER HUNDRED, SIR!" the General yelled. He noticed some of his other subordinates watching him through the office window.

Fuck. I'm losing it. I need to get my control back. It's because I want to fuck him. And I haven't been sleeping well and—

The General could hear his subordinates talking on the other side of the window. One said something and another started laughing.

They're laughing at me. I need to do something. I need to make an example of this guy before I lose control completely.

Without another thought, consumed with his frustration, the General grabbed the soldier by his collar and dragged him past the other recruits.

"Get back to work you fucking *vergers!*" he yelled. "I'll show you what happens when you disobey me."

The communal shower room was in the next building and the General dragged the recruit through the Officer's tent, and into the shower, slamming the door behind him. He pushed him against the wall and gave him a good, hard punch in the gut. The recruit bent over in pain, but refused to cry out. Another punch and he fell down on the cold shower floor.

* * *

The first drops of hot water fell, but they'd barely touched him before Jason collapsed. His embarrassment completely forgotten, he curled up on the ground and allowed his tears to come. As the water poured over him, Pinar called Jason's name over and over to help him find his true self beyond the trauma that had invaded him. Unable to hold them in any longer, Jason's cries carried out into the dark forest.

This is how it was, thought Ash. *I'll be here soon.*

Only rarely did she journey into her future. It was the strangest feeling to relive something she'd already seen, and felt, before. As she had once explained to Pinar, it was kind of like a very intense sense of déjà vu but more real. She had experienced PTSD most of her life, and the flashbacks she used to have, the sudden nightmares that would grab her, kicking and sweating back into the past were similar. But the journeys went both ways through time and not everything she saw was bad.

Still slowly pouring the hot water, Ash looked up as a small flock of crows landed on the roof of the cabin and, in perfect stillness, stood witnessing the ritual.

I was wondering when you guys would get here.

The pot was getting lighter and the steam and smoke were making Ash's eyes water. *Or I'm crying. I don't know which.*

Her arms were tired and she could feel Pinar adjusting the pot and taking more of the weight from her. She opened her mouth to say something and—

Ah, there you are. Ash saw herself appear, ghostlike, in the clearing, perhaps twenty metres from the cabin. She looked surprised and stared back. The present Ash just smiled. *Don't worry dear, it'll all make sense.*

And she silently disappeared again.

Jason was still howling, crumpled on the ground, soaked and steaming in the evening light and Ash lifted the pot higher and returned to her work with new determination.

Thank you, she prayed silently. *You taught me well.*

* * *

"I'll teach you to make a fool of me, *vergent,*" the General barked. The shower was on full and before him, the recruit was soaked, fully dressed, in freezing cold water. The grunt was silent. He just took the punishment, seemingly unaffected by the icy water filling his boots. The General pulled out his cock and hot piss flowed in his eyes, his mouth. Still no sound. The General was angry enough to kill him. He pulled the recruit back up to standing. Shivering and reeking of piss, somehow he still wore that cocky little smile of his.

"You fucked up this time, *verger.* I'm going to make you mine."

The General's cock was hard again. He knew he was stepping over a line. He knew that he had only survived this far by keeping his history, and his secret life at the toilets, totally separate from work. It was one thing to push them around, and punish them—that was his job. But he wanted more than that. He needed more.

The General pushed his subordinate up against the shower wall, his forearm against the recruit's throat. Body pinning him and keeping him from getting away, the General began to taste his inferior, to consume him. He licked his face and pushed their lips together. He was dizzy with power and wanted more. There was even the taste of blood in his mouth. Yet still the recruit didn't resist.

It was then, as the General withdrew slightly, that he saw the grunt was smiling again. Bending forward towards the General's ear, he whispered—

"Caught you, Sir."

There was laughter behind them. The General turned and saw his superior officer standing by the door accompanied by three riot soldiers with handcuffs and batons in hand. They'd been there for a while, silently watching the whole scene.

The General stopped breathing as the riot soldiers forced him to his knees and handcuffed him behind his back. He looked up at the grunt, standing above him, still smiling.

Struggling against the handcuffs, the General tried to get to his feet, but one of the soldiers slapped him back down, slamming his knees painfully against the hard floor. Again, he tried to resist and again he was pushed down. This time his superior took the opportunity to kick him in the gut and the General curled up on the wet tile, his eyes closed tight in pain.

The General didn't rise a third time.

2. Secrets

Chapter fourteen

Jason sat outside the cabin alone, soaking in the dappled summer light and watching a tiny mouse running in the leaf litter collecting food. He was feeling stronger every day. After Ash set his jaw, he was able to eat solid food again and after a few days more he started taking short walks in the forest alone before coming back and curling up on the sofa to rest. Through the care of his new friends, his body was recovering quickly, but trauma was much more than a physical illness and each night his sleep was still shattered by feverish nightmares, cold sweats, and screams which seemed to erupt from his very core.

Pinar knew what he had been through was stored deeply in the tissues of his body and it would take all of his strength to face it. They could support him through the process, but the demons were his to face alone. For six nights, they had performed the cleansing ritual and tomorrow night would be his last.

"Could you bring some more firewood if you see some on the way?" Pinar asked Ash as she was getting ready to leave the cabin. "And maybe some squashes from your garden?"

"No problem," she replied, bending down slowly to lace up her walking boots. Her back was tired and she was feeling her age after so many nights in Pinar's small bed. "I'll be here before dark and I'll see what I can pick up. I'll bring tomatoes too; they should be ready."

"Thanks. Take care."

Ash closed the door behind her and set off for home.

Each day while Ash was away taking care of her garden, Pinar and Jason worked around the house and got to know each other better. He signed for the first few days while his jaw healed, but soon enough he could comfortably speak English again. Pinar found she was enjoying his company immensely. He was enthusiastic and surprisingly sensitive. As she heated some nettle soup over a fire outside the cabin, she realised it was his way of asking questions that she enjoyed most. He always seemed interested, but never invasive. He never pushed her. He in turn found Pinar wise and caring. She was robustly feminine and he could lose hours listening to her stories.

Jason sat shelling peas in the warm morning air. She arrived carrying two bowls of soup and sat down next to him.

"Leave that for now." Pinar handed him a bowl. "Let's eat!"

She started straight away, tucking away her long hair behind her ears, but Jason blew on his soup and waited a while for it to cool—his jaw still hurt sometimes if he ate anything too hot.

After a while, he asked in his strong northern accent;

"Where did you grow up? If you don't mind me asking."

Pinar had found his accent a bit difficult to follow at the beginning, particularly with his broken jaw, but now she found it quite charming.

"I grew up in the City," she replied. "My parents immigrated when I was very young. Me and Ash haven't been back for years though, for obvious reasons."

Jason smiled politely. He didn't need to ask why they had left. The role of A and P—Ash and Pinar—in the Femme Riots of '21 was a well-known part of resistance history. They had led the fights against systemic racism and for trans and Femme liberation in the City. They had been at the forefront of the revolutionary resistance movement that had spread like wildfire throughout the region.

After the purges though, things became worse than they ever had been. It was clear to Jason why they were here and not there.

"You don't really have a City accent," he said carefully and started his soup.

"Yeah, I lost it along the way I guess. I grew up speaking British English and Farsi, but I think I sound more American these days."

"Like Ash."

"Precisely."

"It's funny how that happens—that we end up sounding like our friends."

"It's cute."

"Did she grow up in the States, actually? Her accent's a bit mixed"

"Partially. She grew up moving between the UK and the US." Pinar scraped the bottom of her bowl thoughtfully. "She moved to Europe permanently after the Trump years though."

Without a word, Jason served them both some more food. They sat in silence for a moment, neither of them particularly wanting to discuss the reign of Donald Trump further.

"Do you go there much? To the City?" Pinar asked as she took her bowl from him.

"From time to time—when I need to. In general I avoid it, though. My mum grew up there, but she moved to the *campo* before I was born so I've only really known life as a *campesino*."

He's mixing Spanish into his English, Pinar thought, *I wonder if there's a story there. Or maybe all the young people do that now.*

After the collapse of the Spanish economy and the crisis in Syria, the City—and the resistance—had always been multilingual.

"I pass through sometimes for a meeting or whatever," he continued. "But I'm a country boy at the end of the day—"

He must be at least thirty-five, hardly a boy anymore.

Pinar caught herself looking at his muscled arms as he ate his soup, the deep wrinkles around his eyes as he smiled.

He's a man. Definitely a man.

"Let's get some air," she said after they finished eating. "Are you feeling well enough for another walk? I'd like to show you our little valley."

Jason stood and tested his ankle. It was still sore, but not painful. With Ash's massage and Pinar's herbs, it had healed remarkably quickly.

"No problem. Let's take it slowly though?"

"I'm an old woman," she laughed. "How fast could I go really?"

"You're *not* old!"

Pinar rewarded him with a broad smile.

"Right answer, sweetie. Right answer."

Chapter fifteen

Like every day this week, Nathalie was back in her spot in what she called the cement valley, the abandoned and increasingly forested motorway that bisected the City from east to west. She brought a flask of coffee with her from the office and, as always, she'd eaten her lunch too fast; gulping it down and giving herself a stomach ache.

I can't wait to see her again. I've missed her all day.

It was the sixth lunch date they'd shared in six days. Nathalie had noticed very quickly that Kit kept her private life private. It had taken to the end of the second date to even learn her name. "K", Kit had told her finally, using the State's obligatory naming convention.

K? Nathalie had thought that afternoon back in the office. *Kelly? Kathryn? Kristina? Why won't she tell me more?*

It had taken to the fourth date, and a lot of insistence, for Nathalie to learn about Kit's job.

"A professional dominatrix," Kit had announced calmly as she bit into an oversweet Nutrition bar. "A pro-Domme."

Nathalie just stared.

"Do you know what that is?"

"I...think I do," said Nathalie, taken back and a little lost for words. "You hurt people and they pay you for it?"

"Men specifically in my case, and not always pain, but yeah that's the general idea. There's also ropes and heels and dog collars."

"Wow."

"It's a job."

"Of course, I mean, just wow, obviously I never met a sex worker before."

"Not that you know of," Kit replied flatly fixing eye contact until Nathalie looked away.

"Not that I know of."

In that moment, Nathalie noticed her chest felt tight, her heart was beating too fast.

Am I scared of her now? Of her power?

Taking a breath and looking out over the concrete and trees she began to recognise the feeling in her body.

Actually I know this. It's just like in the park.

Sat now between the trees, Nathalie checked her watch. Kit was late for lunch as she always was.

Maybe this is a domination thing, Nathalie wondered, *to always keep me waiting, to keep me guessing and wanting more. It makes perfect sense that she's a—what did she call it? Pro-Domme? Those graceful, muscled arms, that imposing way she stares you down if you say the wrong thing. Naturally men would pay to be under her control.*

Nathalie pulled out a compact mirror and re-checked her hair and makeup for the third time since she sat down. *I have to look my best for her. I really need to impress her.*

Either from nerves or the midday heat, Nathalie was sweating. She lifted her left arm for an odour check.

God. It's like a rat climbed in there and died. She took a bottle of watered down perfume from her handbag and sprayed far too much on. *Damn. Now I smell like an explosion in a flower store. I can never get it right, I always—*

Her thoughts were interrupted by the unmistakable sound of Kit's heels clicking on the concrete in the street above her. Nathalie checked her hair one more time.

It'll have to do.

She picked up the flask to present to her date. She hadn't touched a drop...

After all, it isn't really mine.

"Hey, *guapa*," said Kit as she arrived. Nathalie blushed as they exchanged the usual formal four cheek kisses.

"Let's go down a bit, into the trees. I don't think you want to be the gossip of the office this week."

Using tree trunks and branches for support, they carefully made their way down into the motorway valley. Nathalie stumbled and fell a few times over roots and upturned concrete slabs, but even in heels and a tight skirt, Kit walked effortlessly down the slope.

She looks so young, thought Nathalie. *Younger than me, but she's done so much in her life. How old is she really? Why is she even here with me?*

Once they were out of view of the street, they sat down on a slab. Nathalie was still holding the flask and passed it to Kit who took it, poured herself a cup of coffee and began drinking without a word. Nathalie just watched her. The way she inhaled the steam with just a hint of a smile. The way she licked her lips after every sip. *She even drinks elegantly.*

"How's work?" Kit asked finally, passing her back the empty cup.

"Boring," replied Nathalie, immediately refilling it and handing it back. "Nothing like yours I'm sure."

"Probably quite different. It must be hot up there."

"Yeah, it really is!"

Nathalie loved complaining about the weather, it was one of the few subjects she felt qualified to talk about at great length.

"Obviously it depends on the season. Right now it's disgusting inside, but at least I can escape at lunchtime. The weather is just so unpredictable. Do you remember last year? This summer is *wild!* I mean I know the climate's changing or whatever, but—"

I'm gabbling again. She makes me so nervous.

Nathalie flashed back ten years to when she was eighteen on her very first date with a woman—H, apparently. That's all she'd ever learned about her. She had been nervous then too and had never seen her again after that night. But Nathalie knew then that she had no other option but to be with women. Every part of her craved it. She had never even so much as kissed a man.

"Anyway, yes," she resumed. "The office is very hot."

"I see." Kit smiled just a little and then looking back down at the steam still coming off her coffee. "And do you do something important for the State?"

"Honestly I have no idea. I redact official papers. It's all kept very compartmentalised of course and I don't really understand a lot of what they give me. Mostly, I just cross out any words that are on the latest prohibited list and file everything away. Obviously it would be much easier with a computer, but the few that are left are all dedicated to keeping the Life Accounts running. Once in a while I get something juicy—military plans, stuff like that."

Her interest suddenly piqued, Kit forgot about her drink and looked straight at Nathalie.

God, those black eyes could actually kill me.

"I want to hear everything."

"Okay. I mean I guess I shouldn't really be talking about it outside of the off—"

"Everything."

Nathalie looked down at the ground. Her chest was tight again.

"But first..." Kit continued, looking up and checking again that they couldn't be seen. She leaned in and signed.

"*I'm working tonight and tomorrow all day so no coffee date. Want to meet at the park tomorrow night?*"

"*Yes.*"

"*Will you miss me?*"

"*Absolutely.*"

"*Come over here and show me how much.*"

Chapter sixteen

Ash arrived home and she was happy to see her vegetables had made it through another hot night and morning. Even with the thick layers of leaf litter mulch that she'd laid and the shading nets that she'd strung over the soil, the summer heat was unforgiving and she needed to water the garden at least once a day just to keep it alive.

She spent a good part of the afternoon carrying buckets of water from what was left of the river and pouring it into the little troughs that separated her tidy lines of cabbages, onions, garlics and tomatoes. As fast as she poured, the water was sucked into the thirsty ground and the soil looked instantly dry again.

I'm barely keeping up. If it doesn't rain soon, we're going to go hungry again.

Once the garden was as watered and protected as it could be, Ash sat on the deck of her tiny houseboat and looked out over the slow-flowing backwater she called home. A noisy group of mallard ducks approached on the river, quacking loudly to each other. Ash watched them as they swam by and smiled.

That's odd. Where have all the drakes gone? It's unusual for there to be none at all in a group.

She looked closer as they passed by the boat. Some of the ducks had orange bills, some olive green.

Of course! It's that time of year again.

Ash knew that every summer, as the males—the drakes—lost and regrew their flight feathers, they could barely fly and so for a time it became safer for them to become camouflaged. Their bright green and black courtship feathers were gradually replaced with mottled brown ones—much better for hiding in the reeds. During this time, known as their 'eclipse,' they looked remarkably similar to the hens who were discreetly brown all year round and unless you were paying close attention, it could easily appear that there were only females and that all the drakes had disappeared.

It seems about a month since the last eclipse, where is time going? Is this what happens with old age?

Watching the ducks, Ash caught a glimpse of her reflection in the still water. Her stubbly beard, her long earrings sparkling in the sunlight. She had experienced this "camouflage as the other sex", as she thought of it, for most of her life. *I was in eclipse my entire life before I came here.*

Out in the forest, she felt freer to be herself. And these ducks, this water, the sound of the wind blowing through the poplars behind her and Pinar of course, *this* was her family, her home.

What else could I need in the world?

* * *

I need more, thought Nathalie. *I want all of her.*

She was under Kit now. She felt herself pressed down between the strong body above and the weeds and the concrete below. They were surrounded on all sides by trees and bushes, but they both knew they were far from safe, the motorway valley was barely two hundred metres from the street. Nathalie tried to lift her head to check for passers-by, but Kit pushed it back down and kissed her again.

Those lips, she thought. *I never want to kiss anyone else.*

She lay her head back down and stopped resisting.

* * *

Nathalie ran up the stairs to the office.

She was late. She rushed in, red in the cheeks, her hair in knots.

I hope they don't notice, she thought looking at her workmates. She needn't have worried. No-one cared enough to say anything.

They look half dead, buried in their paperwork. I'm not like them though, not anymore. I'm alive again.

She put the empty flask and cup on the desk in front of her and stroked it tenderly with her finger. It still had some of Kit's bright lipstick on it.

K's so beautiful, so perfect. I already miss that intense stare. Her voice. Especially when she's angry with me, I feel like I could die. And now I need to wait until tomorrow night *before I can see her again.*

Feeling herself descending into a bad mood, Nathalie picked up the first of a pile of papers she needed to work on that afternoon and began crossing out the prohibited words, most of which she knew by heart. The sex amongst the trees had been amazing, but now she just wanted more. She always wanted more. She pushed down too hard on the pencil and the lead broke with a loud crack smudging the document with graphite dust.

From his desk, B gave her a disapproving look and tutted. "Those are expensive you know," he warned her. "Ever since the mineral scarcity of the 2010's..."

Nathalie ignored him. *I want more from K than she's giving me. I need all of her, I need...*

Yes, Nathalie realised as she reached for the pencil sharpener. *I need her to need me.*

Chapter seventeen

Tonight Danny had escaped the bar. A client he had seen regularly on and off for the last few years was in town and had sent a message that he wanted to book him for the night. They always met at his fancy hotel and ate something expensive on the balcony overlooking the sea, with candles and plenty of wine. Danny didn't even hesitate.

The first part was always the worst, though.

The client had been sucking Danny off for about twenty minutes already. It wasn't bad, it just wasn't good. There was supposed to be some vague role play happening, Danny was 'room service' desperate for a tip and willing to do anything to get it.

Including, apparently, receiving this horrible blow job.

The 'hotel guest' kept looking up and smiling like it was the greatest oral sex anyone had ever performed. Danny, ever the professional, smiled back and made all the right noises. He was good at playing the studly top, although today he was too hungry to really act his best.

This morning's meeting with the sex-work collective had gone on longer than he'd planned and he'd barely had enough time to eat before cycling over to the hotel. He was imagining the fancy dinner they'd eat after all this was over. The balcony, the wine.

Concentrate, Danny. You're being paid very well for all this. Dinner will come soon.

"That's great!" he moaned in his most convincing pre-orgasm voice. "You're so damn *good!*"

I'm so damn hungry, he thought to himself. *Surely this guy's mouth must be getting tired by now.*

"Let's do you now, Sir," Danny suggested, taking control.

The client rolled onto his back obediently and started pleasing himself. It was all over very fast and suddenly Danny's pleasure and unfinished orgasm were forgotten about entirely.

"That was amazing. Let's go again later!" Danny said as he sat, not too subtly, under the little bell which was used to call room service. "Are you hungry, handsome?"

"I could eat. Let's get something and move our little party to the balcony, what do you think?"

Danny was ringing the bell for the *real* room service before his client had even finished the sentence.

While they waited for their meal to be brought up, Danny and his client took a shower together. Somehow in the bathroom, this client always become very attentive and loved nothing more than to soap Danny all over, rubbing the suds over his muscled back and rinsing him off with decadently hot water. Danny found it sweet—strangely unsexual and intimate. He relaxed and even began to enjoy his client's gentle kisses on the back of his neck as he ran the incredibly soft towels over his body. There was a knock at the door and, slipping on a perfectly white robe, the client went to bring them their meal.

Danny's client was rich and dinner, as always, was extremely good. He worked high up in the Life-Accounts department apparently and lived well despite decades of economic depression. The food—real beef and vegetables and not a single Nutrition product to be seen—was excellent and Danny ate and drank as much as he could without seeming rude.

This was always the best part of their nights together. It was romantic, in a way, sitting at the table, looking out over the sea. As always, the surf was thick with dirty foam and even from up on the tenth floor, Danny could see the pile of jellyfish carcasses a metre deep along the beach. Ever since the sea started heating up, and their natural predators were overfished, jelly populations had exploded.

Danny couldn't remember the last time he'd dared to get in the sea for a swim. There was a rumour that as everything else became more scarce, they had become the primary ingredient in Nutrition Snacks.

The food was perfect and there was more than they could possible eat. This client was always generous: Danny earned as much in one night with him as he did during an entire week of dancing. And the day after, he usually found a big tip put on his Life-Account.

Invariably, those tips would go towards buying materials for the resistance—to run the *comedores*, the soup kitchens, to keep the medical supplies being smuggled in from beyond the wall and to keep the underground education system in pencils and paper. At the end of the month, Danny would end up just as poor as ever—but at least he was doing his work, to survive and for the movement. And if he could convince his client to sleep, then he got to sleep in a really good bed for a night.

For all its problems, this is a pretty good job.

"This is delicious!" he said. He was probably over playing it a little, but actually the food *was* really good.

"It's fine," replied the client poking at his steak. "The food's always pretty good at this place. Not amazing, but good enough."

Danny didn't bother to disagree with him. This was the best thing he'd eaten in weeks.

"So how's the office?" he asked with his mouth full of meat.

Work was always an easy topic with this client. He loved to talk about his job, to complain about his workmates and the outdated technology that was holding the whole system together. He was an engineer with the department, or a technician, Danny could never remember the details. It was obviously something well paid at any rate.

As his client talked, Danny enjoyed his meal, nodding more or less at the right times and tutting in appropriate outrage when he thought he should. He realised he was getting a bit tipsy—after a long, hungry day, the wine was going to his head.

I should probably slow down.

Although the client was easy to talk to and their conversations were always fairly relaxed, Danny had to be careful. There were a hundred personal things a resistance fighter couldn't talk to a State employee about.

If he knew almost anything real about me, I'd be in a State prison cell within the hour.

Danny had a whole identity invented for himself, a name, a fake family history, the whole thing. "L" was from *les banlieues*—the poverty-stricken suburbs of Paris. He was an edgy, bi-curious boxer, had worked as a security guard and had a long history of getting into trouble. In reality, Danny grew up in the centre of Brussels in a middle class, diplomatic family and had never been in a street fight in his life. The closest he'd ever been were the demonstrations he went to when he was younger and even that had felt like an orchestrated dance between the police and the protesters. Gentle and political, Danny was nothing like L, but sometimes, he told the story so often he almost started to believe it himself.

When he was with a client, he had to be careful not to use any of the forbidden words. *Struggle, resist, rebel, queer*—and a host of others—were considered too radical by the State and had been banned decades ago, replaced with more innocuous words such as 'to make effort', 'to dispute' and 'to betray'. Queer, having passed through 'LGBTQIA+' at the turn of the century and 'Sexual and gender divergents' two decades later, now had no permissible equivalent that wasn't a slur. As the linguists working in the State knew very well, without a vocabulary to express it, there could be no concept. By banning the very idea of queerness, they hoped that the people themselves would also disappear.

Danny used the forbidden words all the time in his political life, so he had to be careful to make the switch. He could relax here, but he was also at work. *At the end of the day, this guy, as sweet—and generous—as he is, still works for the State.*

Danny saw that somehow his glass was empty again and the client quickly refilled it for him.

I'm still drinking too fast. I should definitely slow down.

* * *

Sweating in his cell, the General was thirstier than he had ever been in his life. He hadn't eaten in days and he couldn't sleep. His body hurt in every place he could imagine feeling pain.

Six days and six nights.

Six days since armed soldiers had dragged him away from the base. Six nights since he had slept on a real bed that wasn't just a pile of filthy blankets on a prison cell floor.

The guards had beaten him when he arrived

—And the perverts loved every minute of it—

and the General hadn't eaten a thing except a couple of Nutrition bars since he got to this tiny, damp cell.

His toilet overflowed onto the floor and there were cockroaches hiding in the shadows. He could hear them crawling all over him as soon as the lights went out.

I'll die here. Like a rat in a cage.

The first two days had been easier. He had been fuelled by his own rage and had spent his hours composing mental lists of the people he blamed and the punishments they deserved. The recruit, the bathroom sex worker, the officers who'd set him up. He had hated them all as deeply as one human can hate another.

Then the anger had passed and the self-loathing had started.

Why am I like this? he wondered. *Why can't I resist all these dirty faggots?*

Then suddenly he was overcome with rage again and wanted to hurt someone, kill someone, smash the people who did this to him like a rat under his boot. He missed the days when he could fuck whoever he wanted, when calling himself 'gay' hadn't meant anything to anyone.

With nothing to do but wait out the hours, days, or weeks until the State decided what to do with him, he lay, oscillating from hating the world to hating himself with no grey area in between.

The General, now Prisoner 7485, curled up into a ball and stared at the wall. He'd been caught red-handed and knew there was no way out. Public execution might well be on the table. He wasn't scared of dying. *Anything has to be better than living like this. Will it be the thirst that kills me. Or the hunger?*

A guard rapped his baton against the cell door and woke Prisoner 7485 up from the feverish half-sleep he was in. He automatically curled up tighter on his pile of blanket and tried to hide.

I never want to see another person again.

But for the second time that day, armed guards came into his cell, dragged him to his feet and made him walk the five flights of stairs down to a massive underground hall where he was being forced to work. Conveyor belts and hand operated machines filled the room from wall to wall attended by prisoners in white paper suits. The Nutrition Factory.

For the last decade, most of the residents of the City had come to depend on the Nutrition Company for food and it was an open secret that the majority of the snacks, bars, and meals produced by the monopoly came from this underground factory staffed almost entirely by prisoners.

Along the back, he could see giant stacks of the boxed final product—sticky bars wrapped in paper with smiley faces stamped on every box. The nauseatingly sweet smell hit Prisoner 7485 like a wall as he entered the vast chamber.

It's like some fucked up combination of decaying bananas and mouldy laundry. The last thing in the world it smells like is food.

"You're on packaging again, prisoner."

He just nodded and walked over to his spot at the end of the conveyor belt. This morning he had tried to resist, had refused to work and tried to escape back up to his cell. The guards, themselves long-term prisoners who earned rewards for keeping the factory running, had beat him for that and he soon learned his lesson. He got to work placing bars into boxes and tried not to think about food. Already the smell—or the hunger—was making him nauseous.

If I was still General I'd have all these guards beaten, I'd fucking beat them myself, I'd take them outside and—

But, Prisoner 7485 realised sadly as he lifted another heavy box, pulling a muscle in his tired back. *I'm not General anymore.*

* * *

Danny was still eating and drinking. After devouring his own steak and most of what his client had left, room service brought up a massive bowl of fruit salad and even ice cream.

Where the hell, do they get this stuff? thought Danny as he took a banana and unpeeled it as slowly and seductively as he could. This was the first real banana he'd seen in many years, since the global monocultures of genetically identical plants were all but wiped out by a fungus and the world's most popular fruit became one of the most expensive. He was so used to the artificial powdered banana substitute that, he noticed, the real thing didn't really taste of much. *What do I care? This sure as hell beats Nutrition bars.*

After dinner, his client ordered another bottle of wine and when it arrived Danny poured himself a large glass.

"Would you like some?" he asked, offering the bottle.

"Maybe in a little while, I'm pretty tired," said his client, pouring himself some water from a carafe instead.

Danny smiled. "I don't know how you can *resist!*" he said and then, just as fast, he realised his mistake.

What the hell am I saying? His heart was racing and he looked to see if his client had noticed. He just stared back at him silently.

Refrain, turn down, abstain. These were the alternatives, he knew them by heart after years of learning to carefully control his speech.

I forgot who I was talking to. A forbidden word! This guy works for the enemy—he is *the enemy. I must be drunker than I realised. Stupid, stupid, stupid.*

Chapter eighteen

I'm sorry," Danny began "I really don't know why I said that..."

His client was still silent. He emptied his glass and pushed his chair away from the table.

"You know? It's been a long time since I've heard that word."

"I'm really sorry. I hope you don't think I'm..."

"What, *resistance*?" He signed the word with disgust. "Of course not! You're too sweet to be with those dogs."

"Well, thanks...I..."

"But you know what?" said the client, glancing unconsciously towards the door. "It did kind of turn me on to hear you speak like a...*dirty rebel.*" He smiled as he signed another of the forbidden words. "Maybe you should say it again, L."

Danny was surprised to see the sign on the well-manicured hands of this State worker.

I might have a way out here.

"Well," he said, dropping his shoulders. "If you ask nicely..."

The client stood up and opened the glass door back into the hotel room. Reflected in the glass, the sky was just beginning to lighten in the east.

"It's nearly morning. Do you want to sleep?"

Danny was tired, but he was used to staying up all night. He shook his head.

"Good." The client smiled. "Because you've given me an idea for a new role play."

Pinar and Jason crossed the dry stream bed and the valley widened before them. The forest filled the horizon and the early sun was just rising over the valley cliff, casting a deep shadow over the meadow where they stood.

There was an enchanted air about the place and, without either of them noticing it, they were silent; their hands barely inches from each other as they walked. This was their second outing together, just the two of them, and they were enjoying each other's company.

Jason felt honoured to be shown around by Pinar.

She's practically a resistance legend, he thought to himself as he caught her smiling at him, her eyes emerald green in the morning sun. *And they brought me back from the edge. I owe them both my life.*

They walked in silence, both just enjoying the fresh air and the sounds of the morning. A high pitched *kee-kee-kee* echoed off the walls of the valley and Jason looked up to see a pair of kestrels flying by overhead and calling to each other.

"Are those falcons?" he asked, pausing and pointing upwards.

Pinar knew before she even lifted her head.

"Kestrels. Actually it's a pair of males that nest together in the valley. They've been together for a few years already. Ash calls them Bert and Ernie for some reason."

Pinar had never watched a lot of television.

"They're both males?" Jason asked, surprised. "But don't they need to breed?"

Pinar smiled patiently. "It's quite common. Neither of them have ever bred as far as we know, although they mate with each other all the time. They built a little nest on the cliff a while back." She pointed. "They seem quite happy there."

They both watched as Bert and Ernie flew by and called to each other again.

"You know," she continued, "this whole idea that animals only have sex and form partnerships to make little animals, it's entirely made up. And it's very heterosexist."

"I had no idea."

Secretly, he also wasn't really sure what heterosexist meant but was too shy to ask. The resistance was proudly fourth wave and trans-feminist and he'd had a good education as a result.

But it's a whole lot of vocabulary and precise terminology. I can barely keep up sometimes.

"Don't worry, most straight people don't think about these things..." She gave him a playful poke in the ribs. "Watch, they're going to do their courtship flight. It's pretty dramatic."

The kestrels flew straight up into the air, so high that they almost disappeared from view then in perfect unison they began to rock from side to side, flying close to each other as they descended. They separated for a few seconds, reunited and finally flew off together towards the cliffs overhanging the valley.

"Amazing."

"It is," Pinar agreed. "It used to be that they only flew like that in the early spring, but things are different now. Climate change or whatever." She turned and gave Jason a little wink. "Now it seems they like flirting all year round."

"So, are there a lot of birds that have gay sex?" asked Jason as they crossed another meadow full of flowers and brambles.

"Of course," said Pinar. "Animal homosexuality is at least as rich and complex as heterosexuality."

Jason couldn't hide his surprise. "Really?"

"Yes, dear." Pinar replied patiently. "Every major animal group has some—at least four hundred and fifty species have been recorded having gay or bi sex, but considering the institutional homophobia in the science world, the real number is probably much higher."

Somewhere at the other end of the valley, they could hear Bert and Ernie calling each other.

"You know, male elephants masturbate each other with their trunks," Pinar said, smiling playfully. "And female koalas mount other females from the side while they hang together on a tree."

Jason looked at her wide-eyed and nearly tripped over a stump as they walked.

I should probably be embarrassed having this conversation, he noticed. *But it's fascinating.*

"Go on," he almost whispered.

"Erm yeah, so other examples...female orang-utans for instance, put their fingers inside their female mates and male macaques sometimes have oral sex with each other in the sixty-nine position."

Pinar was clearly enjoying herself. She'd been considered an authority on 'queer ecology' back in the day, but out here in the forest she rarely got to share her knowledge with other people—Ash had already heard her stories a hundred times and usually checked out when she started talking about them. *But I miss this feeling and I like it. I like being listened to.*

Jason was watching her expectantly.

"And dolphins for example," Pinar continued, her voice more authoritative than he'd ever heard it before, her head a little higher. "Male atlantic spotted dolphins have a special soundwave they can produce to stimulate their partner's genitals and female bottlenose dolphins insert their fins or tails into another female's genital slit. Male boto river dolphins have even been seen inserting their penis into another male's blowhole!"

Jason blew air out of his nose in surprise.

"Amazing. How do you—?"

"I did a Ph.D. in biodiversity in the City back in the day."

"Biodiversity. Isn't that mostly about the number of species though rather than their behaviour?"

"Not when I study it." Pinar gave him a wink. "Behavioural diversity is absolutely a part of biodiversity and serves many of the same functions."

"And why don't more people know about it?"

"As I said before, institutional homophobia and biphobia is still a big deal," said Pinar sadly. "And there's an interesting double-bind. If animals are totally straight and never gay—which is what scientists always assume and what we were always told in wildlife documentaries—then being queer is 'unnatural' and 'artificial'. If animals are sometimes gay and humans are sometimes gay, then human queers are 'beasts, no better than animals.' Either way we lose."

Jason noticed the 'we' pronoun and was curious to ask more. Instead he said:

"I never thought about it that way."

Pinar paused by a particularly beautiful flower meadow to rest against an old Mediterranean oak. She was a little out of breath. *I'm not used to speaking so much! But I like it.*

"Shall we head back to the cabin soon?" she asked after a short while. "It must be lunchtime."

After all the walking and biology lessons, she was very hungry.

"Sure." Jason leaned against the tree with her. "Thank you, for sharing all this."

"You're welcome."

Jason began to look a little awkward and poked at a root with his foot.

"What is it?" Pinar asked. She could already read him like a book. "If you have a question, just ask, hon."

He blushed a little. He loved when she called him that.

"Erm...yeah. I wanted to ask you something about Ash. Erm, something personal if it's okay...?"

"Is it about her being trans?"

Pinar had known Ash for a very long time and she could no longer count the number of people she'd had to give a queer education to on her behalf. She usually didn't enjoy it—*people could be so uncaring, so naïve*—but she knew Ash hated it even more.

"No, no. Not at all!" Jason put up his hands defensively. "That's none of my business."

Pinar looked relieved. Jason bit his lip and poked at the root again.

"Actually I wanted to ask about the two of you...erm...if you, you know...have a thing together?"

Pinar was surprised by the question. She'd never seen Ash in that way, they were best friends, practically sisters.

I can't blame him for being confused though, after all these years, of course we probably look like lovers.

"We have a lifetime together. But we're not romantically attached if that's what you mean. Ash doesn't do that in general. And although I've certainly been with plenty of women, I'm mostly into guys these days." She smiled at him. "Particularly younger, handsome, revolutionary guys..."

Jason blushed and looked at the valley, the sky, a random mossy rock.

Anywhere but those green eyes.

Pinar knew she was embarrassing him, but she couldn't help herself. *He's adorable, far too young for me of course, but entirely adorable. And the resistance has trained him well.*

She remembered when most activist men his age were arrogant and macho.

But that was a long time ago, before the fourth wave, before the Femme Riots.

Pinar enjoyed talking to him, showing him the valley and hearing his stories from the struggle. She knew he would be well enough to go back to the forest soon, that he needed to find his *compañeras* and rejoin the struggle. But secretly, she wanted him to stay for a while longer. She wanted to be close to him.

They pushed off the tree and headed home. They walked in silence for a while and, as they crossed the river bed again, Jason asked:

"Would you mind if I sang a song for you? Something from my village? It's kind of a love song between a man and the land he works on."

Pinar turned to look at him and smiled. It was then that she realised that she badly, badly wanted to kiss him.

* * *

The kiss was as violent as Danny could manage. He lifted his head and said in his most dangerous voice: "Give me the secrets, *salope*. I know you have them."

He was beginning to enjoy himself. He was wearing a bandanna over his mouth and nose and was straddled over his client, his hands on his throat.

Being an angry rebel is much more interesting than being a desperate room-attendant.

His client, sweating in his suit, with his hands and feet tied to the bed rails was the abducted State officer. His eyes were wide open with intoxication and affected fear and he was rock hard with excitement.

"I...I don't know anything Sir."

"Don't give me that bullshit, *pute*," said Danny giving his client a playful slap. "You're going to tell me everything you know." He always swore in French, his mother tongue, and he found it a much more interesting language for domination than English.

"Well, I might know something..." implied the client, coyly. "More wine might loosen my tongue...Sir..."

Danny smiled. His client was terrible at staying in role. He reached for the bottle and took a swig of wine. Below him, the client smacked his lips with anticipation. Slowly and as seductively as he could, considering how much he'd already drank, Danny dribbled the wine from his own mouth into the client's.

Just like a baby bird.

"Now you'll tell me how to shut down the Life Accounts computers, *salope*!" said Danny, getting back into role.

"The computers, Sir?" the client looked a little worried.

Danny wasn't really sure how far he could push the role play. *After all, for me, none of this is that far from the truth—I really* am *resistance and some intel on the State's ancient computer system could be very useful indeed.*

He knew he should be careful, but the sleepless night and the wine were kicking in. He felt like taking risks and besides they were both having fun.

"More wine first, boy. Then you'll tell me how to bring down the computers."

Chapter nineteen

Danny woke up with a blinding headache.

He was alone in the bed.

Suddenly through the fog of alcohol, last night—and this morning—came back to him in a flash. After yet another bottle of wine and plenty of enacted torture, Danny got some very important information out of his client. Something that—if it was accurate—could entirely shift the balance of power in the City.

He rolled over and saw there was a note for him by the side of the bed. Squinting in the bright morning light, he read it.

"Good morning my darling, L.

You were so sweet while you were sleeping, I didn't want to disturb you.

Check out is at 14:00 so just let yourself out when you wake up. Please don't stay later though, I don't want any trouble.

Thanks again for last night. It was very intense. You were amazing as always.

Love, Y."

Danny looked at the small clock on the desk. It was eleven-thirty A.M. He had a resistance meeting that evening and he was desperate to share what he'd learned.

But he was also tired. The hotel bed was seductively soft and he'd only gone to sleep at 9am after his client had finally passed out from the wine.

I can sleep for a couple of hours and still make it out of the hotel and to the meeting in time.

"Just a little hour." Danny mumbled to himself as he lay back on the giant pillow that still smelt like last night's sex and fell back asleep.

* * *

The sun was already above the trees when Pinar and Jason got back to the cabin. They could hear Ash inside clattering around in the kitchen.

"I'll go and get some water from the well and check on your herb garden if that's alright," said Jason.

"Don't you want to eat first?" asked Pinar. "Smells like Ash is cooking up a storm in there."

"I will, I just thought you ladies might like some time alone first. I don't want to be in the way all the time."

Spontaneously, Pinar leaned forward and gave him a peck on the cheek.

"You're a sweetheart. Meet us here in half an hour or so and we'll all eat together?"

"Great," said Jason, still blushing from the kiss.

"Great," said Pinar, also blushing and feeling strangely like a schoolgirl again. She turned abruptly and went into the cabin.

"Mmm, smells good." Pinar stepped into the kitchen.

"It *is* good," said Ash with a twinkle in her eye. "But where's your boyfriend?"

"Excuse me?"

"You know exactly what I mean."

"He's...*Jason* will join us in a little while. He wanted to give us some time alone."

"So he's handsome *and* thoughtful? Quite a catch, Pin..."

94

Pinar didn't say a word. She took the lid off a saucepan and started vigorously stirring the sauce with a wooden spoon.

"Get out of my sauce! You'll make it all sticky again," said Ash, shouldering her friend out of the way and retrieving her spoon.

Pinar pouted and crossed the room to rearrange her herb jars instead.

"He likes you too, you know."

"I know, but..."

"But?"

"But I'm old enough to be his mother," Pinar protested. "Anyway, it's against our guidelines—he's still our patient after all."

"Well, he's almost better," said Ash with a grin as she stoked the fire. "And then he won't be our patient anymore, will he?"

"You're terrible." Pinar opened a jar of dried dandelion and held up a long, tangled root to show Ash. "We could roast this you know and make coffee. I know it's not as good as the real thing, but—"

"It's disgusting and bitter and tastes like dirt. And besides, don't change the subject!" Ash laughed. "He likes you. Do you like him?"

"He's...*charming*."

"With good politics..."

"Yes."

"And hot?"

"Yes," Pinar confessed, fiddling with the roots in her hand. "Fine, yes, he's very attractive."

"He's hot in all the right places, *I'd* say."

Pinar laughed. "I agree, okay? But *seriously* I haven't been with a guy in a hundred years. I've forgotten how it all works. They're so much more complicated than women."

"Shall I draw you a picture?"

"Don't you have a home to go to?" Pinar threw the dandelion root at Ash's head. She missed completely and it landed with a plop into her perfect sauce.

* * *

Danny woke up with a start. Someone was knocking loudly at the door. He looked over at the clock.

14:30. Damn, I overslept!

Panicking, he jumped up and wrapped the sheet around his waist. The person at the door was knocking without stopping, louder and louder.

A voice shouted, "Open up! This is the State. We know who you are. Open this door right now!"

Danny's heart was racing. He looked out the window, at the sea ten stories below. He had nowhere to go.

I'm trapped.

Chapter twenty

ou think we don't know what you are, boy?"

"But I'm not...I..."

Danny was terrified.

I pushed it too far last night and now my fucking trick has reported me to the State troops. I knew I shouldn't have drank that last bottle. And now there's an armed trooper in the hotel room pointing his weapon at me. I've gone too far this time.

"You're one of those whores from down town." said the trooper, poking the tip of his gun into Danny's firm chest.

Danny sighed with relief.

This is about sex work then, not the resistance.

He stood a little taller.

"My work is no business of the State. I am here under the protection of Y from Life Accounts—"

The protection he was quoting was a well-known policy in the City. As much as the State officially hated sex workers, they were still happy to enjoy the services they provided and for that they needed to be protected. For as long as anyone could remember, every State worker with enough power could extend protection over a sex worker under their employ. It was an unwritten law, but everyone respected it.

"Protection ran out at 14:00, boy."

He's bluffing. Protection never runs out.

Several times, Danny had been arrested in the street and taken to the City lock up. One quick message to any of his highest-ranking clients and he was back in the street with a pat on the ass and a nutrition bar in his pocket. Protection never ran out, everyone knew that. But Danny also knew better than to argue with a trooper who thought he was in the right.

"How can I apologise...Sir?" he said in his most subservient tone.

Well if nothing else, I'm good at playing roles.

The trooper touched his crotch where he was hardening by the second.

"There might be a way."

Danny wasn't particularly surprised. This certainly wasn't the first time.

* * *

That night when Kit got off from work, she cycled to the City centre to meet Nathalie near her office. She arrived and pushed her bike down into the wooded motorway valley to their usual spot and waited for her hidden amongst the trees and bushes.

Nathalie hated to cycle, but she had obediently brought her bike to work that morning so they could go together to the park. One minute after five, she left the Admin building and pushed her bike across the street.

"Hey," she whispered into the valley.

"I'm down here."

Nathalie clumsily climbed down through the trees pushing her bike until she found Kit leaning against a concrete slab. Her hair as always was immaculate, freshly shampooed with a mix of herbs she made herself and pinned on one side in the City fashion.

She looks fucking hot today, Nathalie thought, *of course, she's been at work.*

She looked around to check that they couldn't be seen from the street and, as soon as she was sure, she put down her bike and allowed Kit to pull her into a hard and passionate kiss. It was still a risk for Nathalie, so close to her job.

But it's worth it. Who could resist those lips?

"I need more of that."

"Then let's get moving," said Kit, pushing her bike down the slope to the main part of the motorway.

"The highway will take us nearly to the park and it's safer than the street."

Nathalie followed and nodded her consent although she didn't really need to. She always did whatever Kit told her to and they both knew it.

For Nathalie, cycling to the park was hard going. The motorway was only just intact and they had to navigate their way constantly around tree trunks and gaps in the concrete. When they arrived at the park, she was completely out of breath, but as she looked over at Kit, already getting off her bike, she saw that she'd barely broken a sweat.

They pushed their bikes over to the area of grass which served as a bike park. A volunteer stood nearby watching over the twenty or so bikes already left there.

Kit, suddenly overcome by impatience, grabbed Nathalie and gave her a forceful kiss on the lips. Nathalie kissed her back just as passionately.

I've needed this all day.

The moment consumed them and they stayed there holding each other for a long time, oblivious to the other visitors who arrived. Then they parked their bikes and headed out into the bushes to find some action of their own.

Her breath smells like coffee, Kit noticed. *Since when did that become a turn on for me? And since when did I start getting into apolitical, insecure girls? But hot is hot and besides, if her job gets me some good intel on the State, it'll definitely have been worth it.*

"Let's go in," she said finally, pointing towards the bushes. "I have so many dirty, beautiful things I need to do to you right now."

Chapter twenty-one

Prisoner 7485 longed for a bath, but at least he wasn't hungry anymore. For each shift that he laboured at the factory conveyor belt, collecting sticky, warm food bars, wrapping them and piling them in boxes, he was rewarded with a bar of his own. As a General he had never lowered himself to eating Nutrition bars.

Crap food for the stupid masses he had called it, back when he'd been able to get whatever food he wanted.

But now, he thought, *I think these bars might be the best thing I've ever tasted.*

Down in the factory, he was losing all sense of time and his mind was increasingly numb with each passing hour.

How did it ever come to this? I was a great man. I was a fucking king.

He remembered back to the days before the Crash and the Improvement. Back before he had come to the City and became a soldier. Back when he was the happiest he had ever been.

He lived in Berlin for most of his life and he had fond memories of that cold, bustling city. His good looks and powerful intelligence carried him through economics school and he became successful faster than any of his classmates. PhDs, job offers, he was spoilt for choice.

His first real job was at a multinational bank in the 2010's. He was open from the beginning about his love of men and—as he kept reminding his workmates—he was just like everyone else so they had nothing to worry about.

In Berlin he had a good place to live and he paid his taxes. Gay rights were already forty years old by this point and gay men married, had kids, and served in the army. Once middle class, cis, gay, white men like him had their demands met, identity politics were declared officially over. Mobilising around sexuality and sexual freedom became passé as the most powerful of the queer hierarchy got everything they'd ever wanted.

He remembered his promotion to 'sexual minorities liaison officer'. His job, as he saw it, was basically to hijack LGBT events in order to promote the bank. At one Pride, they'd even sponsored a giant, inflatable pink bicep on wheels with the bank logo printed all over it.

It was stupid as hell, he remembered, *but people loved that shit.*

He could clearly remember his first meeting with the board. The bankers scheming around the oversized conference table, minimum wage servants bringing him his coffee just how he liked it. Like all successful businesses, the bank was being accused of various financial evils—settlement construction in the West Bank, mineral exploitation in the Congo—and there were protests almost daily outside the Berlin headquarters. He learned that day, through six hours of powerpoint presentations, that it was the liaison officer's job to give the bank a friendly face.

"After all," they had said. "How bad can we be if we support the gays?"

Three months later, the bank was the main sponsor of Pride and, again, the bank was plagued by protests, this time by queer activists who began regular protests, die-ins, and blockades against what they called 'Pinkwashing'—the deliberate exploitation of LGBT+ struggle for commercial gain.

The bank was rapidly losing face so the handsome, acceptably conservative Sexual Minorities Liaison Officer was sent to give a string of media interviews, publicly calling out any criticism of the bank's sponsorship as radical homophobia.

"It's the radicals, the muslims and the transsexuals" he had said.

"They want to take away our hard-earned freedom."

The media took the bait and from night to day, the bankers gathered in their corporate tower became beacons of LGBT+ freedom, and the rabble of queer activists down in the street became homophobes. As a final coup de grâce, the Liaison Officer passed a motion that strictly forbid the use of the word 'pinkwashing' in all official bank discourse. It was a perfect scheme—the bank went from strength to strength after that and the Liaison Officer earned himself a hefty bonus.

Those were the good days. He had all the sex he wanted, all the coke and GHB and poppers and methadone he could use. And he slept very well in his luxury apartment overlooking the park.

"You're moving too slowly! Are you asleep or what?" One of the other prisoners was shouting at him from behind the conveyor belt. Prisoner 7485 saw there was already a big mound of nutrition bars piled up at the end of the belt waiting to be boxed up.

"Yeah!" joined in another prisoner from the next belt over. "You're not dead *yet*, faggot!"

"Maybe he's too busy checking out your ass 7340!"

"Well, who can blame him?"

They laughed and Prisoner 7485 put his head down and worked faster. He just wanted to be back in his cell.

But this was all his fault.

The Improvement had destroyed his comfortable life, but he had survived it. *Like a fucking phoenix, I rose from the ashes, worked my way to the top as a decorated General, went back in the closet so I could be the best.*

He hefted another box of wrapped bars over to the delivery bay. His back was killing him and he leaned against the boxes for a moment to rest.

But I just couldn't keep it in my pants.

"Keep moving!" shouted a guard.

The prisoner kept moving.

I had it all, he thought miserably to himself. *And this time there's no way out.*

* * *

Kit was at the point of no return.

She rarely came with other people. Although she faked orgasms almost every day and had become quite the expert at it, she usually kept her real climaxes private and just for herself.

Tonight, though, she couldn't hold back.

Nathalie was going down on her, tasting her, thrusting her tongue deep. The chemistry between them was palpable and within minutes they were surrounded by spectators.

Nathalie, she noticed, enjoyed having an audience and the more people were watching, the harder she seemed to work. Kit didn't mind, she even wanted to invite some of their watchers to join in, but it was already too late, she couldn't hold back anymore. She'd been on the edge already for at least half an hour and she had to let go.

She grabbed Nathalie's hair and screamed.

* * *

The guards were yelling again.

"You're too slow, prisoner," shouted an older, white guard with facial tattoos. 7485 had heard he was in for killing his wife. "I'm moving you onto Inspections, you lazy little—"

The guard grabbed 7485's wrist and dragged him over to a pile of boxes of nutrition bars like the ones he'd been packing all day. He pushed a small letter opener into his hand.

"You open, you check. Do you think your little *verger* brain can handle that?"

"Yes."

The guard lifted his hand to hit him.

"Yes...*Sir*."

After another two hours of work, Prisoner 7485 was desperate enough to try anything.

A guard near the door rang the bell to signal the end of shift and the new prisoners lined up to be returned to their cells. As they left the factory, they were handed a single Nutrition Snack to take back with them.

Prisoner 7485 knew that if he was going to get out of here, he'd have to work fast. So, as discreetly as he could, he slipped the little letter-opener into the pocket of his filthy overalls.

I'll take it back to the cell, cut my wrists open when the guards are gone and put an end to this. It won't be easy, it's not very sharp, but I'll do it. Another thirty minutes and it'll be over. I'll be out of here.

Despite his exhaustion, Prisoner 7485 realised he was grinning.

I always find a way out.

Chapter twenty-two

Prisoner 7485 joined the line at the door and shuffled forward patiently. When he reached the front of the queue, he put out his hand to receive the snack from the guard, but from behind him he heard a familiar voice yelling. Before he could even turn his head, a massive, meaty hand smashed against it. In blinding pain, he fell to the ground.

"Where is it, prisoner?" shouted the tattooed guard. "Did you think I was stupid, or what?"

Prisoner 7485 reached into his pocket and held up the letter opener. The guard grabbed it, giving him a kick in the stomach.

"No snack for you, prisoner. And two extra works shifts tomorrow."

Prisoner 7485 tried to reply but his mouth was full of blood. He tried to nod, but his vision went blurry. He tried again and the room went dark.

* * *

Night was over. The first light of the morning began to cast shadows slowly across the park.

What an evening! thought Nathalie as they walked hand in hand back towards their bikes. It was only walking together that she noticed how much taller she was than Kit, her paler hand wrapped around Kit's darker hand effortlessly.

The perfect fit.

Nathalie had to go to work in the morning and she knew she'd be exhausted all day.

But I'll only need to think about tonight and what we did here. I'll know it was worth it.

They collected their bikes and were about to start heading back into town, but somehow just weren't ready to leave yet. They were in the zone of new lovers where time becomes slippery. Entire nights together could disappear in the blink of an eye. They stood for a while with their bikes, but neither of them got on.

"Let's sit," said Kit, putting her bike back down in the grass.

They walked over to a bench near the cliff that fell dramatically down from the park to the sea and, still holding hands, they sat. The sun was just appearing over the horizon and the breeze coming off the water was deliciously fresh.

"This was amazing, thank you," said Nathalie.

"It was." Kit looked thoughtful for a moment, unconsciously fiddling with her hair.

She never does that, Nathalie noticed. *That's my thing, not hers. Is she nervous?*

"My name's Kit by the way," she declared with just this hint of nervousness in her voice. The State had a strict policy of naming and revealing her true name was a great sign of trust.

"Kit. It's a beautiful name. I'm Nathalie."

"Nice to meet you, Nathalie."

"Nice to meet you, Kit."

They sat silently for a while watching the sun rise.

"We need to protect these places, you know," said Kit finally. "The parks, the sea."

"Of course."

"And the forest…"

Nathalie stared back in surprise. *We've never talked about the forest before.*

Like most people she knew, Nathalie had never left the City and what she knew of the world outside, she'd heard mostly from rumour. It was taboo to talk about anything beyond the City walls, in particular the forest. *The guerrilla war, the resistance, defending the earth and all that, we just don't talk about it. Kit knows that.*

Kit continued, "Because if we don't, there'll soon be nothing left." She looked Nathalie directly in the eyes and continued in USL, keeping her hands slightly hidden and her gestures discreet.

"*The resistance needs people like us, you know.*"

Nathalie was too shocked to speak.

K—her darling Kit—was...*one of them.*

Chapter twenty-three

Prisoner 7485 woke up back in his cell.

There was blood in his mouth and he was pretty sure he'd pissed himself. As he lay on the concrete floor and stared at the blank wall feeling sorry for himself, somewhere beyond the walls of his tiny cell, he began to make out the sounds of birds calling. *A flock of seagulls maybe. They must be loud for me to be able to hear them in here.*

The sound grew louder as if they were right above the prison.

I wish I could see them flying and see the sky, just one more time.

Prisoner 7485, curled up perfectly still, listened to the birds in wonder.

* * *

Kit and Nathalie sat quietly listening to the waves when suddenly a massive flock of gulls filled the sky. Squawking and whistling, they gathered together over the cliffs of the park and headed out to sea in search of a meal. With everything that had happened to their populations—climate change, overfishing, pollution and hunting—the birds were finally reclaiming these abandoned parts of the City.

Just like us, thought Nathalie. *We're taking these places back too.*

She wanted to respond to Kit's revelation, but needed to find the words. She was just getting up the courage to speak when Kit stood up abruptly. She yawned and stretched and then announced loudly:

"This was *fun!*"

"Err yeah it was—"

"We'll do it again soon."

"I hope so—"

"Definitely. But for *now* let's get you home and ready for your long day at the office!"

Nathalie didn't know how to respond. She nodded and obediently followed.

* * *

At Ash's boathouse, her guests had arrived and dinner was served. It was going to be a feast. Pumpkin soup, fresh flat breads and a massive salad that they'd never finish even between the three of them.

Jason and Pinar sat waiting at the little table on the deck. They held hands and chatted softly about the day they'd shared together. Ash was still inside, busy in the kitchen.

"Ash, are you coming?" Pinar called.

"I'll be there in two seconds."

Jason squeezed Pinar's hand and asked:

"Can I hear some more stories while we wait?"

Pinar smiled and nodded.

"Well, ahem." She cleared her throat. "I guess we were talking before about gay sex in other animal species, but obviously, homosexuality is much more than just sex..."

Jason leaned forward, listening intently.

"Bert and Ernie's courtship flight for example. It's bonding. For kestrels, that's normal behaviour for straight couples as well, but many species have special courtship and bonding behaviour only for gay and lesbian pairs. A lot of homosexual bonding is technically non-sexual," she continued. "Male mountain zebras 'kiss' each other on the mouth for example and male bonobos do the same but with a lot of tongue."

Jason smiled shyly.

"Male bonnet macaques spoon their partners sometimes even holding on to their mate's penis while they're sleeping."

"Cute!" blurted Jason.

"Totally."

"And it's always in monogamous partnerships?"

"Not at all. There's every imaginable combination of multiple males, multiple females, two of one and one of the other, heterosexual 'primary' partners with homosexual 'secondary' partners—and the other way round. Not to mention the orgies and the self-masturbation."

"Seriously?"

"Have you never seen a dog rubbing against a lamppost?" Pinar laughed.

"Well yeah!" Jason loved these conversations. Every minute he spent with Pinar, he felt like he was learning something new, seeing the world in a slightly different way.

"Also..." continued Pinar, enjoying being back in her educational role. "Savanna baboons have been known to masturbate with their own tail and perform auto-fellatio. Walruses use their flippers. Female orang-utans make dildos out of vines, penetrate themselves with them and rub them against their clitorises."

"Orang-utans have a clitoris?"

"Every mammal species on this planet has a clitoris dear."

"I..." Jason was lost for words. "Oh."

Inside the boat's little kitchen, Ash was deep in thought, mindfully lighting a candle at her altar as she always did before dinner. On the shelf in the kitchen, she had several important objects from her life laid out—photos of her teachers, a stone from the Femme Riots amongst others, and now she was putting out something new.

In a box of her things, she had recently found a small framed photograph of a heroine of hers, someone who had changed her life in more ways than one. She placed the photo on the altar next to the candle and lit a bundle of dried sage leaves which burned gently, releasing their fresh, clean smoke into the kitchen.

She had taken several pebbles from the river bank that morning and to complete her shrine, she started to lay them around the photo in a semi-circle. She brought herself into the moment, took a deep breath and—

Suddenly—

She was gone.

Chapter twenty-four

A sh stood in a massive, screaming crowd. Thousands of men and women in a park somewhere. She could smell their tension, excitement, and nervousness. She felt instantly overwhelmed, bombarded with sounds and smells and sensations. She was jostled by people on either side and someone near her was blowing a piercing whistle. She could smell popcorn. The sun was high and bright; it was summer.

As she squinted against the sunlight and looked around her, Ash realised that she remembered this park. She remembered this day.

Somewhere at the back of the crowd, she knew a seven-year-old version of herself must be right now eating candy and holding hands with her mother, equally scared and excited to be in such a large group of people. Ash looked around but couldn't see herself.

She already knew that while she was here she was almost unnoticeable to the people of this time. As if to prove the point, someone bumped into her violently and someone else pushed past her towards the stage.

They look right through me as if I'm not here, but maybe it's better that way. What if I changed something?

Suddenly there was a tussle on the stage and one of Ash's greatest heroines stepped out and grabbed the mic.

Sylvia Rivera.

She looks just like the photo.

Sylvia Rivera. Latina, transgender and homeless from the age of ten. Radical in a world of people trying to hide and assimilate into the mainstream.

Uncompromising, outspoken and committed and furious at the betrayal of her so-called community.

I remember this day perfectly.

It was 1973, barely four years after Stonewall: the Christopher Street Liberation day rally.

Ash watched on as Mama Rivera—as she would one day be known—gave a speech that would rock the young Ash to the core.

Sylvia Rivera, a vision of fury on the stage, called out the gay and lesbian community for ignoring their trans siblings in prison, for ignoring the violence that she, and others like her, experienced daily at the hands of the police.

"You all tell me go and hide my tail between my legs! I will not any longer put up with this shit! I have been beaten. I have had my nose broken. I have been thrown in jail. I have lost my job. I have lost my apartment for gay liberation. And you all treat me this way? What the fuck's wrong with you all?"

Her voice was hoarse from screaming over the boos and hisses launched at her by the crowd.

This crowd who were supposed to be her community and family. The same people who enjoyed the privileges they did only because of the hard work and fighting of drag queens and trans women at Stonewall and the other riots.

This crowd who were only too eager to leave trans people behind, only too keen to denounce Mama Rivera as a 'man' and to keep her from the stage or put her at the front of the most violent demos until the press arrived and they took the mic back into cis-white hands.

Ash was breathless as she watched. She remembered this speech by heart although for her it had been a lifetime ago. Years later, watching the videos recorded on the day, it had become a major step in her radicalisation, a log on the fire of her fury that would fuel decades of activism and hard work, of uncompromising confrontation.

She blinked back a tear and took in the moment.

I'm so glad to relive this again. Even if only for a short time. I could stay here forever, so many things happened at this time, so much changed.

But already the world was fading in its familiar way. The colours of the park and its people started to disappear. Sounds became more distant and she felt herself spinning, falling. Ash reached out to steady herself, but what she grabbed was the kitchen counter. *Her* kitchen. Ash stood perfectly still, the final smooth pebble of her shrine still held tightly in her hand.

Pinar and Jason were standing with her in the kitchen and Jason looked terrified.

Chapter twenty-five

E verything okay, hon?" asked Pinar.
"I was...I was with Sylvia!" she replied with tears running down her cheeks. "Can I be alone for a minute?"
Pinar took Jason's hand and lead him out to the deck.

Ash touched the photo frame tenderly. Not for the first time, she felt a deep appreciation for her gift, a deep gratitude for the memories that it kept fresh for her despite her ageing mind. She placed the final smooth pebble down and completed the circle.

"What...what just...?" Jason attempted as he closed the door behind them.

Pinar gestured towards his seat at the table.

"Sit down. We need to talk."

* * *

The evening meeting was about to start and Danny was actually on time for a change. Since he left the hotel, he had thought of nothing else but getting to the meeting and reporting on what he'd learned the night before from his drunk client.

He had asked the facilitator to put him at the front of the agenda, but he was still third in line. He tapped his feet impatiently and waited for the meeting to begin.

"Evening everyone," said a young trans guy Danny vaguely recognised. "I'm afraid the official agenda has been cancelled as we've just received some serious news from the forest."

Danny was immediately concerned.

These people love their protocols. For them to cancel the meeting at the last minute, it must be something really serious.

A woman across the circle began to talk. She was covered in dirt, and looked like she hadn't slept in days. Danny figured she must be from one of the 'shoals' as the resistance groups in the forest were known.

"Hi, everyone," she said, smiling weakly, "My name's Michal. Most of you know me I think. I've been out with one of the forest shoals in the south for the last month, securing the wells. I just got back an hour ago. Sorry to interrupt the meeting, but I have bad news I'm afraid—three nights ago our shoal was attacked by State troopers."

The room was silent.

"We were okay," she continued. "We got away. A couple of us even managed to track the troopers for a few days and we overheard them talking. From what we could gather, we're not the first—another shoal was attacked about nine or ten days ago. We haven't heard anything from them."

There were murmurs of concern around the room. Danny knew people out in the shoals.

"There's more, I'm afraid," continued the woman. "The State seem to be planning a more comprehensive attack on all the shoals they know about in the next few days and they want to bring the fighters in to work in the factories."

"How many of the shoals do they know about?" asked someone from the circle.

There were around thirty shoals in the forest protecting the forest communities, but several of them had split into smaller groups and even the resistance wasn't quite sure how many there were anymore.

"Right now, we don't know enough. Just that a major crackdown is being planned. Obviously, I got here as fast as I could. We don't have much time to plan a counter action. I propose we split up into working groups and..."

In the shocking revelations, Danny's news was forgotten completely. He knew that an attack on the shoals took priority over everything else. *Without the resistance fighters, the communities in the forest will be unprotected. The forest itself will be unprotected.*

Danny leaned forward into the circle to hear better.

I'll help if I can. I just hope we have time.

* * *

"So you're a...*time-traveller?*" asked Jason, still visibly shocked. He ran his fingers through his thick hair and tried to avoid meeting Ash's eyes.

She sighed. She hated having these conversations.

"Sure, kind of."

"Wow."

"Well, it's not all that."

Ash had only come out intentionally, or like tonight, been outed accidentally to a few people in all the years that she had been journeying.

It's always the same process. Confusion followed by denial.

Then later come the arguments for why such a thing definitely, absolutely can't exist. Why I can't exist. And finally, some kind of acceptance usually tainted with a search to explain me. They always want to pin it all down to biology, socialisation, mental illness or a mixture of all three.

Ash had once described it as being exactly the same as 'the trans conversation' which she hated just as much.

Jason was currently at the confusion stage.

"I...had no idea such a thing was even possible," he said. "Are you...sure. I mean, it's not some kind of—"

He didn't have to finish the sentence, everyone knew he was going to say "delusion."

Pinar touched his hand gently and gave him a cautious look. Ash was famous for her short temper and nothing made her angrier than being accused of being delusional.

She had known and worked with plenty of delusional people in her time—through her clinic, through mental health support work in the City—and although she learned to respect their alternative views on reality, she knew her journeys weren't tricks of the mind.

Besides I have evidence.

Almost every 'vision' she'd had of the future had come to pass exactly as she'd experienced it.

Not least this guy himself turning up on our doorstep.

There wasn't a doubt left in Ash's mind that it was all real.

"Sorry," said Jason. "That was rude of me. I guess I'll need some time to adjust my understanding." He looked at Ash and said gently "Would it be easier for you if I continued this conversation with Pinar privately? I don't want you to feel like you need to educate me. And honestly I probably need some educating..."

"That *would* be better, yeah," said Ash. "Pin?"

"No problem." She gave Jason a generous smile and a squeeze on the leg.

Such maturity from someone so young—I knew I chose well.

"But later, okay?" said Ash. "I'm starving!"

Chapter twenty-six

That night would be Jason's last cleansing.

Ash scrubbed the dishes while, on the deck, Pinar prepared the hot water with rose petals she had brought from the tenacious old plant that grew all over her roof and fresh *yerba buena* from the garden. Jason prepared himself and the space near the boat. He knew tonight was important. He knew he had to be ready.

As he cleared the space and lit candles, he became aware of something he couldn't quite explain. A pulse of life within the land and within his own chest. Something new, and yet something very, very old.

Ash stepped onto the deck and gave Pinar a silent hug. Without speaking, they stepped over onto the river bank and began the ritual again for the final time that week. The forest itself seemed to fall quiet for the event. This time in spite of the wood smoke and the fresh bite of the mint leaves, Jason's eyes were dry. He had cried enough. He had moved through.

Later that evening, as Ash and Pinar cleaned up, Jason took a walk alone along the riverbank watching the ducks and the still, low water. He heard a loud *kee-kee-kee* echoing through the valley and didn't need to look up to know it was one of the kestrels. *I'm so lucky to have been in this place. I'm so glad that I got to meet these women.*

Jason paused for a moment at a curve in the river before turning and heading back to the boat.

And now I'm ready to leave.

Night fell and that meant it was time for Jason to return to the forest. He and Pinar stood together by the river, and could hear Ash off in the distance, watering her garden.

"Are you sure you don't want to stay another night?" Pinar asked him. "I know you said you always travel at night, but it wouldn't hurt to rest your ankle a while longer."

"It'll be fine," he said. "I'll be fine." He moved a little closer to her. The moon was up early tonight and her eyes looked even more beautiful in the pale light. "I'd love to stay longer, but I have to get back. I have to meet my shoal at the *rendez-vous* tomorrow."

"I know." Pinar looked at the moon thoughtfully. "Come visit us sometime?"

"Of course. I'll be back as soon as I know everyone's okay. And I'll send you a message soon."

Pinar smiled, but her heart was heavy.

I'm worried about him. And I'm going to miss him.

They fell silent for a while and listened to the rhythmic buzz of crickets.

"Can I give you a hug goodbye?" he asked.

"Please do."

They hugged then for three long breaths.

Pinar pulled away just a little to look into his eyes.

Wise beyond his years. I'd happily stare into those eyes forever.

She moved forward to lightly kiss his cheek.

Suddenly and violently Jason recoiled as if from a burning flame. Some memory had appeared, had forced itself upon him. For a few seconds, he was miles away in another time and another place—his heart pounded in his chest and his face was frozen with panic.

Pinar stood still, unsure what to do. After a few seconds, he shook and came back to her.

"*Perdón,*" he began, "I don't know why—"

"Don't apologise. It's not your fault. I didn't mean to push you."

"I guess I'm not a hundred percent better yet, I just..."

"None of us ever are. It's okay; I understand."

"Yeah. Thanks." He stood awkwardly for a moment then held her dark hands in his. "But, I'd like to continue this someday. With you. If you—"

"Yes. I'd love that," said Pinar. Despite herself, her eyes were watering just a little. "Take care of yourself please. And if you need anything, just come back, okay?"

She blinked back the tears.

"*I'll miss you,*" she signed.

"*Me too.*"

Chapter twenty-seven

Desperate and half out of his mind, Prisoner 7485 searched the room for something to kill himself with. The pain and humiliation were all he could think of. He had to make it stop.

He bashed his head against the wall. If he could do it hard enough he figured maybe he'd die. Or at least pass out.

After the third time, he stopped. He had a brutal headache, but he was still very much alive. He needed something with more of an edge, something more efficient. The room was empty except for the broken toilet which still overflowed onto the floor. He held his breath and knelt down next to it.

He gagged, almost threw up from the smell, but it didn't matter. It would soon be over. Dramatically he lifted his head and prepared to bring it down with all his strength against the metallic edge of the bowl. *Enough, enough of all this.*

He slammed his head down, but before it reached the bowl, his knees slipped on the filthy floor and skidded out from under him. He smashed down on the floor, landing painfully on his shoulder.

Blinking and stunned, he stared at his reflection in the underneath of the bowl. He was wet, covered in his own shit.

I'm too pathetic to even die properly.

And yet, as he lay there for what might have been minutes or hours, something began to shift in him, something at his very core. He was too exhausted for anger, too broken to be scared. He had never cried in his entire life. Not since that time when he was a little boy. Not since his dad came home that afternoon...

He had nowhere to go and no way out. Somehow as he lay, with his head practically in his own waste, he realised he was beginning to feel something new and unfamiliar.

He felt grateful that they'd caught him.

He had lost everything that he'd ever had, his money, his power, his dignity.

But I don't have to hide anymore.

The door to his cell opened. A trooper looked like he was going to step into the cell, but seeing him lying there, semi-conscious in his own shit, he thought better of it and stayed in the doorway.

"7485. Execution's set for next Tuesday. Public hanging."

The trooper turned and left, slamming the cell door behind him.

Chapter twenty-eight

A week later, Ash was taking the long walk back home along the river. She was tired and sweated in the morning heat. She passed an area where the bank had been washed away during floods last winter and plants were still recolonising. *Forty days of rain without stopping! And now it's almost completely empty. I don't know if this summer will ever stop.*

She passed tiny otter pups playing on the river bank, oblivious to her careful footsteps. She heard the sounds of woodpeckers and wrens rattling through the trees. This land she belonged to was bursting with life, even with the drought, and she drank it in. She was happy.

But she was also distracted. Days had passed since Jason had returned to the forest and they'd received no word. Pinar was putting on a brave face, but Ash knew that she was worried. There was nothing either of them could do but wait.

Ash arrived home. The boat was deliciously warm inside. She curled up in her little bed for a siesta. *All this walking is taking it out of me.*

She listened to the buzz of insects and the gentle splash of the river until she fell softly asleep.

* * *

Ash was standing at the base of a cliff. A sweeping landscape opened up before her. She didn't know this place, yet it felt familiar. She also knew that it was full of death.

A waterfall cascaded into a valley burned red by the setting sun. Rain fell all around her.

So much rain.

She could never have imagined so much water pounding the earth. Buried rivers exploded from beneath the concrete. Their sounds deafened her.

She watched as an army of ghosts walked across the land. Ancestors, armed and furious, the extinct, the forgotten, wave after wave invading the City and reclaiming what was theirs.

Ahead of her stood a terrifying thing. The absence of a thing rather than a thing in itself. A shadow cast by no-one; the brightest of holes, a gap in the world itself.

The no-thing was growing and as it became bigger it spun around, greedily sucking the world into its own emptiness. With a deafening roar, the trees, the buzzards, the land itself were consumed by its nothingness, pulled irresistibly into its whirl.

Ash felt that pull. She was being dragged in, too. She knew there was nothing good left here. There was nothing for her to do. She stopped resisting and allowed herself to be taken.

She woke up gasping for breath and drenched in sweat. The sun was setting.

I must have slept the entire afternoon.

As she caught her breath, she began to feel the knowledge of what she had witnessed aching deeply in her bones. *Something's coming. Something that has been consuming this land for longer than anyone could remember. Something that will take all of us unless we can keep running.*

She got up and quickly pulled on her shoes. She had to get to get back to the cottage.

She had to tell Pinar right away.

Chapter twenty-nine

An hour later, panting and sweating from the run, Ash arrived at the little cabin in the woods. But Pinar was nowhere to be seen. She looked inside the cottage, near the fire circle, in the herb garden. There was no sign of her friend anywhere. It was almost completely dark and Ash was more worried by the second.

Where is she?

The family of crows were back on the roof and as, she looked at them, the oldest, a female, called out. A deep *craaawk* that went straight to Ash's old heart. And she knew.

She heard the crack of a twig near the edge of the woods signalling someone's approach. It was Pinar. She looked awful. Her long hair was in knots and her eyes were red from the tears that streaked her face. She carried a large bottle of water filled from the well, but she hadn't closed it properly and it was leaking all over her dress.

"My darling, they took Jason, didn't they?"

Ash held her close and Pinar collapsed into tears. When she could speak again, she stepped back a little, stared at the floor and spoke frantically.

"A runner from the resistance arrived this morning just after you left—the State took him—he's being taken to prison. That's all I know. I never should have let him leave. I have to go right now. *I have to help him.*"

"Slow down, *breathe*. Did the runner leave directions to the camp?"

"Yes."

"Then we'll find him. We'll find him together."

Pinar looked up through her tangled hair, with something like hope in her eyes.

"You'd go to the City for me? You'd really do that? But you swore you'd never go back. I could never ask you to—"

"Honey," she said, softly, embracing her friend. "Let's go before I change my mind."

3. Journeys

Chapter thirty

It was barely dawn and most of the village was awake. A cockerel called incessantly from his favourite tree as a gang of squealing children took turns throwing each other into the warm, shallow waters of the river.

Elias was beginning to hate them. He rolled onto his back and rubbed his eyes.

Every damn morning it's the same. I need to get my boat moving and get as far away as possible.

But with the drought, Elias' boat home was thoroughly stuck in the river bed and, until it rained again, he wasn't going anywhere. A splash of water hit the window closest to his bed.

Enough is enough.

Elias got out of bed and, still in his pyjamas, climbed out onto the deck.

"It's the middle of the night!" he shouted. "Go and help out in the kitchen or something, you noisy little—"

"But Mr E," a wet child called back from the middle of the river, "it's *morning!*"

"For the hundredth time, my name is Elias. El-i-as. Now go away!"

"Yes, Mr E. Sorry, Mr E."

Still squealing and giggling, the kids climbed out of the water and ran towards the kitchen tent.

"I still hate them," he mumbled to himself.

They don't even call me by my real name.

Elias had been called Elias for the first five decades of his life, but just over twenty years before, in response to massive economic collapse, the State began to lose control over its subjects and a crackdown began. Like an abusive lover who gripped ever tighter the more it lost control, the State began imposing a whole swathe of restrictions on society, eventually coming to include language and naming.

Just the previous week, Elias had taught a class about the Franco dictatorship of Spain which in 1938 banned all names that weren't religious or traditionally Spanish from being given to newborns. For a while, Basques and Catalans could no longer call their children Basque or Catalan names and, as a result, Maria became such a common name that it received its own abbreviation: M⋅.

Franco knew that nothing was as important to people as their names. Following a long history of similar repression, the State reduced the name of everyone in the land down to one single letter of the English alphabet and overnight, Elias had become E.

After all this time, he still found it ridiculous. *Out here in the forest we're free from all that nonsense. Why can't we go back to using our real names?*

But Elias knew as well as anyone that culture can be stubborn and no matter how much he tried, everyone in his village was used to having a letter for a name. Anyone under the age of twenty had never known anything else. *So I'm E, or Mr E, whether I like it or not.*

The cockerel was still calling from his perch.

We should just eat the damn noisy thing already.

Elias wouldn't go back to sleep now so he stretched out and put on his glasses. Tied together with string, they had been fixed more times than he could remember.

As battered and useless as I feel.

"I'd kill for a coffee." He scratched his grey beard, stood up and started looking for his clothes.

* * *

The kitchen tent was already full by the time Elias got there. Adults and children spread out under the shade of the tent and pine trees, signing and eating and sharing their dreams from the night before. The sun hadn't even climbed above the mountains yet, but it was already hot and the Sett, as the resistance village was known, was buzzing with life. Colleagues and friends swarmed around Elias before he even sat down with his breakfast.

"Another hot one, eh E?"

"Mm."

Elias was doing his best to ignore everyone around him, but seemed to be failing.

"What are you drinking there? Herbal tea of some kind?"

"Hawthorn. Or mud, it's hard to tell the difference really."

"For your heart?"

"Mm."

It was only a small attack and even that was two years ago. Why does everyone keep making such a fuss about it?

"It's good that you're taking care of yourself. You're important to us, E."

No matter how much Elias tried to avoid people, they always wanted to be with him. He knew he was considered an elder by much of the community, but as far as Elias was concerned, he was a grumpy, old man and had no idea why they should love him so much. The others chatted around him while he ate in moody silence.

"I'm *so* excited about Harvest Day. I hope L makes her famous squash soup again."

"She always makes it. It wouldn't be Harvest Day without it. Though the gardening group actually harvested everything nearly two months ago."

"I know! Another year like this and we're going to have to rewrite the calendar. It barely makes sense anymore as it is."

"It seems to be a bit worse each year. I honestly remember when climate change wasn't even a thing. Or it was a thing, but no-one wanted to talk about it—"

"—Things only ever get worse!" grumbled Elias, suddenly joining in the conversation with his mouth full. "That's the whole of history *right there*. No-one cared enough about the planet when they could have actually changed things, when things still worked. It all went to shit, and now here we are stuck out in the dust eating sticks and drinking mud."

He took a loud sip of his hawthorn tea to make his point.

An awkward silence followed his outburst. Everyone had too much respect for Elias to contradict him so they focused on their food instead. Eventually one of his colleagues tried to change the subject.

"So E, I heard you're teaching about the history of USL today? That sounds like a fun class."

"It'll be fine." Elias pushed his wooden stool out and stood up. "Excuse me."

He escaped the kitchen tent and headed back towards his boathouse. It would probably be too hot in there by now to sleep, but he wanted to rest before school started.

I need all the energy I have to face those damned kids.

As he stepped out into the clearing between tents, he saw how perfectly blue the sky was and felt himself relax a little.

I probably shouldn't complain so much. My colleagues aren't really so bad.

Eight years ago most of these people had still lived in the City and were total strangers to one another. Some had worked placements; some had lived in the street. Some, like Elias, had fought with the resistance. But in the end they were all forced to leave, to escape to this sanctuary in the forest.

It certainly beats being locked up in a State cell. Which would have been the best of the other options.

Despite his complaining, Elias knew he was lucky to be part of this community. Part of living in the Sett was giving back valuable work. Elias had decided he was too old for anything physical, so helping out with the small primary school seemed like a good compromise. In no time at all, he was designated the main history teacher and was giving classes every day.

He adored history. In many ways he considered it his one true love. His goal was to train the kids to think critically, to analyse things for themselves, to never trust the official version of events.

They're so impatient, though. Too full of energy to concentrate. Not like when I was young.

Thinking of the chaotic class ahead of him, Elias descended into a bad mood again.

"Things are always worse," he mumbled as he kicked a pebble out of his way. "We're so fucking screwed."

Chapter thirty-one

The forest looks half dead here," said Ash, pausing to look out at the dry brush and fallen pine needles around her. "Are we nearly at the camp?"

"I hope so," said Pinar. "Are you tired? We could rest a bit?"

It was their third day hiking through the forest towards the resistance camp and, according to the directions the runner had left them, they should nearly have been there. Both exhausted from walking in the heat, they tried to rest during the hottest part of the day. Carrying heavy packs was hard work and, despite her best attempts to tie it up, Pinar's hair hung over her face in a sweaty, tangled mess.

"I've been tired for as long as I can remember," grumbled Ash. "Let's push on. I do wish we had brought more food, though."

"I can actually hear your stomach grumbling!" Pinar laughed. "Don't worry, we'll get there by this evening and I'm sure they'll have something ready for us."

"I'm not quite as optimistic, but I hope you're right. I kind of wish the runner had stayed a bit longer to take us to the camp. Are you sure we're going the right way?"

"She had other people to alert." Pinar held up an ancient compass, one of the few objects given to her by her father before he passed away, and looked at it thoughtfully. "Anyway, we'll be fine. I'm pretty sure of the way."

"Well as long as you're *pretty sure,* then I feel much better."

"Want to turn back?"

"No way. This is an adventure. Let's go rescue your boyfriend."

Pinar didn't respond.

She's just teasing me, just hiding her exhaustion in humour like she always does.

But when Pinar thought about Jason, about what the runner had told her, she felt sick to her stomach. Apparently, he had been abducted in the night, taken by the State from where he was supposed to be meeting his friends. And from one moment to the next, he was no longer free.

We had better arrive soon, she thought to herself. *We're not any safer ourselves out here alone.*

For another hour, they pushed on through the dry forest until finally they heard voices and the sounds of cooking. The air was thick with wood smoke and the smell of nettle soup.

"Las prímulas lucharán—!" Ash shouted as they approached the camp.

"—And the land will be defended!" came the response.

"Ready for some terrible resistance cooking?" Pinar whispered as they entered the camp.

Ash's stomach growled.

"I've never been more ready in my life."

* * *

"Alright, alright. Settle down. Settle...would you sit down already?!"

Elias' history class wasn't off to a great start. While he was underslept and in a particularly bad mood, the kids were as full of energy as ever.

I swear there's more of them than yesterday, he thought to himself. *Sometimes I think people here do nothing but breed—there's never a time when* someone *isn't pregnant. We're eating sticks as it is, how many more of these screaming little monsters do we really need?*

He finally managed to get his class sitting down in a teaching circle.

"Right, that's better. Ahem. So today we're talking about USL. Who can tell me—"

"Universal Sign Language!" three of the children called out in chorus.

"Yes, very good. But who can tell me why it's a misnomer—an...inaccurate name?"

Silence.

"Because it isn't really universal and it isn't really a sign language."

The kids sat and stared at their teacher. Signing was a big part of their lives. For once, he had their full attention.

"*Why isn't it a real sign language? We use signs, don't we?*" a young girl said and signed at the same time to illustrate her point.

"We do, but USL is just like English, only in sign. Real sign languages are totally different, different grammar, different word order and they grow from within deaf communities."

"What's universal, Mr E?" asked one of the younger children.

"Something universal works everywhere. So, a universal language, for example, can be used by everyone. USL isn't more universal than any other language though. Some people use it and some people don't."

"Why is it called *universal* then if it isn't universal?" asked the same child.

"There's an interesting story there that I'll get to later. But, in fact there *is* a Universal Sign Language which deaf people developed for meeting other deaf people who speak other sign languages, at international gatherings for example. You wouldn't understand a word of it, unless you speak a real sign language."

"Do you speak a real sign language, Mr E?"

"It's Elia—oh never mind. I do, actually. My mother was deaf and I grew up speaking to her in LASL. Levantine Ar—"

"And, and, and!" interrupted one of the youngest boys enthusiastically. "You speak Arabic too, don't you, Mr E?"

"Yes, until it was forbidden by the State. Which brings me back to USL…"

Once they got started, the class went better than Elias expected. He explained how, back in 2019, the State imposed a ban on Arabic, Spanish and all the other spoken languages the State considered 'local' or 'migrant' and soon, English became the only State-sanctioned language. The only *spoken* language at least.

The State, as most hearing institutions do, forgot entirely about sign language.

"So back in the early 20's—" Elias said standing, surrounded by his students "—The resistance, which from the very beginning had deaf members like my mother, started using something called Manually Coded English as a secret language. Who knows what MCE is?"

Silence again.

"When I was young, before speaking people recognised sign languages as real languages, deaf schools worked mostly in MCE. It's basically English coded into sign—just like USL—and it was easier for hearing English speakers to learn than real sign languages. Pretty soon everyone in the resistance learned it and were using it to sign secret messages to each other. We called it RS, Resistance Sign."

One of Elias' older students, one of the few that he really liked and who always paid attention, was waving her hand in the air.

"Yes, erm…H?" He was guessing really, he never managed to remember all their names.

"And didn't the State know?" asked H. "Didn't they realise what you were saying when you were signing?"

"I think it took a long time for them to realise that it was even communication. I'm sure they saw us signing, but just ignored—"

"But, but—" another student interrupted "*Everyone* speaks USL!"

"Not at the beginning, as I say. At that point, it was only really used and understood by deaf folks and the resistance and we only used it very carefully. Eventually, the State figured it out and co-opted...that is, they *stole* it from us."

"Why?" asked H again, her eyes bright with curiosity. "Why didn't they just ban it like all the other languages?"

"Good question. Well this was at the end of the Coffee Wars and, as I told you last lesson, the State was becoming more and more economically isolated as other countries stopped trading with it because of its terrible human rights record.

"When the State saw RS, they thought we had created some kind of brand new sign language that everyone could learn easily. The State figured that they would present it to the world as a new *lingua franca*—do you know what that means?"

No-one spoke.

"It's kind of the same as a universal language, one that everyone can speak and use for trade and commerce. Well, the State figured they would present this new universal language to the world, the other states would stop freezing them out and there would be trade again."

"And did it work?"

"Not at all." Elias scratched his grey beard thoughtfully. "Well, partly. They co-opted RS, renamed it USL and enforced a strict education programme until everyone under State control had learned it. That part was a huge success. I remember that, within a few years, almost everyone could sign. It was a really impressive transformation."

"So you didn't always sign USL, Mr E?"

"Not at all. Anyway, in 2024, amidst great pomp and ceremony, the State announced USL to the world and—"

H was waving her hand around again.

"Yes, H?"

"But, didn't everyone already speak English? Wasn't that already the, erm...*lingua franco?*"

"*Franca,*" Elias corrected. "Yes, precisely. USL wasn't really anything new. English was already the global language. And in fact, there was already a Universal Sign Language, only the State hadn't heard of it.”

“And then what happened?”

Of all the possible questions about history, Elias always dreaded this one. Sometimes he felt like he was just a glorified story teller. As if history, *his* history, was just a series of events, one after the other to be recounted in order.

These aren't stories for me though, they're memories.

“Well,” he continued as patiently as he could. “The State looked pretty stupid and their big plan to restore diplomatic ties didn't work. They retreated back inside the City walls and a year later the crash hit...”

“Tell us! Tell us!”

From outside the tent, the lunch bell rang and Elias sighed loudly with relief.

“That's for tomorrow, I think.”

I've spoken more than enough words for one day.

Chapter thirty-two

As usual, Kit had a full schedule that afternoon. Self-defence class at the warehouse followed by a special emergency resistance meeting called to discuss the forest raids. Danny went over to pick her up from her house so they could go together. He found self-defence class too emotionally intense so he avoided it when he could. He had conveniently booked himself in for a few dances at the bar just a block away from the warehouse and planned to meet Kit again later for the meeting.

"Hey, *darling!*" she said loudly as she opened the door. She grabbed Danny and ruffled his hair. "It's been *ages*. How've you been?"

"I'm good. I—ow!" he said as she rubbed her knuckles against his head.

"Let's go?"

"Do you have anything to eat?" he asked peering over her shoulder towards the kitchen.

"I packed us a little something something," she said patting her shiny leather handbag.

Danny saw she was wearing only leather today—knee high boots, a leather jacket, a short skirt.

How does she even get away with it?

They both knew that following the Femme Riots, the State had imposed strict rules on appearance. But like many of the sex workers, Kit, lived under protection and was happy to flaunt that fact in the face of ever trooper who dared to stop her.

Also, as she'd pointed out to him more than once:

"Society is profoundly racist. If *you* change your clothes, people see your white face and you won't get profiled. I don't have that luxury, so I might as well look totally fabulous and bad ass."

Danny could see her point.

"*Kit, I have something exciting to tell you!*" Danny signed in case the neighbours were listening. Even with protection, they were always careful when discussing politics. "*I got some really interesting information out of my client the other night. I really want to tell you about it.*"

"I'll hear it at the meeting tonight. Come on, I'll be late for my class."

"But—"

"Let's go already!"

Danny knew there was no point arguing.

"Going, going..." he agreed obediently and they headed down the stairs. "But can we eat on the way? I'm starving."

* * *

"This food is truly awful," Ash complained. "Who could mess up nettle soup?"

"Ssssh!" Pinar switched to USL. "*Maybe you should cook next time.*"

"Maybe I should."

A tall black woman with tight braids came over to where Ash and Pinar were sitting by the fire.

"Hey, I'm V—or Vicki—one of the runners," she announced and they both stood to give her four formal cheek kisses. Ash always tried to avoid the four kisses when she could—she had never enjoyed such close proximity to total strangers—but there were some social obligations that just couldn't be escaped.

"I've heard about you ladies," said Vicki as she brought herself a log to sit on. "Ash and Pinar from the Femme Riots, right?"

"The same," said Pinar.

"You're quite the superstars of the resistance, you know!"

Ash squirmed.

"I heard you came because of Jason. Are you friends of his?"

"Something like that," said Pinar with an edge in her voice.

"Ah, ok. Have you been debriefed yet?"

"Not really—"

"Let me get some soup and I'll catch you up."

As Vicki explained over dinner, Jason wasn't the only fighter who had been abducted. Six from their camp alone had been caught out in the forest that night and taken to the City, presumably to jail.

"There are signs that the State's beginning some kind of wider crackdown on the resistance shoals," Vicki said between mouthfuls. "Without their protection, the communities are also going to be under threat pretty soon."

Ash thought about the Sett. Neither she nor Pinar had been back in years, but they still had good friends there.

"Tonight we'll break camp and head to the City," Vicki continued. "We're meeting the rest of the resistance and the other shoals there. By the time we arrive, there should already be some kind of plan in place to free the prisoners."

"What would that look like exactly?" asked Pinar.

"It's not clear yet—even after all this time, the resistance is still pretty disorganised. Either way though, we'd be honoured to have you along with us."

Vicki got up and stretched.

"This soup is kind of awful isn't it?"

Ash smiled. She was beginning to like this person.

"We should reach the City wall by tomorrow night. We'll avoid the East Gate as it's guarded round the clock these days and we'll take the tunnels to get inside."

Ash and Pinar knew about the tunnels. They were practically a resistance urban legend—a system so vast they formed a city under the

City all centred around what used to be an underground shopping mall. With electricity so limited, the mall and tunnels had been left dark and the State had stopped using them. For the resistance though, they were a lifeline to the outside world.

"We'll approach the walls from the south west, quite near the sea, where there's a few tunnel entrances close together. Then we'll head into town."

Vicki picked up her bowl and looked ready to leave the conversation.

"We'll be moving out in a couple of hours—if you're not too tired?"

Despite her complaining, Ash was already eating another bowl of soup.

"No problem for me," she said with her mouth full. "Pin?"

Pinar nodded her consent and looked out into the forest with a serious expression.

I know that look, thought Ash.

She had seen it before in the countless demonstrations, meetings, and actions they'd organised together over the years. *Nothing in this world will stop her now.*

* * *

After class, Elias escaped the school tent and headed for the river. It had been a long day and a dip in the water—what was left of it— seemed very inviting. He walked through Central Square and paused, as he always did, at the Memory Board.

The Board had been at the very heart of the Sett from the beginning. Now though, it looked more neglected with each passing season. A vertical wooden notice board sheltered from the weather by a wide sloping roof, it was covered in photos, hand-written accounts, and the detritus of people's former lives.

This was their collective history, a reminder, when it was needed, of what had happened to bring them here, and that it could always happen again.

Elias noticed a newspaper clipping had fallen onto the ground below the board and he slowly bent down to pick it up. It was from 2033, just before the expulsions had begun, and was so faded and covered in dirt that it was barely readable. Sadly and carefully, he pinned it back onto the board.

"No-one gives a damn about history anymore," he grumbled. "They'd all much rather just forget."

"What's that Mr E?" asked H, appearing from the other side of the board.

"Oh...hello, H. I, ah, didn't see you there. I was just thinking to myself that the Memory Board doesn't seem as important to us as it used to be. We're forgetting about our history, about how we got here."

"Well *I* think it's important," she replied. "If we forget history then it repeats itself. We make all the same mistakes again."

"Well yes, well said, H. How are old are you again?"

"I'm nine, Mr E. You know that. I was three when my mum brought us here. Just after the Improvement."

"Yes, of course."

"When did *you* arrive, Mr E? What did you do before the Improvement?"

Elias cleared his throat and leaned against the Memory Board.

Well maybe I have one more story left in me today.

"I was one of the first to arrive here, you know..."

H sat down cross legged in the grass and settled in to listen.

"I was here before there were boats or tents, back when it was nothing but pine trees and the river and the mountains. After we escaped, after we became *exiliadas*, we walked for weeks. I remember being so hungry I couldn't see straight. We walked and walked and thought we'd never find a place safe enough. Nowhere that the State hadn't already destroyed."

"Who were you with Mr E?"

"My friends Ash, Pinar, and Oscar. We escaped the City with nothing but the shirts on our backs and Oscar used a wheelchair so we took turns pushing him. I remember how hard it was for him, how the chair kept getting stuck in the dirt."

Elias stared off into the distance for a while.

"Anyway, eventually we came here and found others like us. Luckily we found the wells within the first week and for a while we survived on food the others had brought from the City—"

"It sounds hard, Mr E."

"It was the hardest thing I ever did. News got round pretty quickly though and suddenly we were some kind of a community. Your mum arrived with you in tow a while after. We built our homes, grew our food and stole what we could from the State—"

"—Like the houseboats?"

"Precisely. Years after we came here, one of the scouts found them abandoned downstream, a few miles from the City. They still had fuel and everything, though there's not much of that left anymore."

"And what did you do before, Mr E? When you lived in the City?"

"Well, I worked of course and lived the best I could with the resistance. It wasn't an easy time for me."

Lost in his thoughts, Elias ran a wrinkled finger over another of the curled and faded photos pinned to the board. It showed a smiling white family playing in a city park. He vaguely recalled being in that park with his own family, before they were hunted down. Before he'd lost them all.

"No wonder we try so hard to forget," he said quietly to himself and H nodded sadly.

After a while, Elias looked down at his student. She still sat patiently waiting for him to continue.

"Ahem. Where was I?"

"The Improvement."

"Yes. Well, to be honest none of it surprised me very much. My family immigrated here when I was four and I grew up surrounded by racism and hatred. The Improvement was really just the same thing on a bigger scale. As you say, history always repeats itself."

"And are you happier now, Mr E? Now that you live in the Sett?"

"Happy is a big word, H. I miss my friends. Ash and Oscar. You're too young to remember either of them, I guess. Oscar died a year after we arrived here. And Ash just woke up one day and sailed her boat downstream."

"Why?"

"She'd had enough of collective living. She lives near Pinar, I heard, out there now—" He pointed vaguely into the forest. "I miss them sometimes. They always looked after me."

H stood up and suddenly grabbed Elias around the middle in a hug. "I'll look after you Mr E!"

Elias was too surprised to speak. He rarely touched anyone. He patted her head instead and silently blinked back a tear.

Chapter thirty-three

Kit's eyes were burning with sweat. Her black hair was tied up in a ponytail and she was punching and kicking as hard as she could. She yelled and cursed and, when she finally stopped, she heard applause.

She was teaching self-defence class.

"Okay, she said, stepping away from the home-made punch bag suspended from the warehouse roof. "Who's next?"

Three women stepped eagerly forward.

"One, two, three." Kit put them in order. "Five minute each without stopping, please, while the other two give feedback." She turned to the other twenty people in the class and said "The rest of you practise the grabs and releases from last week. Remember to check consent from your partner before you do anything, especially the grabs." Nods all around. "And...if your partner forgets to check, I give you permission to punch them in the nose."

Kit's students laughed and paired up to practise. She was only partly kidding: Kit couldn't count the number of times she'd been grabbed in a class by some overzealous guy without proper consent or discussion. Luckily she was really, really good at defending herself.

She circulated amongst the pairs, but they were well trained and didn't need much correction. After a few minutes, she went to rest against a wall for a while and watch her students. Watching them practising and taking care of each other, she couldn't help but smile.

The door at the far end of the warehouse opened and Kit saw someone come in. She recognised Nathalie's skinny hips, expensive haircut, and nervous walk instantly. Kit noticed she was wearing tennis shorts and a tight top.

Much sexier than her work gear.

"Hi...erm...K," Nathalie arrived and stood awkwardly with a gym bag full of her work clothes on her shoulder. Kit put her arm around her and pulled her in for a kiss.

"I'm glad you could make it, Nathalie."

"Thanks, me too. I'm glad to be here."

"Any problems with security?"

"No, the person at the door said you'd told her I'd be coming."

"Yeah, cool. Hold on a sec; let me introduce you."

"Nice work everyone," Kit announced to the class, "Gather round please, I'd like to introduce my friend, Nathalie. She's new to the resistance which is why you won't have seen her in meetings yet."

Nathalie went round the group giving cheek kisses to each and every one of Kit's students.

She's still so formal, Kit reflected, watching her. *but I kind of like it. And her legs look amazing. She should wear shorts every day.*

Although this was her first self defence class, Nathalie had already been to a few introductory meetings that week through Kit's connections and Nathalie's promise to bring the resistance anything interesting she might come across at work. She had been given access to the lowest security level spaces. The evening after next she was already signed up to volunteer at one of the soup kitchens and Kit couldn't have been prouder.

Kit had the class gather closer together in a circle and sit down.

"The physical techniques are really coming on well. It all looks great. This afternoon I'd like to come back to the vocal work some of you started a few weeks ago. Using our voice as a weapon and learning to keep it strong even in scary situations. Who would like to present to the group what we lear—"

Kit saw someone else had come into the warehouse and stood quietly near the door.

"Come on in!" said Kit. "Don't be shy."

"Hi," said the person so quietly Kit could barely hear. "I was wondering if I could join the class...Sorry, I know you're in the middle."

"No problem. Tuesdays and Thursdays are a closed group, but today you're more than welcome to join us."

The person came over and joined the circle. Kit didn't recognise them; they had short brown hair and wore tight jeans and glasses.

"Thanks," they said. "My name's Rhona and..."

One of Kit's students, a fiery young woman called Alex stood up. She looked furious.

"Alex?" asked Kit. "Everything okay?"

"We're allowing *men* into the class now?" she blurted out.

"I'm trans..." said Rhona softly. "I'm a woma—"

"You're a *man*." Alex was shaking. "We've heard it all before, you know? Putting on a nice dress doesn't make you a woman. It makes you a man trying to colonise our spaces."

Rhona sat in silence. Her arms had unconsciously wrapped around her knees for protection.

"I...don't—" she began, but her voice broke and she couldn't continue.

Kit stood up and met Alex's glare.

"Alex, I think you need to shut up now."

"Fuck you!" Alex shouted back. "I'm not going to stand here and be told to shut up for protecting this space." She glared at the group still seated around her that she had been training with for months. They glared back at her. She felt suddenly exposed until two of her friends stood up and came over to join her.

"We'll be bringing this to the *meeting*," one of them said, spitting out the threat.

"Let's go," said Alex, gathering her friends and pushing them towards the exit. Before Kit could say another word, they had stormed out of the warehouse and slammed the door behind them.

The group sat for a moment in shocked silence.

"I'm really sorry..." Kit began softly. But Rhona, still grabbing her knees was already in tears.

Chapter thirty-four

That afternoon, after Kit's self-defence class, the squatted warehouse became a meeting room. Nearly a hundred people crammed in, sitting in concentric circles. At the top of the agenda were the raids in the forest and preparation for a counter action.

Only five minutes in and the meeting had already been derailed. Kit sat as calmly as she could with Danny on one side and Rhona on the other who was already back in her defensive knee hugging posture. Kit would have liked to have Nathalie there for support, but it would be months before she would have access to this level of meeting. Alex stood across the circle practically screaming at her.

"The self-defence class is supposed to be a *safe space.*" Alex yelled. "A women-*only* space. How can I feel safe when I train if there's a *dick* in the room?"

Kit was trying very hard to keep calm.

"This isn't the time or the place for this discussion," she said. "But actually—"

"Well *of course* it isn't. No-one ever wants to talk about these things."

Kit continued as if she hadn't been interrupted.

"But actually, I've never declared it a women-only space, just a consensual, respectful one. How people identify is none of my business."

"But it *is* a women's only space. The guys have their class on Fridays."

"The point is moot," said Kit calmly. "Rhona is a woman."

"*He's a man in a dress!*" shouted Alex. Her friends stood next to her now.

"*A man in a dress!*" they joined in.

Kit glanced over at the facilitator, an old friend of hers who already looked exhausted and overwhelmed by all the shouting. Kit's expression clearly asked permission and the facilitator nodded. Kit stood up.

"Okay Alex," she said quietly. Danny recognised that tone immediately.

"*This Alex person had better be careful,*" he signed silently to Rhona who nodded in agreement.

"Let's make this perfectly clear," Kit continued. "Rhona is welcome into my class any time she likes. She has been nothing but respectful. You on the other hand have been offensive, obnoxious, and—by calling yourself the authority on what women should look like and reducing women to our genitals—downright fucking *misogynist—*"

Alex looked too shocked to speak.

"You will *not* be welcome in my class again."

Kit sat back down next to Danny and caught her breath. She knew she was overstepping meeting protocol, but this meeting was already a shambles. "*And...*" she continued in USL. "*If you go on like this, you and me are going to have problems.*"

"She's threatening me!" Alex cried, still standing. She looked at the facilitator. "Are you going to just sit there while this *tranny* threatens me?"

The room fell suddenly, completely still. Even outside, the birds seemed to stop calling for a moment. In her twenty years with the resistance, no-one had ever publicly discussed Kit's trans-ness. Most people assumed she was cisgender. She had never brought it up, not once. Danny put his hand comfortingly on her knee and was about to say something, but Kit stood up, her arms open, eyes glaring.

"Excuse me?"

"You heard me!" said Alex, her voice entirely out of control now. "We all know what you are!"

Kit was about to speak when, to her surprise, Rhona stood up next to her. In a powerful voice, entirely unlike the quiet, shy one Kit had heard that afternoon, Rhona shouted loud enough that her voice echoed off the walls.

"That's *enough!*"

Alex's mouth was open.

"Sit down and shut the hell up because no-one wants to hear your vicious bullshit anymore." shouted Rhona. "If you want to beat on women and hate on oppressed minorities, go join the fucking State already."

Alex paused for a moment. Then before she could think better of it, she was running towards Kit and Rhona with her fists out.

In a flash, Danny was on his feet. Kit bent down and took off her heels—her very dangerous heels—and held them in one hand. Rhona braced herself and clenched her fists. People instinctively began clearing the floor as Alex stormed across the room. Kit lifted her heels ready to strike.

"Wait!" someone shouted from the back of the meeting. Alex paused barely two metres from Kit and turned to the voice. "I'm trans too!" they announced. "And if there's a fight, then bring it!"

A woman stood at the other end of the room.

"I'm not trans," she said, "But count me the hell in."

"Me too," said a third also standing. "I'm genderqueer and I defend my trans sisters' right to be here."

One by one the entire room got to their feet.

"I'm *done* with this shit," shouted another. "Get the hell out of our space."

"This isn't feminism, it's a *witch hunt*. Go join the State."

Surrounded by a room full of enemies, Alex and her friends stood frozen, suddenly looking terrified. They paused for a moment, looking around them. They were entirely alone. Then without another word, for the second time that day, they ran out of the warehouse.

* * *

Out in the forest, the resistance shoal was getting ready to move. The camp was loud and stressed. People shouted back and forth as they took down tents. Pinar wanted to leave immediately, but they were going to move as a group and breaking camp for thirty people would take time.

She directed her impatience into helping pack up the camp. Ash watched her sweating and lifting logs with her long hair tied in a bun. She moved like a woman half her age, a fierceness to her movements that was new and yet familiar.

Just at it was getting dark, everyone sat down for a final moment of calm before the long walk. Ash and Pinar sat next to each other as the entire camp came together in a large circle around the fire. A gentle silence fell over them.

Each person sat for a while with their thoughts and their worries. They were held by the circle, by this determined group so dedicated to their cause and their missing friends. There was a collectivity here, a group living that Pinar and Ash had known in days passed. Something familiar embraced them and held them close.

The moment ended. The fire was put out and the camp was ready. Silently, as one, they moved out into the dark night.

* * *

In the warehouse, the facilitator, finally reprising his role, stood up and cleared his throat.

"I'm afraid we're out of time for this evening. I propose we postpone until tomorrow morning at six A.M. We still need to discuss the forest situation and Danny apparently has some very interesting intel for us."

Danny rolled his eyes and groaned. For him, six a.m. was basically the middle of the night.

After the meeting, Kit dragged Danny to the bar where she worked. A loud pub was the last place he wanted to be on his night off but he rarely got the chance to spend time with his friend and after all the drama, she wasn't taking no for an answer.

"It's so ridiculous!" she shouted in his ear. He had to lean in close to hear her. "What the hell were they even *doing* in our groups for all that time? And *outing* me in public. I actually wish we'd had the chance to fight."

"I'm glad you didn't. You would have broken her, K."

"She deserves it. Who the *fuck* is she to talk about occupying space when her and her friends occupied *my* class."

"I know, I know." Danny answered, barely suppressing a yawn.

I really need to get more sleep.

"Well, they're gone now."

Kit still looked angry as she drank from her bottle of beer. Danny seized the opportunity to speak.

"Oh wait! I still haven't told you what I found out from my client!"

She gave him a stern look.

"This is important. Don't change the subject."

"Sorry," said Danny, glancing down at the floor.

"You're forgiven." Kit looked up at the clock. "Anyway it's fine, my girlfr—erm...N will be here soon, I'm excited for you to meet her—She's so incredibly hot!"

"Erm...great," said Danny doubtfully. "But I can't stay long. The meeting was postponed until tomorrow morning at seven, right?"

"Six, dear."

Danny made a face of disgust.

"Let's drink! I want to get you *so* drunk tonight. "

Danny wasn't sure he liked the sound of that.

* * *

While the entire village was preparing for Harvest day—hanging streamers from trees, preparing the kitchen stage for performances, and cooking up a huge feast—Elias took the opportunity to be alone. The water was low, but the perfect temperature. He had an hour or so before the festival began and he planned to thoroughly enjoy it cooling off in the river. When he lowered himself in from the bank, he had to sit on the river bed just to submerge himself.

Elias was worried. *It's not right that the water's so low. If it doesn't rain soon, the wells will dry up. When that happens, there really aren't any good options.*

Elias placed his glasses on the river bank. Pinching his nose and holding his breath, he dipped his head under the water. He loved the silence and calmness of being below the surface. It was perfectly dark down there; cool and still. He felt like he could stay forever.

A minute, two minutes, and his lungs began to hurt in a familiar way. *If only I didn't need to breathe, I'd stay down here in the quiet. Away from people. Away from so much painful history.*

His instincts were stronger, though. He burst out of the water. He gasped for air. He took a deep breath and another, but his lungs were still burning.

Smoke, he realised. The air was full of smoke.

He coughed. This wasn't the gentle smoke of a camp fire. He could smell burning grass and bush. He could already hear the roar of flames coming from the direction of Central Square.

The forest, his home, was on fire.

Chapter thirty-five

P anicked voices shouted out in the darkness and Elias ran towards them, pulling on his clothes and his glasses as he went. He could see the fire in Central Square, light flickering off the pine trees standing all around the clearing. As he got closer, he could see the Memory Board already engulfed in flames.

"My god, what happened here?" he shouted as he joined a line of people passing buckets of water from the river. "How did this start?"

"No idea!" shouted a colleague from school as she passed Elias a heavy bucket that sloshed over his trousers. "I was just walking home when I saw it. We're so careful with the cooking fires. This couldn't have been an accident."

The fire in the square rose ten metres into the air, dangerously close to the lowest branches of the pines, which sizzled and popped from the heat.

"And the Memory Board," Elias said sadly. "It's completely destroyed."

"Just be grateful it hasn't reached the trees. If it does, there's no way we'll be able to stop it."

Elias passed the buckets even faster.

The community sweated and doused the flames into the night until slowly they began to overtake the fire. Another hour of hard work later, Elias watched as the last flame was stomped out barely a metre from the edge of the clearing.

This can't have been an accident. Someone set this fire intentionally. Someone wants to destroy the village.

Chapter thirty-six

N, this is D."

They hadn't moved from the bar and Danny was already dizzy. As always in public spaces, they used their State names: full names were strictly for resistance or in the privacy of the home.

"I told you about him. The stripper."

"*Dancer,* actually. Nice to meet you, N." They exchanged kisses.

"Hell no!" shouted Kit, far too loudly. Danny noticed she was a little drunk. "I've seen you dance, boy. You're a stripper through and through. My old grandma could dance better!"

"What's gotten into you, K?" Danny laughed, "Is this what you look like when you're in love?"

She gave him a hard poke in the chest.

"Shut up!" she said, but smiled.

Danny noticed that the two women were standing as close to each other as they could get away with and looked at each whenever they could. He had never seen Kit so excited about someone before.

"I'm just kidding." Danny turned to Nathalie. "Careful with this one, she's gonna work you hard, you know."

Nathalie replied with just a little sass:

"Yes, I've noticed..."

"*Anyway...*" Kit continued. "I didn't tell you yet, did I? *N joined the erm...thing that begins with R.*" she said in a conspiratorial whisper. "And she's already got a full schedule of meetings and barely any time to sleep—so now she's officially part of the family!"

Danny looked confused.

"The thing that begins with R...oh!" He almost said 'resistance' out loud. "Erm. So welcome to the family I guess?"

Nathalie smiled politely. "Thanks. It's just one more reason I'm glad I met K." She turned to her. "Hon, could you get me a drink? I'm just going to the bathroom."

"I'll get you two. You have some catching up to do."

Nathalie smiled and left.

"She seems nice," said Danny. He was slurring a little from the gin. "Less pushy than you described her..."

"I never said she was pushy, just...you know...a bit in love with me."

"Which doesn't seem to be a problem anymore."

"Well, no. I admit, I'm pretty into her. And look, she's already joined the erm...*R—thing*," Kit said, looking around suspiciously at the other people in the bar.

So many skills, Danny thought to himself, *but subtlety is definitely not her art.*

"Well, I'm not surprised that you'd find an obedient partner..."

"She *is* quite obedient. That's definitely one of her charms."

"It's a little fast though, isn't it? From Admin worker to being part of the R-thing in a few weeks."

Kit had excellent selective hearing.

"Another drink?"

"Erm...I should probably get going..."

Kit continued to ignore him and ordered four more shots from the bar.

"Cheers!" she said enthusiastically as Nathalie came back. They raised their glasses.

"Here's to too many meetings and not enough sleep!"

Danny's glass nearly slipped out of his hand as they clinked glasses. *I really should go to bed.*

* * *

The shoal had been walking for hours, following a dry river bed through the valley towards the City. Ash and Pinar had been in almost constant movement for days and were beginning to feel weary from their sleepless nights on the ground.

"Are you okay? You look exhausted," Pinar asked gently as their path started climbing up the side of the valley.

"I'm fine," said Ash, almost slipping on a rock.

"Is your arthritis playing up?"

"Let's pretend it isn't." Ash clambered over more rocks and loose scree. "Let's pretend we're at home drinking tea."

"Sure thing, hon. Whatever helps."

They climbed uphill for another hour until they found themselves high on a dusty cliff, a sweeping panorama before them of the moonlit valley and forest.

The shoal stopped to rest.

Out of breath, Ash sat down near the cliff edge amongst the dust and pebbles to take in the scene.

From here, it seemed to her that the whole world was dry and dead. Even the forest itself, which had survived so many droughts and floods over the last decades, looked like it was finally giving up on life. Down below, in the canopy, she could see great gaps—old oaks and pines felled by winter winds but never replaced. She rubbed her fingers in the soil. It was bone dry, practically dust. No wonder nothing could grow here.

Pinar joined her.

"It looks bad, doesn't it?"

"Yeah," Ash replied sadly. "It's gotten so dry out here, I didn't even know. Our valley's really escaped the worst of it."

"And tomorrow we'll reach the Ring. I heard it's even worse than when we left."

The Ring was the name given to the dead zone surrounding the City walls—a swathe of burned, eroded forest destroyed by the State.

"It's wider every year and they're still burning," said Ash angrily.

"Just to make it easier to spot resistance groups. They don't even use the wood, they're just killing the forest for politics."

"It's always been for politics. That or money, which is almost the same thing."

"Yeah." Ash looked over the dry canopy below them. "In the end though, it won't be the State that kills the forest but this fucked up climate. All that oil and gas and power gone up in smoke. What a waste."

Pinar took her friend's hand. There was nothing she could say that didn't sound like a platitude so they sat in silence, looking out over the land.

After a while, she noticed a small herd of red deer had appeared in a clearing below them. They moved silently, nibbling on leaves, silver in the moonlight. Pinar turned to point them out to her friend, but Ash had already been watching them for a while. Her face looked calmer than it had in days.

After an hour of rest, they heard Vicki calling. It was time to move out.

Chapter thirty-seven

Harvest Day was officially postponed until the following night. No-one felt like celebrating while there was still smoke in Central Square. The Sett was alive with speculation and fear. If the fire *was* an accident, who could have been so careless? If it wasn't, then something very serious was happening. The Sett itself might be in danger. People were frantic, meeting after meeting was called through the night.

"E? E?"

"What, what...?"

It was Elias' neighbour from the next boat along. He was shaking him awake.

"You fell asleep, mate."

Elias looked around at the faces gathered around him. He had dozed off in a meeting.

"Go to bed already," said his neighbour softly. "We're not even nearly finished and we'll still need teachers in the morning."

"Okay, thanks—"

"Rest well, E."

"Night."

Elias dragged himself back to his warm little boat and was asleep within seconds.

He slept fitfully that night. He dreamed of a fire that could not be extinguished. An unbearable heat that threatened to consume the world. He fought and ran, but there was nowhere to escape. He woke just before dawn, covered in sweat, his heart pounding in his chest.

The sun appeared over the trees just as the shoal arrived at the edge of the forest.

"My God," said Pinar.

Ash was silent. It was even worse than she'd expected.

They stood at the boundary between two worlds, behind them the forest, dry as it was, still alive with trees and deer, squirrels and nettles. Ahead, spreading out as far as they could see was only charred soil, felled trees, the total destruction of the Ring.

Vicki came over.

"It's not pretty, is it?" she said. "We made good time so we're going to set up camp down in one of the *arroyos*—the dry river valleys—and get some sleep. You two must be exhausted."

"We're pretty used to walking," said Pinar more cheerfully than she felt. "But sleep does sound good. Show us the way!"

Although Pinar was showing a brave face, reaching the Ring marked the end of four tortuous days and nights for her. Since the moment she'd found out about Jason's abduction, she'd been racked with guilt, with self-doubt, but most of all with fury at those who had penetrated their sanctuary and taken away someone already so dear to her. *I've only just met him, but I already miss his smile. How is that even possible?*

If she was honest, she thought about Jason, and the others like him, constantly. The walk, first to the camp and now to the Ring, had been hard going and that at least had kept Pinar focused and able to hold it all together.

As she helped Ash set up their little tent, she had the impression that her feelings could burst from her chest at any moment. She wanted to scream and cry and let it all out. Instead, as she always did, she smiled. She smiled and hid her pain and carefully unrolled their sleeping mats.

* * *

Danny was in a meeting again.

Sometimes it feels like all I do is go to meetings, work, and sleep.

This morning, though, he was glad to be there—despite his hangover. After two failed attempts to bring his news to the *mesa*, he was finally at the front of the agenda. As usual, he sat next to Kit. The warehouse was packed.

"Good morning everyone," said the facilitator cheerfully. "Thanks for getting here so early. I've been asked to keep the meeting focused today after our *small tangent* yesterday."

Danny gave Kit a smile, but she didn't see it. She was thinking about Nathalie.

I wish she had her clearance already. I want to see her in meetings, to see how she is with other people, learn what else she can bring to the resistance. She's so shy, insecure...almost like my clients. And she worships me like they do. But I'm not sure if I want that. Maybe I want her to stand up for herself more. Maybe I want—

She realised the facilitator was still speaking.

"First on the agenda, postponed from last night, is Danny with some interesting intel."

Despite the fact that he performed for an audience every night at the bar, Danny hated public speaking. He was wearing a tight white t-shirt and, without looking, he knew he was sweating under his armpits. He stood up and cleared his throat several times.

"Ahem. So yeah, hi everyone."

"Hi Danny," teased Kit.

"Yes, hi Kit. Ahem. Well, basically, it's this, one of my clients—he calls himself Y, but I doubt it's his real name—works for Life Accounts. He's an engineer of some kind and erm...under some *very specific conditions*, he told me that there was an electric surge last month which has left most of the State servers fried to hell. Since

163

then, the Life Accounts system—basically the entire State economy—is being managed from a single warehouse of computers."

He looked around the room, people looked both surprised and intrigued.

"We all know the protocol—obviously he could have been lying and as usual we'll need to check everything," he continued. "But anyway, he said that more parts are being brought in from outside the City, but that'll take a week or two which means that for the next week at least, if he was telling the truth, then the State's vulnerable. If we're thinking of attempting some kind of large-scale action, at the prisons for example, this is the time."

"Thanks for that, Danny," said the facilitator. "We'll need to verify the intel, but this sounds very exciting. Okay, next on the agenda..."

Danny sat down, his hands were shaking.

"*Why didn't you tell me about all this before?*" Kit signed to him. "*This is really big news!*"

"*Well,*" he replied. "*I did try.*"

Chapter thirty-eight

A sh and Pinar managed to sleep for about six hours before the heat became unbearable. Pinar climbed out of the tent looking dishevelled, her long hair in knots. Ash tried to hide from the morning a bit longer, her head stuffed under a blanket. The camp was already wide awake.

"Morning," said Vicki, cheerfully. She was sat by a small fire stirring a pot. Pinar hadn't noticed before how beautiful she was. Her brown eyes sparkled in the sunlight.

"Hey," replied Pinar, she smiled and came over to sit next to her.

"Did you sleep okay?"

"*I think Ash's still sleeping,*" Pinar signed. "*Let's sign. What are you cooking?*"

"*Porridge. Or something like porridge. It's kind of goop really.*"

Vicki signed an unfamiliar word for goop. It looked like she might have just invented it.

"*Can I help?*"

"*Please do. I hate cooking and I should go prepare for the morning meeting.*"

"*Let me take over then and I'll call when it's ready.*"

"*Perfect, thank you.*"

Finally, after another half hour, Ash emerged from the tent. Her beard had reached the scratchy phase again so after breakfast she went off to a private spot in the woods to shave.

When she came back, the shoal were gathered in a circle for morning meeting. Ash saw Pinar was already engaged and she silently sat down next to her. Someone she didn't know yet was speaking.

"We'll cross the Ring tonight, enter the tunnels and—all things being well—we'll be in the City by tomorrow morning. We'll *rendez-vous* with the City resistance and see where things stand."

Pinar spoke next. "If it's a good time, I'd like to discuss what will happen when we get there, how we're planning to support the prisoners and protect the forest communities."

"Good idea," said the first speaker. "Let's move onto that..."

Pretty soon, Ash drifted off into her thoughts. She knew that Pinar found all this analysis gave her somewhere to put her energy and helped her to focus, but Ash found it exhausting. After an hour, she excused herself and went to sit alone with the forest plants.

She found herself filled with familiar doubts. Strategies, tactics, political analysis, direct action. It all seemed crucially important and yet Ash had never felt a part of it. Her brain just didn't work that way.

She never had the feeling she had useful things to say, or a good idea of the big picture. Back during the urban uprising against the State, this doubting had been her undoing. She had felt like she could never do enough, never knew enough, never *be* enough. She had been a shadow of herself, trying to fit in where she didn't belong. She and Pinar had become leaders—the mythical 'A and P' of the Femme Riots, leading protest after protest and uniting coalitions. Together, they practically founded the resistance, and all along, Ash had been secretly dying inside.

A group of long-tailed tits flew overhead, their contact calls resonating through the trees as they made their way through the forest. Ash couldn't help but smile.

Those years were past her. Out here, she had found her niche. She knew who she was—a part of this place, this wildness which embraced her complexity and love and returned it without condition.

The same wildness, she realised, that they would soon be leaving, perhaps forever. Panic welled up inside her when she thought about the City and threatened to overwhelm her. She put her hands on the ground and swallowed it all down.

Sometimes it isn't actual death and violence that holds us back, she reminded herself, *but the threat and fear of those things. That's how they control us. That's how they stop us from fighting back.*

This is no time to panic, Pin needs me.

Chapter thirty-nine

Sun streamed in through the high windows of the squatted warehouse. Inside, Kit's students were already gathered for self-defence class.

"Hi everyone, thanks for coming." Kit had spent more time than usual in front of the mirror this morning. Her hair was boldly pinned on one side and she wore the dark purple lipstick she kept for special occasions. She was wearing the highest pair of heels she owned. She wore heels even in self-defence class—*especially in self-defence class*—and considering how the last lesson had ended, she wanted her students to see her at her best.

"Great to see so many of you here."

This must be every student I've ever taught. Nothing like a bust up in a meeting to boost numbers.

"Today we're going to be practising a few different techniques in preparation for a street roleplay which will involve several aggressors against one defender on the ground."

A few of the students looked excited, a few looked nervous.

"Of course, like all roleplays, this might bring things up for people and it's absolutely okay to opt out at any point and you don't owe anyone an explanation. If you can though, I'd ask that you check in with me quickly before you leave the space. I just like to know that everyone's okay."

Nathalie watched Kit with admiration. She loved seeing her taking a powerful position, controlling the room. She imagined submitting to her, being under those heels, following her every command. She played with her hair unconsciously, twirling it around a finger back and forth.

It must be love if I'm willing to join these people. A resistance den is the last place I ever thought I'd end up.

Kit stood abruptly. "Get into pairs and let's get warmed up."

Nathalie silently obeyed and quickly found a partner. As they went through the compulsory check-in and began their warm up exercises, she looked discretely over her shoulder to check if Kit was watching her. She wasn't: she was talking to one of her students. Nathalie felt a rush of envy.

Pay attention, Kit, she thought to herself. *I'm only here for you, you know? I would do anything for you, go to any class, serve any amount of slop to these resistance idiots. But you could at least notice me.*

Ten minutes later after warm up was complete, still focussed completely on her teaching, Kit began the class.

"Ok everyone, let's start the roleplay..."

* * *

Ash was back in The City and she was terrified.

She was in the street and she saw herself, her body hidden by baggy, dark clothes, her hair short, her gestures understated, her hips frozen.

It was nineteen years ago, but she was back there, reliving every second; a frightened shadow who could only watch and remember.

"There he is!"

The shout came from the other side of the street and both Ash and her shadow looked up in fear.

The gang came then, the regular people overcome by mob adrenalin. The shadow from the future watched on as Ash's body was thrown to the concrete, as her disguise was torn away despite her screams, as her tiny, red nightdress was revealed to the world.

* * *

"...Now using all the techniques we've practised today, the defender's role is to get off the ground and get away from the group as quickly as possible.

You have the right to protect yourself and you have the right to get out of this. I'll demonstrate first..."

* * *

"Fucking tranny!"

Ash still clung to her nightdress. She remembered its every detail perfectly. It had been her one magical garment and she had worn it every day, underneath her guy's clothes, close to her breasts and hips to keep her connected with who she really was. And now she watched on as this tiny piece of silk—and with it, her identity—was violently exposed to the sky.

* * *

"...Working on the assumption that it's too late to avoid this conflict and that the aggressors are beyond reasoning, my only responsibility now is to my own safety. To get free and get away by whatever means possible..."

* * *

Ash from the future watched on. She tried to look away but she could still hear her own screams as her body, two decades in the past, was exposed to the kicks and slaps of the angry mob. Gobs of spit rained down as her past-self curled into a tight ball, her only thought to protect the shreds of her precious, silk dress.

Finally, mercifully, the scene began to fade.

* * *

"...In this situation, the defender's body will be filled with adrenalin, poised for the flight or fight response. The hardest and most important thing is to use this for our own advantage, to strike out against our attackers, to keep our voice strong..."

* * *

"Hon, are you okay? You looked far away..."

Ash tried to focus on the face in front of her.

Pin, my darling Pinar.

"Were you...? Is everything alright?"

Ash was sat a hundred metres away from camp, her face was wet with tears.

"I'm perfect!" she snapped, standing abruptly; her heart racing, her body still filled with the chemicals of fear. "Everything's just perfect!"

"I'm sorry, I just..."

"Well sorry doesn't help me, does it? You'll *never* understand what I go through—how *could* you? How *nice* to be you. How *nice* just to forget!"

Ash stormed off into the forest leaving Pinar alone, shocked and hurt.

Chapter forty

An hour later Ash reappeared. She looked calmer, but her eyes were bloodshot from crying.

"I'm sorry..." she said, sitting near to where Pinar was preparing dinner. Her friend didn't respond at first. She was cutting vegetables loudly on a chopping board, the knife moving fast and steady. "Let's talk later. I'm not ready yet."

Ash stood up to leave.

"Sit down," Pinar said abruptly, changing her mind.

Ash obediently sat back down.

"It's...fine." Pinar continued chopping. "Apology accepted. Let's face it, it's not the first time you've shouted at me."

"Sorry..." repeated Ash, weakly. She sat quietly for a moment and watched as a group of sparrows chased each other across the forest floor, chittering loudly as they went. *A quarrel*, she thought to herself, *a group of sparrows is called a quarrel.*

"When were you?" asked Pinar. "Do you want to talk about it?"

"Maybe later."

"When you need to, I'm here." Pinar picked up another knife and handed it to her friend. "Want to help with dinner? We're leaving in about four hours and we should really get some sleep before we head out."

"Sure thing."

* * *

After they ate dinner and Pinar was finished with yet another planning meeting, she climbed into their small tent. Ash was already curled up on her mat.

"Are you awake?"

"Yeah...sort of. How was your meeting?"

"Good, I'm getting a better sense of it all. There's a lot of the recent repression that I didn't even hear about. I've been pretty disconnected I guess."

"I miss being disconnected..." Ash mumbled still curled up and hidden in her thin blanket.

"You're scared of going back to the City, aren't you? Scared of what you'll find there? Talk to me, I want to be there for you."

"I'm not sure I can yet, but thanks."

Ash rolled onto her back. As she often did when she was nervous, she gently took a handful of Pinar's long hair and curled it up in her fingers, teasing out the knots. It was something she'd always done with her own hair before middle-age hormones had kicked in and she'd starting balding. Pinar loved the gentle pulling on her hair and was happy to share.

"I don't know, Pin. Some of it's practical, you know? I'm going to have to wear my...guy's stuff again." Ash cast a glance to where her backpack was stuffed into a corner of the tent. "It's been a long time—I'm not sure I'll even fit. And you know, I'm not sure what use I'll be when we get there. What can *I* do in the City?"

"It's a huge deal that you're taking care of me, hon. And the others. I know you know that, but please don't forget it. It's everything to me."

"Thanks."

Ash rolled over again and curled up small. Pinar curled up with her and wrapped her up in her long arms.

"I'm just a bit nervous is all," Ash said through the blankets. "The Ring, the tunnels. But it's fine, I'm fine."

But Pinar knew it wasn't. The City was an ugly memory for both of them, a wound that would take a lifetime to heal.

"If you change your mind, I would never hold it against you. Really. Go back if you need to."

"Not an option. Anyway...sweet dreams, hon."

"Sleep well."

Two sleepless hours later, just as they finished packing up their tent, a young white guy came over to talk to Ash and Pinar.

"Hey, I'm Mike. I'll be accompanying the two of you to the City walls."

Pinar smiled politely. Ash barely acknowledged him at all.

"It's easy to get turned around in the Ring and I recently came through the tunnels so...stay close to me. We just need to stay in the eroded gulleys and stay off the horizon. As you can see, there's really nothing else out there to hide behind."

"I'm sure you'll get us there safely, Mike," said Pinar kindly. "Are we leaving soon?"

"Everyone's already split into their groups, so whenever you're ready."

"Let's go."

Over the next half hour, group by group, the resistance shoal reluctantly stepped out of the sanctuary of the forest and entered the Ring. They all knew there was no going back from here.

Chapter forty-one

In groups of three, the shoal head out across the Ring, dead soil crunching under their feet. They could already see the City walls up ahead and before that lay three kilometres of nothing but deforestation and erosion.

Ash and Pinar were among the first groups to leave and although the moon was covered by clouds and the night was dark, they felt suddenly vulnerable.

"*I hate it here,*" signed Ash to her friend. "*I see why they keep expanding the Ring. I feel like troopers could appear at any second and we'd have nowhere to hide.*"

"*We've avoided them so far,*" Pinar replied. "*Let's hope our luck holds out.*"

"*Ever the optimist.*"

"*Keep moving please, ladies,*" signed Mike. "*Not far now.*"

Ash ignored him. She was too impatient to deal with other people's impatience.

After nearly an hour of clambering through gulleys and running in the gaps, a tiny breeze blew over them, bringing a fresh smell which Pinar recognised immediately. There was the faintest sound of gulls calling far away.

"*The sea!*" she signed with a twinkle of nostalgia in her eye.

"*We're close,*" Ash signed back and pushed on, her face and her gestures revealing nothing of the fear that was slowly filling her heart.

* * *

They were a hundred metres from the walls of the City. Two concentric circles of concrete blocks built decades ago formed a sheer cliff face separating the outside world from the City.

Some kind of stone barrier had existed here since ancient times, but faced with continual attacks from the outside, the State had ordered prisoners to fortify the walls by hand. Every year, the walls were at least a metre higher.

"*I certainly didn't miss* that *sight.*" signed Pinar. "*I'd forgotten just how big they are.*"

"*I hoped I'd never see this again,*" Ash replied.

They stood for a moment, awestruck, but were soon rushed forward by Mike who was much more used to the sights of the City, including its walls.

"*Let's get to the tunnels,*" he signed impatiently. "*We stick out here like a sore thumb.*"

As they got closer to the walls, the huge vertical surface soon filled their field of vision. Ash noticed that, like some of the oldest trees in the forest, it was impossible from this position to see both the top and the bottom of the wall at the same time. The effect made her nauseous.

Following their guide, Ash and Pinar soon came to the base of the wall and the entrance to the tunnel. They had made good time and were the first group to arrive.

"*The tunnel is under here.*" Mike signed, pointing at a pile of sticks and leaves. To the women, it looked like pretty much every other pile of dry brush in the Ring. "*Help me pull these branches away from the entrance.*"

As they pulled the sticks aside, a metal hatch was revealed. Mike slid the hatch to the side, and in the moonlight they could see a gaping hole with a rusty ladder leading down into perfect darkness.

Ash felt sick. Her heart was racing.

* * *

The air coming up from the tunnel smelt all wrong. For Ash, it was the smell of death, of imprisonment, of the City. Her lungs begged for better air and unconsciously she took a step away from the dark hole. Pinar noticed immediately.

"*Everything okay?*"

"No, no it's not okay," replied Ash, her throat catching. "I don't think I can go down there. I don't think I ca—"

She was cut off by an urgent sign from their companion. His eyes were wide with fear.

"*Horses!*" he signed. "*I can hear horses! We have to get in right now!*"

Chapter forty-two

The hooves were getting louder by the second.

Pinar looked across the landscape at the remaining small groups making their way towards them. The last group—just now climbing out of a gulley carrying tents and equipment—were still at least five hundred metres away.

"*But what about the others?*" signed Pinar.

"*There's no time! We can't give away the location of the tunnel,*" Mike replied, his hands shaking as he signed. "*We need to get in!*"

Pinar saw the other groups ducking down into an *arroyo*.

They must have heard the horses too. There's nothing else we can do now! Damn!

Pinar got onto the ladder and started her descent into darkness. She looked back at Ash who stood perfectly still at the edge of the hole.

"Ash!" she said, gripping onto the rusty rungs of the ladder. "We have to go!"

Ash said nothing. She was frozen.

"Ash! Get in!"

Mike was terrified and angry.

We're completely vulnerable out here, and this old woman's putting us all at risk.

He stood between her and the hole and taking hold of her shoulders he gave her a hard shake.

"We have to get to the tunnel," he said sternly. "We're running out of time."

Slowly a look of recognition came to Ash's face and she snapped back to reality. She looked back one more time to where the other groups of resistance members had been moving across the land. There was no one to be seen.

Are we really leaving these people behind? What choice do we have?

The thunder of horses grew louder around the curve of the wall. Ash climbed onto the ladder and followed her friend. Rung by rung, she disappeared.

Chapter forty-three

Above his head, Mike pulled the metal hatch closed, blocking out the moonlight and plunging the three of them into total darkness. Normally he'd pull the branches back over the cover, but there was no time. They'd just have to hope that the troopers wouldn't come close enough to notice it.

Hanging on the ladder, they paused for a moment. They listened for any sound—of the others arriving, or the thump of horses—but they heard nothing except their own panicked breathing. Either the hatch was too thick to hear anything, or the others had managed to hide.

Or something much worse has happened.

Ash didn't want to think about what might be happening up there. Below her, she heard Pinar start making her way down the ladder and she followed, her sweaty hands grasping to the rails as firmly as she could.

Will the others be okay? Will they make it to the City? Will any of us?

Breathing heavily from the effort, Pinar finally reached the bottom of the ladder and carefully stepped on to the ground. It was perfectly dark. As she waited for Ash and Mike to arrive, she began to explore. Following the brick walls with her hands, Pinar could feel that it opened up into two—no, three—different directions. She hated that she didn't know the way. They were completely dependent now on a guy they'd barely known for an hour.

She heard Ash meet her on the ground.

"Okay, hon?" she whispered.

"How could I be okay? We just left them out there!"

"I know. But we didn't ha—"

Pinar was interrupted by a loud cracking. She gasped as green light flooded the tunnel.

Her eyes adjusted and she saw that Mike was holding something bright in his left hand. It took a second to realise what it was.

He's holding a glowstick!

"Where does the resistance even *get* these things?" she asked. "I haven't seen one of those in...at least twenty years!"

"We have our sources..." Mike smiled back. "But it's one of our last."

He paused to listen, tilting his head up.

"I still don't hear anything from above. We'll have to assume the others made it to another entrance and we'll meet them in the City."

"That's one possibility..." said Ash, grimly. "We shouldn't have left them."

"Shall we go back up?" suggested Pinar.

"It's not safe," said Mike. "I left the hatch unlocked for them if they make it. But if the troopers find it, we're screwed. We need to get going."

Ash gave him an unpleasant look. Pinar sighed in defeat.

"Which way?"

"Follow me," said Mike, confidently taking the left exit. Ash and Pinar followed him and his otherworldly green light into the tunnel.

* * *

They were directly under the City walls. Ash could clearly see two white lines of chalk crossing the floor of the tunnel to mark the point.

Why would anybody even bother? It's so meaningless down here.

Still, as she stepped over that line, it felt significant. It might just be in her head, but the air felt thicker now, the darkness even more oppressive. They were going downhill and she began to imagine the tonnes and tonnes of rock above her head. And she couldn't stop thinking about those that they had left behind.

We have to get out of this claustrophobic hell as soon as possible.

After an hour or so of walking, the tunnel opened into another large junction.

"Can we rest a second?" Pinar panted, leaning against the wall.

"Sure, but just a second," Mike replied as he pulled a hand-drawn map out of his pocket and checked it. There were four other tunnels running off from the junction and they were all perfectly identical.

Suddenly there was a sound. They could hear footsteps and voices, and they seemed to be getting louder.

Mike pushed the glowstick into his trouser pocket blocking out the light and plunging them back into darkness.

"Should we run?" he whispered.

"No," replied Ash. "If we run now, they'll hear us for sure."

"Stand against the wall and stay as still as you can," whispered Pinar. "If they don't have lights, hopefully, they'll walk right past us."

Holding hands, they pushed back against the wall. To Ash their quiet breathing suddenly seemed painfully loud.

Chapter forty-four

People were definitely coming towards them. The voices had stopped, but the footsteps rang out and echoed. It sounded like a large group.

Ash, Pinar, and Mike held their breaths as the strangers arrived into the junction. They had no light and, in the darkness, Pinar could hear hands rubbing over the walls, presumably looking for the entrances to the tunnels.

One of them walked very close to her. She could hear their hands rubbing against the wall, moving towards her. She still held her breath. They were less than a metre away. Pinar tried to push herself back even further into the wall, but there was nowhere to go.

Her lungs burned. Any second now, she'd have to breathe.

Chapter forty-five

W ait a second!" A voice boomed out breaking the silence. "Pinar, is that *you?*"

The voice was familiar. Familiar enough for Mike to pull out the glowstick again, filling the cave with green light and illuminating the group of people standing in it, their eyes wide with surprise.

"It *is* you!" It was Vicki, grinning. "I'd recognise the smell of lavender oil anywhere!" She laughed as she scooped up all three of them in a warm embrace. The junction was instantly filled with whoops of excitement and laughter from the shoal behind her.

Ash sighed with relief.

Now let's get the hell out of here.

* * *

The Sett was celebrating. After a day of meetings, a general decision was taken to reinforce security of the village; to send runners to other villages to warn them. But all that could wait until tomorrow. Tonight was for relaxing and despite the fear and paranoia left over from the previous night, the entire community were out of their houses preparing for a great evening.

Harvest Day was the most important day in the Sett calendar and even Elias was getting into the mood. First came a massive meal in the kitchen tent, followed by music. The kitchen pulled out all the stops and, as predicted, L, the head chef, had made her famous squash soup.

Elias was glad to see that the kitchen had been hard at work with its home-made still. There was a small bottle of gin on the bar with his name on it. Everyone knew about Elias' fondness for gin.

He wasn't the only "E" in the Sett, but the other one was three years old, so he figured it was for him. He poured himself a glass.

I probably shouldn't—with my heart and everything—but I'm not going to worry about that tonight, it's Harvest Day after all.

"Hey E, Happy Harvest Day!" It was L from the kitchen. "Cheers."

They clinked glasses together and watched as a band stepped out proudly onto the wooden stage. They had been in Elias' class a few years back.

They must be in their teens now, he realised, *and apparently, they think they're rock stars. What a noise!*

Within five minutes of him sitting down, Elias' friends had arrived and he was surrounded on all sides by gossip.

"They're getting pretty good!"

"Well, they *have* been practising all week. I swear the only thing these girls will wake up early for is their band practice."

"Rumour has it that *you* used to sing, E. Is it true?"

"Nope. No way," Elias refused flatly. He had heard that rumour too, several times, in fact. In truth, he had once been well known for his rich, tenor voice, but he kept it a carefully guarded secret. Of course, living in a community, there were no such things as secrets. "It's a lie."

"Really? I can *totally* imagine you on stage, singing and danc—"

"Nope."

"Oh."

"Another gin, E?"

"Why not? But I won't sing for you. No matter how drunk you get me."

"Of course not, dear..."

* * *

"So what happened up there?" asked Pinar. "I'm so sorry we left you behind. We really didn't know what else—"

"You had to protect the tunnel," said Vicki touching her shoulder lightly. "You were just following protocol."

"It's still not okay," said Ash.

"All's well that ends well. Although it got a bit hairy there for a moment, I must admit. We headed for a different entrance, about twenty metres from the one you used, and we were nearly all in—I was the last—but the troopers arrived before we closed the hatch."

Pinar and Ash listened intently.

"I'm a resistance runner, you know, I spend my whole life running and delivering messages so I ran back to the forest to distract them. I think I ran faster than ever before. I had to forget all my training—running quietly, pacing myself, all that—and just go for it. I ran as loud as I could—shouting and making a racket. And those jerks followed me right back into the forest."

"And then?"

"Once I was back in the trees, I could outrun their horses. I looped around and made my way back to the tunnel entrance. The rest were still waiting for me inside."

"You must have run six kilometres!" said Pinar, clearly impressed.

"That's what I do. We nearly got lost a few times in the tunnels though," Vicki continued. "Next time, *I'm* taking the glowstick!" She poked Mike playfully in the arm.

"Next time, you should keep up!" Mike joked back.

"If we weren't carrying all *your* supplies, we would have! Come here!" Vicki grabbed Mike again—she was so tall he barely came up to her armpits—and she gave him a long, hard kiss on the lips.

"I'm glad you're okay, sweetie," she whispered to him. "I would have missed you."

* * *

Elias was on the stage. The whole room was clapping and whistling. His students—who Elias thought surely should have been in bed already—were lined up at the front calling for him to sing.

"Mr E! Mr E! Mr E!"

He was a little drunk, to be sure, but he also just felt too old to care.

If these people want me to sing, why not? After all, I might be dead tomorrow.

Elias began his song, a soft lament in his native tongue. It was a love song he had learned decades ago, a young man singing for his love. If only he hadn't lost him. If only their love hadn't been forbidden. If only the world was a different place.

It was a song that had sung to a generation of forbidden lovers, a song that Elias held closest to his heart. His voice was deep and powerful and as he brought the song to a crescendo, holding a single high note for one long breath, a tear fell from his cheek and the Sett cried with him. The silence that followed was unbroken and Elias sat back down and continued his drink as if nothing had happened.

Later, the teenagers started playing again and Elias managed to slip away for the night. As always, the walk home took him through Central Square—*what's left of it*—and his feet crunched through the blackened grass.

Elias stood by the pile of ashes of what was once the Memory Board. He could still hear the music and laughter from the kitchen.

How quickly we forget, he thought to himself and turned towards home.

* * *

The shoal walked on for another half hour until Vicki stopped abruptly.

"I think we're here—"

Ash and Pinar stood beside her expectantly.

"—Should be just around this corner."

In the light of the glowstick, they watched as she pushed open a heavy metal door. They stepped through it and the ground ahead of them sloped away opening into a massive cavern. The walls of the cavern were so far apart that the light didn't reach the other side, but in the semi darkness Ash could just make out what looked like tables and plastic chairs and...*what's that?* From a shop window, a wigged mannequin stared back at them illuminated faintly in green.

Ash took a step back.

"What the *hell?*"

"Of course!" Pinar exclaimed. "The Mall!"

"Welcome to the City!" said Vicki, beckoning them forwards.

Chapter forty-six

Elias was glad to be back on the deck of his boat. Somewhere in the woods he could hear owls calling to each other, there was a soft humming of crickets bringing the cool night and above the mountains he could see the light of the full moon peeking between clouds.

He sat back in his folding wooden chair and sipped from another glass of gin he'd snuck out of the kitchen. The third glass was always better than the second and he enjoyed the burn it left in his chest as it went down. He relaxed a bit more and listened as the owls kept up their calls.

Despite everything, it's not really so bad here, he thought to himself. *There are worse places to be and here at least I have a family. And I'm well fed and taken care of.* The cricket song began to fade and the owls moved to another part of their territory. The night was left silent, perfectly still.

No, Elias thought to himself, *this life isn't bad at all.*

* * *

The raid happened just before dawn while the Sett was sleeping. They were completely unprepared.

4. City

Chapter forty-seven

The General rolled onto his back. He was covered in sweat and smelt awful, but he was undeniably alive. He lay on his back, staring up. The air was hot around him and his head was pounding. He blinked to clear his vision. He could see the sun blazing in the sky and was shaded by something.

My God, trees!

His memory was messed up. He could remember being back on base. And the shower—the grunt—and the prison cell. He could remember the factory. And then he was here. Somewhere outside, under a tree.

Where the hell am I?

He tried to get up, but he was too weak. He felt like he'd been drugged. His arms and legs weren't responding in the way they were supposed to. His head was heavy and groggy. He lifted it a little but could only see trees. There were trees in every direction he looked.

Is this some kind of game? Some kind of punishment before they kill me?

His headache was worse. His vision was swimming and his eyes watered. He lay back down and gritted his teeth against the pain and the heat. The world went black.

* * *

Elias awoke with a start, his heart racing.

The morning was filled with screams that turned his blood cold. Before he could think, he was out of the door and standing on the deck of his boat.

There were uniformed state troopers everywhere kicking down doors and smashing windows. The kitchen tent hung at a wild angle and the burned square was a mess of running children. Troopers were arresting and handcuffing everyone they could catch. Elias saw two running towards his boat.

He kicked off the little plank that connected him with the riverbank, but the boat was too close to make a difference and the river was far too low to escape. The soldiers jumped easily onto his deck and grabbed him, forcing his arms behind his back and handcuffing his wrists. He couldn't even resist.

What's the point? They could snap me like a twig.

The tallest of the two effortlessly flipped Elias onto his shoulder and carried him over the gap to the river bank. He was made to walk again and, still in his light blue pyjamas, they marched him to the burned grass of Central Square where most of the community was already kneeling, hands tied behind their backs.

Elias hadn't seen and heard so much fear in many blissfully long years. The troopers handcuffed him, forced him to his knees and left him surrounded by his adopted family. All around him he could hear the panicked voices of his neighbours, his colleagues, his students. But he couldn't look anyone in the eye. The smell of fear, the cries and tears.

It just makes all this worse.

He looked on as the troopers trashed their home. They had no reason to be quiet and seemed to be taking great delight in destroying what had taken years to build.

They dragged people out of their beds and through the dust. They pissed on mattresses and tore what was left of the crops from the gardens.

Elias felt nothing but numbness. He had seen all this before.

* * *

The troopers were efficient and merciless.

Looking at his community traumatised around him, Elias did a quick head count. Around thirty people were missing, including some of his students. They must have escaped, probably fleeing up into the mountains.

Elias knew this would happen one day. The fire, he saw now, must have been a State operation to flush out the community. When that failed, they simply sent in the troopers.

The Sett was totally unprepared. Elias remembered in the first few years after exile, they had stayed constantly ready for an attack and eviction. They had been proud of their self-defence training and round-the-clock vigilance. But over the years they had become complacent.

We committed the greatest sin of all—of allowing ourselves to relax and to forget the past. In this world, for the kinds of people who live here, moving on will never be a possibility. Forgetting is a luxury we can never afford.

Once the boats, tents and little wooden houses had been wrecked to their satisfaction, the troopers began to line up the prisoners and tie them in two long lines to march them to the City.

"Where are you taking us?"

"What's happening?"

Every question was answered with a slap or a kick and people soon fell silent, resigning themselves to whatever the State had in store for them.

Elias and a few others were still kneeling and four troopers approached them to add their chains to the growing line. One grabbed Elias under the elbows and expected to lift the frail older man easily. But the trooper grunted in frustration.

"What the fuck?" he said. "He's as heavy as a rock!"

His eyes vacant, his face expressionless, it was as though Elias was somehow stuck to the ground. The trooper braced himself, planting his boots firmly into the dust and tried again, but Elias wouldn't budge.

This is my home. I'll die before they take me from it.

Chapter forty-eight

Another soldier joined in and even together they couldn't lift Elias from the ground. His friends looked on, confused, as three more troopers tried to move the old man still mysteriously bound to the earth.

Everyone else in the square was already chained to the marching lines and watched on as for twenty long minutes the troopers tried to lift their friend. Forgetting their fear for a moment, they began to shout and jeer at the troopers, at once both begging them to leave him alone and hoping desperately for Elias to somehow stay rooted to this land, their land, forever.

But his tired body could only take so much. Suddenly a look of agony flashed across Elias' face and with a long, low groan, he fell to the ground, his arms still handcuffed behind him.

"My arm!" he shouted and the troopers stepped back in surprise. Elias' friends pulled desperately at their chains to try to reach him.

"Elias!"

"Are you okay?"

Elias writhed for a moment, his face pushed into the dust until he fell silent, his body, completely limp.

It's my heart. They've finally broken it one too many times.

He felt it slowing in his chest, wanting badly to stop beating, to give up on this life.

Beyond the square, he could see the forest canopy. And he saw crows, so many crows, gathering around them in the branches. They were beautiful, he noticed. They were watching him. But his eyes had seen too much beauty in this life and he let them fall closed.

One last time his heart pulsed with pain and Elias sighed with relief as it stopped.

Chapter forty-nine

The General woke up and vomited.

Wiping his mouth, he noticed the air was cooler now, the sun less intense. It could be dawn or dusk.

His brain was still pounding in his skull, but he could see a little clearer and managed to sit up. He looked around slowly. Still trees as far as he could see. Birds were singing all around him, the air smelled of leaves. The only thought that made sense: somehow, he was in the forest and he was free.

He had absolutely no memory of how he got here, but he was no longer in a State cell and he wasn't going to die.

I'm outside, I'm under the sky!

He stood up and wobbled. He still felt a bit drugged, but was elated. A roar of laughter overtook him and hands on his hips, he doubled over until he vomited again. He didn't care. None of that mattered. He had survived.

* * *

"This is so surreal."

"I hate it. Can we leave now?"

Ash and Pinar stood with their shoal deep underground in the great Mall. The single green glowstick created more shadows than light and the effect gave Ash chills.

"Did you ever come here?" Pinar asked her as they crossed the main concourse together.

"Never. Why would I?"

"For a while, I think pretty much everyone came here." Pinar pointed at the abandoned shops, the closed-up restaurants. "As the weather got worse each year, the Mall and the tunnels became the best way to get around. I used them sometimes, remember? And most importantly it was free, as long as you didn't mind seeing all the miles and miles of commercials."

"That was too high a price for me. Give me the sky and the heat any day."

"I get it. It was convenient to get around, but totally creepy. And now it's abandoned it's even weirder. It smells awful."

Without electricity and without air conditioning, the air was thick and smelt like oil, gas and mould.

"It's more than creepy, it's *sad*," Ash declared. "Whole generations considered this their public space. Forget about parks and plazas and street life, *this* place, this *private temple to capitalism* became their place to hang out."

"Now it's just for the rats." Pinar watched as a colony of them ran by, squeaking.

"They're welcome to it."

Vicki came over smiling.

"Don't worry, we're not staying. Not the friendliest place in the world, is it?"

Ash made a face.

"Kind of hard to believe that people ever came to these places of their own free will," continued Vicki, "At least the tunnels have some fresh air from time to time, but the Mall is hundreds of metres underground. This air hasn't moved down here for decades."

"Can we leave now please?" said Ash.

"Let's go. It's not far."

Vicki gathered up her people and led the shoal up a dead escalator. Ash took a final look back at the Mall and they entered a narrow tunnel. Every wall was lined with photographs of smiling white people advertising toothpaste and instant coffee and washing powder and all the other things that no longer existed. At every tunnel corner was a smashed-up café or a shoe store, long ago raided and emptied. Small armies of mannequins stood in shop fronts and Ash could swear she felt their cold eyes on her as she walked by.

Here, for some reason the shoal—even Pinar—seemed to be speaking louder and more excitedly than they had in the forest.

They're actually more relaxed, Ash observed. *They're more at home here.*

But for her, down beneath the centre of the State, far from her precious woods, she couldn't remember a time when she had felt less safe.

She trudged along past more advertisements and up another escalator with her mood as heavy as the hundreds of metres of rock that lay between them and fresh air.

I'm so done with this.

Harsh and unexpected, sunlight suddenly flooded into the tunnel as Vicki cracked open a door. After hours of darkness, they were all blinded and Vicki took a few minutes to let her eyes adjust before she opened the door further and peered through. She looked from side to side and silently slipped out.

She was gone a few minutes and the whole group, lining the service stairwell that led up to the door, stood in total silence. Eventually, her smiling face appeared around it.

"All clear!" she called out. "No-one's here yet, it's just us."

And up and out they went.

They were in an abandoned warehouse, a large open space, impossibly bright after the tunnels. Ash looked up to the ceiling where early morning light poured in through massive windows in the roof. The sky was still red with just a few fluffy clouds. She had never been so glad to see it.

Chapter fifty

As he looked around him, the General noticed that it was getting warmer by the minute and the sky was reddening. Through a fog of confusion, he reasoned that it must be dawn. *I can't stay out here forever. That much is clear, but which way to go?*

His empty stomach cramped and made his decision for him. He turned east towards the rising sun—towards the City and food—and started walking.

* * *

As soon as they arrived at the warehouse, the shoal became busy, preparing the space and setting up a kitchen. City collectives began to arrive and Pinar went off to ask for news about Jason. Staying alone, Ash curled up on an old futon in a corner to rest. She was exhausted and badly needed to sleep.

"Hi, my name's Sandy. What's yours?"

The voice was loud and penetrating.

"I'm...err...Ash. Nice to meet you," said Ash as politely as she could. Before she could say anything else, the stranger was holding her shoulder and giving her four—loud—formal kisses.

"Hi 'err-Ash' I thought I'd come over to say hi while you weren't busy."

"Well actually, I—"

"I'm curious about new people. *I saw you over here and thought we should talk.*"

Sandy sometimes spoke and signed at the same time for emphasis. Ash noticed she was signing in female.

One of the things she had really enjoyed about USL as it evolved was its self-identifying gender. The first-person pronoun—the equivalent of I, me and my in English, could be gendered female—if signed with the left hand, male—if signed with the right, or just dropped from a sentence completely. On the other hand, unlike English, there was no gender in the third person—he, she, it and they all used the same sign—so gendering, at least linguistically, was designed to be always consensual.

Ash, of course preferred signing in female or occasionally she would drop the pronoun in the street if she felt like the apparent discord between how people read her and the gender of her sign might be dangerous. After Resistance Sign was co-opted by the State, it became obligatory to use the first-person pronoun in every sentence and avoiding self-gendering by dropping the pronoun was no longer optional. Ash got into the habit of switching into English when she needed to. Anything was better than pretending to be a guy.

"Well, okay...what would you like to talk about?" This person, Sandy, grinned at Ash enthusiastically and she already found her too intense.

"Being trans-feminine for example?"

Ash's hands immediately lifted to touch her hoop earrings and stroked them defensively.

"Is that a problem?" she asked.

"Not at all, I'm trans myself."

Sandy signed every word a little too large, her pale hands flashing in the bright morning sunlight.

"But I still, you know, live in the City I haven't met so many of the...exiliadas. I'd hate to leave. It has its problems or whatever, but for me it's home."

Ash already didn't like this person. She knew it wasn't fair to judge someone within ten seconds of meeting them, but something about this Sandy didn't feel right. Over the years, people had often criticised Ash for being so judgemental, but this sixth sense, this intuitive feeling about people, had saved her skin more than once.

"I...didn't feel that way about living here," she said diplomatically. "Or particularly have a choice. Honestly, I wouldn't be here now if I had a choice either."

"Because you don't pass?"

"*Excuse me?*"

"As a woman, I mean. Because you're pre-op or whatever."

God!

Ash felt herself getting angry, she switched to USL and signed uncompromisingly in female.

"*I pass just fine,*" she signed, emphasising the pronoun with her left hand. "*As myself, as a trans woman. I may not pass as a cis woman because I couldn't afford medical transition—or particularly want it—while there was such a thing.*"

"—But—"

"*My body is my body and the only thing that doesn't work is society. Who the hell are you to comment on it? Why would a trans woman want to judge me when you know from your own experience how hard it is?*"

"—What I meant was—"

"*And another thing. 'Passing' means nothing at all when it relies on other people to decide who I am. I know who I am, I pass perfectly.*"

"—Relax, relax! Don't be so defensive, sister!"

"Please don't call me that."

"Okay, look, I think we've gotten off on the wrong foot. I didn't mean for you to feel criticised, I just, you know, was curious is all. It's nice to talk to other queers sometimes."

For Ash, the fact that they both seen by society as queer was most likely irrelevant. Back in her City days, she had often been introduced to random trans people she had nothing in common with except that they were both not cis-gender. She always reminded those well-meaning friends that, although she appreciated the thought, she was so much more than her gender identity. And really, what would she have to talk about with accountants and architects anyway?

She shuffled awkwardly and looked for a way out of the conversation.

Where's Pin gone? I have to find an excuse to escape from this terrible person.

Unabated, Sandy with her loud voice and dramatic urban sign continued to probe into Ash's private life.

"I'm one of the main organisers of the sex work collective," she announced proudly. *"There's a few of us queer folk in the collective. Did you do sex work, you know, before you ran away?"*

"No."

"I see. So what do you do, out there in the forest? You're not a fighter—not at your age."

"I look after people. I grow vegetables and herbs. I serve the forest."

"Ah right. Cool. Plants and stuff.

This is going nowhere.

"Well, I've got to go to work now," said Sandy leaning in to give Ash more kisses. "Let's continue this another time, yeah?"

Ash was finally left alone and sighed with relief.

My God is everyone like this in the City?

* * *

The General had been walking for hours through the forest with nothing except the clothes he was wearing and a vague sense of heading east. He was desperately thirsty. He couldn't remember the last time he ate. In fact, he couldn't remember much at all.

He stopped to drink from the remnants of a stream but as he

cupped the water in his hands and brought it to his lips, he noticed it had an iridescent shine to it; an oily, shimmering rainbow. He drank it anyway, but within a minute threw up violently. His empty stomach twisted even more.

He was covered in sweat and his clothes still stunk of his own dried excrement.

Despite all this, the General felt strangely at peace. His only thoughts were about getting to water and food and surviving. His mind was uncluttered, undisturbed.

Nothing else matters. I just have to keep walking.

Chapter fifty-one

The warehouse was busy and loud and Ash was overwhelmed. Watching the hundreds of people around her coming and going full of purpose, with their blueprints of the prison system, their high-octane meetings, activist vocabulary, and urban slang, Ash began to feel like a different species.

I miss the forest. How did we even end up back here?

She needed to keep herself busy and decided to set up a clinic in a quiet corner to give bodywork to those who needed it. Within an hour, she had a stream of people coming to her with various aches and pains from sleeping on the floor, dislocated shoulders or other injuries from street altercations, headaches, exhaustion—all things she could help with.

Ash was busy doing what she loved, but she daydreamed often about the river, about her home. Surrounded by people, she realised that she felt more alone than she had in a long time.

That afternoon, Ash found herself cleaning a small mountain of dishes, her arms deep in greasy, soapy water. She had already been cleaning for more than an hour and muttered to herself as she slammed the dishes onto the drying rack.

Why does 'punk' always end up meaning 'unhygienic'? Most of these people are young, able-bodied, certainly fitter than me, but they live like poor people—like it's a damn aesthetic. How did they even survive without me to clean up after them?

She looked up and saw a familiar smile. It was Pinar and she was bearing gifts.

"Ash! You look exhausted. Have you been outside yet?"

"No, not really—"

"—Look, I brought you something! I found *real* coffee at the illegal market by the motorway. The beans are probably not too fresh, and we had to bargain hard for it, but here, I thought it would make you happy."

"It's perfect, thank you."

Ash dried her arms on a small, dirty towel.

"It's a beautiful day out there, and the motorway—or what used to be the motorway—is really nice, lots of trees. We could take a walk if you like, before the *mesa* this evening."

"No...I...I have things to do."

"Hon, I'm not stupid. You're nervous about being in the street. But I also know you're missing the birds and the sky. Let's go out, just a short walk."

"Okay, okay. Let me just get changed and I'm ready. I'll leave this little disaster—" she indicated the dish mountain. "For the young people."

* * *

His legs were bound, rope burned against his wrists.

I shouldn't want this, but I can't help myself. This is everything I dreamed of.

Naked but for the layer of mud on his ass and the candle wax covering his nipples, the man was completely blinded by the scarf tied around his eyes.

Each time, the loud snap before the cold and the pain as strips of leather cut deep into his back. His skin tore open and, one by one, his fears were released. He wanted to scream, to tell her how much he loved her, but only moans escaped his taut lips. Snap then pain. Snap and pain. His boundaries broken down. And he was hers.

I love you, Mistress.

The room became empty, the air suddenly silent. Blood pounding in his ears, the man felt darkness closing in around him as he sensed her absence.

This is the perfect moment. This is the moment I see the root of loneliness.

He saw with a vision born in the dark, a clarity of endorphins. And for a moment there was nothing in the world except the sound of his own breath.

Then she was there again, embracing him, scratching him, smothering his skin with hers, absorbing him into herself. And he was ready to share his pain with her once more.

"Thank you, Mistress. That was incredible."

"I'm *always* incredible."

"Of course, Mistress."

"Lick the other boot clean now."

Kit was enjoying herself immensely. She hadn't met this client before, but he seemed very willing to please her.

And he has a high pain threshold which is always fun.

"Five minutes left, sub."

The client gave her a look that reminded Kit of a lost puppy.

"Come."

She allowed him to put his head on her lap and she stroked his hair. She rarely allowed such intimacy, even if sometimes she wanted to slow down a little and just enjoy the physical contact. *He did work hard to please me though and it's a nice way to close a session.*

"Thank you, Mistress. It's been such a difficult week, I really needed this."

Kit didn't want to hear about her client's boring work for the State. Normally she'd just tell him to be quiet—that she was the only person in this room who had anything worth saying—but she was distracted. She was thinking about Nathalie.

"—It's been so hard getting the new recruits trained up," the client was saying. "My superiors put so much pressure on me. It's impossible to please them—"

I miss her. It's strange. I haven't felt like this about someone for a long time. I don't think it's love or anything, but I'm feeling ready to be more vulnerable with her. To open up a bit more.

"—And there's a lot going on this week. Those resistance rats have been fighting us out in the forest—"

Every time we've met so far has been so...violent. I love that of course, I need it. But maybe something more tender would be nice, too, at some point. I should bring it up with her next ti—

"—And then there's the raid tonight—"

Kit snapped suddenly back to the present.

"What? What raid? What are you talking about, sub?"

"Erm...at an old warehouse down-town, Mistress. We think there's resistance using the space for their meetings and erm..."

"Tell me more."

Her client blushed.

"I shouldn't say too much about it, Mistress. My superiors would kill me if they knew I told anyone."

"Then do something more useful with your tongue boy. Lick my boots clean and get out of my sight."

"Yes, Mistress. Thank you, Mistress."

Kit's heart was racing. *I have to get over to the warehouse. I have to get everyone out.*

She looked unconsciously towards the door.

I just hope I'm not already too late.

Chapter fifty-two

I t *is* beautiful out here."

Ash and Pinar walked along the motorway, the concrete valley slowly being reclaimed by the squirrels, birch trees, and primroses.

"I didn't realise the City had places like this."

"Well, there were always parks for what they were worth," Pinar replied. "But without cars, there's a whole lot more space for things to grow back. Not everything will, of course, and the concrete's here to stay. Still, even if the State tried to clean it all up, they just don't have the machines to do it anymore."

"It's beautiful, but it just reminds me how far we are from home," said Ash, casting a disdainful look down at her jeans and dark t-shirt. "I hate wearing all this masculine crap, you know…"

She had always refused to call jeans 'gender-neutral'. In her opinion, jeans were no more neutral than dresses. Calling jeans, t-shirt and a short haircut, 'androgynous', just centred masculinity even more.

"I know hon, I'm sorry."

"Well, anyway—" Ash lowered her voice. "How are the plans looking? Are we making a move soon?"

"It's not clear yet. There's talk of making this a wider action against all the prisons—there are so many people in there, this could really be—"

Pinar stopped talking and pointed across the motorway where four armed soldiers were walking by, slightly hidden by the trees.

"Just keep walking straight ahead," she whispered. "And let's sign."

She switched to USL.

"*Oh, I* know, *it's been so hot recently. I can't wait for winter. They say there might be a storm coming this weekend. I would* love *some rain. Anyway, we should get back to the office soon, we're probably late...*"

"*Err, yeah, I have to get some work done...mate.*" Ash was signing with male pronouns and felt entirely uncomfortable. "*It's so hot in there this time of year. I don't know how you can cope on the top floor. With the sun and the erm...heat...*"

The troopers passed by, uninterested.

"It's okay," Pinar laughed gently. "Please stop acting—that was truly painful!"

"Uff. I hate this. Why would anyone live here? Let's break Jason out already and get back to the real world!"

"Well, it may not be that simple, but we'll do what it takes. Let's sit here, it's a bit more hidden from the street."

They sat down on a soft piece of ground under the shade of a young oak with a good view of the motorway forest.

"I miss him, you know? Jason..."

"I know..."

"And I never even got the chance to tell him, that I, um—"

"—That you have feelings for him."

"Yeah." Pinar looked thoughtful. "Was it that obvious?"

"After all these years, I should hope I notice when you're in love or not."

"But it's so fast. I mean, I barely know him."

"Well, it happens that way sometimes. I'm happy for you...Shh...look!"

Ash switched back to signing silently.

"*There's a fox, over there, do you see? Down behind the services sign.*"

"*Amazing.*"

"*Yeah.*"

They sat for another hour together, watching the fox, the squirrels playing in the young trees, the clouds of nettle pollen exploding into the breeze. This concrete valley wasn't their home, not even nearly, but as long as they were together, home was never far away.

The sun was close to setting so Ash and Pinar headed back to the warehouse building. As they arrived, they expected to see people discreetly coming and going, subtle candlelight flickering inside the windows, a guard from the security collective near the door checking the people arriving. There was nothing at all. The building was completely quiet.

"*I don't like this, Pin. This isn't right,*" Ash signed in the fading light as they circled around the building together. "*Where did everyone go? Was there a raid? My god...was there a raid?*"

"*Don't panic. Just stay in the shadows, we'll find out what happened.*"

Someone appeared out of the trees behind them. Pinar opened her mouth to scream but before she could, the stranger put his gloved hand over it.

Immediately, Ash took a step forward and prepared herself to kick him, bite him, scratch his eyes out—*whatever it takes to save my friend.*

Chapter fifty-three

As the stranger stepped out of the shadows, his hand still muffling Pinar's screams, Ash realised she recognised him. She'd seen him this afternoon in a meeting at the warehouse.

"Sssh..." He released Pinar. "I'm really sorry to scare you."

"What the f—"

"My name's Danny, I'm part of the sex work collective," he whispered. "I think we met yesterday. Ash and Pinar, right? The patrols are still nearby, that's why I couldn't let you scream. I'm really sorry."

"*What happened?*" Pinar stepped away from him, her heart still racing. Realising it was already too dark to sign, she whispered as well. "What happened here? Where is everyone?"

"We're not safe. Come with me and I'll explain everything."

* * *

The music was loud. Louder than anything Ash had heard in years. *I can barely think like this. My head is killing me.*

They were hidden in the back of a bar in the small, dark room where Danny offered his special services after a dance. It was the closest place to the warehouse with a discreet entrance.

"*Sorry about the noise,*" Danny signed to Ash and Pinar who were sat opposite him on a small, cramped sofa. "*It's always like this in the evenings. I sometimes wish the solar panels would just die already.*"

211

Pinar replied politely. "*No problem. So what happened, back at the warehouse? We were only gone a couple of hours at the most.*"

"*It happened really fast. My friend Kit got word that a raid was being planned for tonight and within an hour we were packed up and gone. I'm pretty amazed we got out in time. Most of the others went to a different location a bit out of town. I stayed behind to let people know, but I think you were the last ones back.*"

"*Thanks,*" signed Pinar. "*We'd have been screwed without you. We actually don't have anywhere to stay in town now. Is it possible for us to get to the new location tonight?*" She looked over at Ash who looked drained and overwhelmed by the noise. "*We should sleep soon.*"

"*It's probably too far for tonight. I've been asked to dance, for just an hour. I'm short on food money so I should probably do it. Then, if you like, I can take you both to my place. It's just around the corner. It's very small, but I'll take the sofa, and you two can have the bed. We'll need to avoid the neighbours but you're very welcome to stay.*"

"*Thanks, that'd be great.*" Pinar turned to Ash who gave a tired nod.

"*Cool, so I'll go get the dance out of the way, and I'll be back soon.*"

"*And what do we say if someone comes in here?*" asked Ash.

"*There's just enough room for Pinar to hide in the bathroom over there.*" Danny pointed at the tiny cubicle in the corner. "*And...Ash, you could say you're waiting for me to come back. That you're my—*"

"*—client?*" Ash signed, frowning. "*Because I look like a guy?*"

"*Err, sorry, I...*"

Pinar put a comforting hand on Ash's knee. "*We'll be fine, Danny. Go dance and we'll see you in an hour.*"

Ash didn't say anything.

I hate everything about this damn city.

Just then, the DJ put on another thumping tune and her headache got even worse.

212

There were so many voices, languages and sounds in the kitchen, Nathalie was instantly overwhelmed.

She had just arrived five minutes before, coming straight from work to the busy squatted building barely a kilometre from her workplace and she already regretted her decision.

Why did I say I'd come? Kit won't even be here tonight. Work. It's always work, or class, or a meeting. Just about everything is more important than spending her precious time with me.

She looked around at the people she'd be working with this evening.

And now I'm stuck here, with these weirdos.

She had rarely seen so many kinds of people in one place, certainly not since the Improvement. A person in a wheelchair was laying out the tables assisted by someone using crutches. Someone else was balancing on a chair and hanging streamers. Each time she needed to hang up another strand of the streamer, the person was forced to get off the chair and pick up more tacks. Nathalie stepped forward to help out, but then thought better of it.

She's obese, Nathalie, thought to herself. Not 'fat', the word that fat activists had politically reclaimed in the 20s, turning it from a slur into a simple descriptor—like 'tall' or 'slim' without all the associated judgement. Not 'weight divergent' as the State-accepted term had become for a while before divergents of all kind were driven away. *She's obese,* thought Nathalie. *And probably sick and too lazy to look after herself properly.* Repelled, she stepped further away from the person and didn't offer to help.

As she continued to scan the room, she noticed a couple signing to each other over by the serving bowls, communicating with hands and faces. Nathalie didn't understand a word.

That's not USL, she reasoned. *They must actually be deaf. Didn't these people leave the City? What is this place?*

White, middle class, skinny and able-bodied, Nathalie stood in judgement of everyone around her, forgetting for a moment that she was herself a kinky lesbian dating a trans woman of colour. Cocooned in privilege, she ignored the fact that if it wasn't for her ability to escape the State's arbitrary profiling, she'd be amongst the first against the wall.

The makeshift kitchen which at some point had been a pizza restaurant was particularly full that night and volunteers ran back and forth shouting orders. Out beyond the front door, Nathalie saw the long queue of people waiting for their meal.

She stood awkwardly for a long moment, curling a strand of her hair around her finger, trying to decide if she should actually get involved or make a break for it.

I can always tell Kit I helped out, she'll never know the difference.

One of the deaf couple came over to speak to her. Tall and beautiful, Nathalie noticed.

"Hey," signed the volunteer.

"Hi," replied Nathalie smiling nervously. *"Do you...erm...sign USL?"*

"This is USL. So yes."

"Ah," said Nathalie out loud before switching back to sign. *"Erm...my friend Kit sent me here, to help out with the food. Do you know her?"*

"No clue. But as you see, security's always pretty low here. Do you want to help out?"

"Sure."

The volunteer lead Nathalie over to where the food would be served and without a word handed her a serving spoon. She showed her how to arrange a plate—first, salad from the secret City gardens in the south, then pasta, from the resistance stocks down-town, one Nutrition bar per plate and hand it to the person waiting.

"We're opening in five minutes," signed the volunteer. *"Will you*

be ok?"

"No problem. Do you...always come here?"

"Every week since the Improvement. Without this place, these people would literally not have access to food. No employment for people like us, you know."

"People like us..." Nathalie repeated just as the doors to the restaurant opened and the first hungry visitors arrived. She lifted her serving spoon and didn't put it down for another three hours until the very last mouth was fed.

* * *

Either from thirst or the sedatives wearing off, the General's head was pounding as he walked through the dark forest.

I think I'm actually beginning to imagine things. There's another one. I see it. I'd swear that's a bear hiding behind that tree.

He stopped dead still and held his breath until it passed by, but a moment later he realised his mistake.

All the bears are long dead.

Minutes or maybe hours later, he was shocked again from the rhythm of his walking by the penetrating call of a wolf.

Or I guess that's what wolves sound like—calling to the moon or something. I must have seen it on TV once.

But again, they'd all been wiped out decades ago.

I'm delusional—it's the dehydration—I'm actually going to lose my mind out here—this dusty forest will be the last thing I see.

He needed to rest. He curled up under a particularly big tree—he figured its thick canopy would give him some protection when the sun came up—and he tried to sleep. He heard voices whispering around him and the wolf—*or whatever the hell that is*—was still calling. The General was too tired to be scared. He slept.

* * *

Danny's bed was comfortable, but tiny, and it was a tight squeeze for Ash and Pinar to fit in together. It was already the middle of the night and they were so exhausted they fell asleep instantly. Danny curled up on the sofa—which is where he usually ended up these days anyway—and they slept deeply until just before sunrise.

They were all awoken suddenly by a loud knock at the door.

Chapter fifty-four

Thees things always take me ages to work out," signed Danny. "Do either of you remember the key for this week?"

He held in his hand a note from the resistance. As usual it was printed out in Braille and encoded with the key they had all received the night before.

"Don't look at me," said Ash, sleepily. "My brain's so old, I barely remember either of your names."

Pinar laughed. "I remember the code." She took the piece of paper. "*It's the first time in ages I had to memorise a transposition key—or anything really. Let's see if I can remember...*do you have a pen?"

Danny passed her one from his drawer. Pinar started reading with her left hand, her index finger running over the tiny dots while she noted down the letters they represented, converted them in her head and wrote down the un-encoded message. It said simply:

Dignity. Tonight. Sundown.

"Dignity?" asked Pinar.

"Dignity Park I guess. It's quite a long walk from here, it's out in what used to be the suburbs, next to the sea."

"I've never heard of it," said Pinar, "Who'd build a new park since the crash?"

"Ah, you probably knew it as Independence Park. Since it was...*reclaimed*...everyone just knows it as Dignity."

"*Will that be the new location for the mesa then?*" asked Ash.

"Seems like it might be. These days it's a...erm...*cruising* park..." Danny said tentatively. "Cruising is when people erm—"

"—We know what cruising is, sweetie," Ash interrupted. "We weren't always old you know."

She gave Danny a playful wink.

"Of course. Err...well, anyway, *the State never steps foot there. It's been a safe zone for as long as anyone can remember. So far, at least.*"

He opened the drawer of his desk and pulled out a map of the City. It was at least twenty years old and bore almost no resemblance to the modern layout, but the park was there and he pointed it out to them.

"Yeah, seems a long way from here," said Pinar, running her finger over the map. "*Maybe it is a safer place for the mesa.*"

"Or it's a great place for the State to set up an ambush." Ash stood up and stretched. "We have no way to know who left this message. We might be walking straight into a trap for all we know."

"We don't have much choice," said Pinar, also getting out of the tiny bed. "*We'll just have to be careful.*"

"Cool, so let's head out this evening," said Danny. "I have a cleaning shift now and a client to see. Help yourself to food and I'll leave you the spare key in case you want to go out. When I get back we can go together if you like?"

"Perfect," said Pinar, "We'll be here."

They decided it was safest to wait for Danny in his apartment, so they spent the day quietly sleeping, signing and watching the sunlight move across the wall.

Ash was hungry and decided to cook something. She got up and dug around for a while in Danny's empty cupboards.

"How does anyone live like this?" she said louder than she intended.

"*Sign, don't shout.*" Pinar giggled. She had accidentally quoted a USL promotion campaign from the twenties. "*Sorry! Didn't mean to speak State at you...*"

Ash didn't look amused. "There's nothing here but Nutrition

snacks and one dusty old Nutrition meal and a bottle of beer which must be older than I am."

"Nothing's older than you are, dear. This is what people eat in the City. There aren't any vegetables...and after all, *'Everything nutritious starts with Nutrition,'*" signed Pinar, quoting another commercial, this time for the monolithic company that controlled the City's food supply.

"Please stop doing that!" Ash sat down on the bed, exasperated. "*This stuff is made by City prisoners, for City prisoners. And who knows what they put in it?*"

"*Rats, I heard.*"

"*I miss our gardens. Well mine at least,*" Ash signed, allowing herself to relax into the banter. "*Yours is just a big mess. I hope my squashes are okay.*"

"*All standing in a row like little State soldiers? I'm sure they'll be fine. I'm hungry. Let's eat Danny's rat bars.*"

Ash made a face. But she stood up anyway and went back to dig them out of the cupboard. Her stomach was growling. She was hungry enough to eat just about anything.

* * *

The General opened his eyes. The sun was bright and high in the sky. His head still hurt and his entire body was screaming for him to drink something—anything—right now.

He guessed he must also still be hallucinating. As he blinked his eyes to see clearer, he saw people around him—five or six in a circle, talking with their back to him. He could smell food and wood smoke.

He tried to lift himself up to cast away the images, but he was too tired. He had walked too much, suffered too much. He wanted to die here surrounded by dirt and trees.

One came over and spoke to him although he couldn't understand a word. It held a cup to his lips and suddenly he felt cold, crisp water in his mouth. He swallowed without thinking. If this was just a dream, he would at least enjoy it. He drank more and nearly retched. The imaginary person was telling him to sip slowly, so he did. He felt a little better; his stomach was knotting less. Gratefully, he put his head back down on soft leaves.

Chapter fifty-five

They were still there, the hallucinations.

They saw that he was awake again and came over with more water.

They were asking him his name.

"G," he said instinctively, which was true although he had only been called the General, or Sir, for as long as he could remember. Or Prisoner 7485, but that was in jail and he was a free man now. So, he was G. The name of his proud past. And here he was, talking to imaginary people. "My name's G."

"I'm Olly, good to meet you," said the hallucination softly.

A resistance name, the General noticed vaguely.

"Are you feeling a bit better?" Olly asked him.

"I'm...are you real?" G asked, his dry lips mumbling the words a little. "Did you come...with the wolves?"

Olly's face creased with concern.

"We found you yesterday—you were severely dehydrated. You're doing better though, G. I think you'll be fine. Here—" he said as he offered more water. "Small sips remember..."

G drank as slowly as he could. His vision was clearing and the people seemed to be staying with him.

Could they be real? Have I survived again?

He drank and ate some bread that the one called Olly gave him.

He was still weak, but he was beginning to feel whole again. *I'm going to be okay. Of course I am. I'm a fucking warrior.*

* * *

Nathalie's heart was racing. She had a meeting scheduled with Kit. In fact, it was a 'date' with her 'girlfriend', but she no longer liked to think in those terms. Every time they'd hooked up, it had been rougher and sleazier than the last time. And Nathalie was loving every second of it.

They were meeting at Kit's place for the first time and after checking repeatedly that the neighbours were absolutely, definitely not in, Nathalie walked quickly through the corridor and knocked on Kit's door.

She waited. There was no sound from the other side and Nathalie looked around the corridor nervously. She really didn't want to get caught: Kit was protected by her job, but Nathalie wasn't. Besides gossip was just never a good thing.

She knocked again, just a little louder this time, still trying not to draw attention to herself. She heard sounds from inside and after another minute's pause, the door swung open, the person behind it standing just out of view.

Nathalie stepped in and the door closed behind her. The apartment was dark and humid. Shutters blocked out the afternoon sun and two red candles were lit by the bed.

Kit stepped out in front of her, completely naked and without a word, began to kiss Nathalie, her lips soft and tender. As Nathalie's clothes fell silently into a heap on the floor, Kit got down on her knees and began tasting Nathalie's breasts, drawing a line down across her belly, the dampness she left behind, cool in the afternoon heat.

What the hell? Nathalie thought. *It's never like this.*

Until today, they'd only met outside, in public, but Kit was always forceful with her, even violent.

And that's just how I like it.

But Kit was different today—tender, even—and as she climbed onto the bed, lying on her front, her arms spread out, she gestured to Nathalie, inviting her to lie on top of her. Nathalie obeyed, climbing on, straddling her naked body.

This doesn't feel right. I wanted to be below her. I'm always below her. This isn't what my fantasies look like at all.

"Pull my hair," said Kit. It wasn't an order, it was a request, a polite suggestion. Nathalie complied and gave her black hair a little tug, but only just.

Since the day she had learned about Kit's profession, every night in bed and every day at the office, Nathalie had fantasised about her lover dressed in leather and heels, brandishing a whip, surrounded by her lucky subs. She dreamed constantly of giving the gift of total submission.

It looks nothing like candlelight and kisses on the bed.

Kit rolled over. They kissed and held each other tight, fingers exploring, penetrating. Kit pulled her close and began stroking her skin.

Stroking not scratching.

A while later, Kit began her climax, an intimate, shaking orgasm that tore out of her mouth in muffled moans. Her expression was one of pure and total bliss, her eyes were wet.

Nathalie followed, but hers was faked. There was something missing. This was all too gentle, too *real* for Nathalie. She wanted violence and tears of pain. She wanted to be pinned down and be given no choice.

All this emotion. Maybe next time, I should piss her off somehow. I'll find a way to provoke her into giving me a good, hard slap.

Kit curled up and invited Nathalie to join her. She complied.

This isn't how it's supposed to be, Nathalie thought as Kit was dozing off in her arms. *I joined the resistance for her. I'm risking my job hanging out with those people. I deserve more than this. Because, after all...*

Kit began to snore lightly.

...I'm dating a pro-Domme for a reason.

Chapter fifty-six

My name's Gus actually. Sorry about before, I didn't know if you might be State. We can't be too careful these days." Gus meant 'revered' in German and that pleased him a lot. The General—prisoner 7485, G, Gus—sat surrounded by the resistance shoal who had saved his life. They hung on his every word as he effortlessly invented himself a new history.

Sometimes lying is just as easy as breathing.

"I lived in the City before, you know, with my boyfriend. He was a pianist with the State, one of the few musicians still around, and— uff...you had to hear him play. He has such an amazing passion, like you've never heard before. The first time I heard him he was playing under the escalators in Central Station, all the other commuters rushing by to get their trains and ignoring him entirely but I just stood there. I couldn't take my eyes off of him. He was so young and handsome. So...intensely focused. I watched his entire set and, of course, missed my train. As soon as we spoke I knew he was the man I wanted to spend the rest of my life with."

Gus took a dramatic pause.

"We moved in together that same year and were together for nearly fifteen years. But we should have known we wouldn't be able to survive the Purges. We should have been more careful. We were caught out—our neighbours knew about us, I mean, at some point everyone did and, I don't know, I guess they had to cover themselves or something so they turned us in. Anyway, when the troopers came to our house, Tom—my darling Tom—was out at work, at the admin office and...uff...

Gus looked around to check his story had everyone's full attention.

"...I kissed him goodbye barely an hour before. The bastard troopers knocked down our front door. Literally, they smashed it off its hinges. And...I was lucky, I suppose. I managed to escape by jumping off the balcony. Almost broke my ankle, but I ran and I ran and I got away. Eventually I joined the exodus—and even saw those same damn neighbours who turned us in—I guess they really had something to hide and tattling on a couple of gays wasn't enough to protect them. Anyway, I escaped through the tunnels with the rest of the *exiliadas*. We walked for days and I've been out here ever since, just getting by. Going from well to well, trying to survive. And Tom, I don't know. Prison maybe? Or something worse..."

Gus caught the eye of the older woman who looked like she was about to cry. He could already see his future opening up before him.

This is almost too easy. Suddenly being a vergent makes me a victim in need of help. Here, it's actually a good thing. I'll be back home in no time.

"...I miss him so much."

"And now?" an older woman asked softly. "Are you heading back to the City? We're only a few hours walk from the walls, you know."

"Really? So close?" Gus kept her eye contact with false sincerity. "Yes, I want to see him again. I know it's dangerous and crazy, but I just want the chance to kiss him just one more time."

There were understanding nods around the circle.

"I must have gotten turned around. I've been walking for days and finished up all my food and water. I would have died here if you hadn't found me."

The group fell silent.

I'm not sure what life I have waiting for me in the City, but I'll find something. Anything has to be better than this resistance-infested forest. I'll start from the bottom and rise, just like I always have.

The grey-haired woman looked like she wanted to say something. *It's coming, I know it is—*

"—We'll need to discuss it, of course," she began, emotion catching in her throat. "But maybe, if you'd like to, you could come with us back to the City?"

There was a murmur of agreement around the group.

"We could help you find your dear Tom again."

"Thank you," said Gus, his eyes watering on cue. "That would be so wonderful."

* * *

Breathless, Danny arrived home. Ash and Pinar sat on his bed with expressions of total boredom on their faces.

"Sorry it took me so long. I had a client who just took *ages*," he said, unlacing his sneakers. "I think he really believes I'm his boyfriend or something…Anyway, look!" He pointed at his bag with his chin. "I brought Nutrition Snacks! I'll just shower, and then we can leave if you like?"

"Sounds good, Danny," Pinar yawned and stretched. "Thanks again for letting us stay."

"Any time. It's always nice to have guests."

Danny went into the bathroom, stripped and climbed into the shower. In truth, he knew they weren't just any guests. He had learned about A and P and the Femme Riots as a kid—They were heroines to him and he had recognised them immediately although no-one had heard word from them since the Purges. Danny was even a bit starstruck, but he kept his mouth shut.

I don't want to embarrass them, but I can't wait to tell Kit that they slept in my bed—She's going to be so jealous!

* * *

After Gus had told his story and the shoal had tidied up their camp in the forest, they met briefly to discuss their new travelling companion. The decision was unanimous and took only a few minutes. Olly came over to deliver the good news.

"It's decided—you can come with us, Gus!"

Gus smiled his warmest smile and even managed to squeeze out another tear of joy.

Chapter fifty-seven

Kit opened her eyes slowly. The afternoon light flickering through the curtains was soft and warm. Nathalie's long arms were still wrapped around her. For the first time in a very long time, she had opened herself up, really relaxed in front of another person and she felt safer than she could ever remember.

She rolled over to kiss her lover. Nathalie was awake and had a peculiar look in her eyes. Something strangely like boredom.

"What a wonderful sleep," Kit smiled and stretched.

"Yeah you seemed to enjoy it."

"You didn't sleep?"

"I didn't sleep."

"Everything okay?

"Everything's perfect."

"So kiss me."

They kissed and lay for a while, Kit running her fingers over Nathalie's pale skin. The warm afternoon had made them both sweat at the points where they touched.

Like we're melting into each other, thought Kit.

It's a bit disgusting, thought Nathalie.

Nathalie still had a distant look in her eyes and through the fog of sleepiness and love, Kit began to sense that something wasn't right. Their connection, their chemistry had gone cold. She shivered.

"Nathalie, sweetie, are you sure you're okay?" Kit said, stroking her curly hair gently. "Did I do something wrong?"

"No, you were perfect. Aren't you always perfect?"

"Erm...I don't really know wh—"

"*Perfect* Kit, with her *perfect* body."

"I'm not—" Kit felt nauseous and confused. *Where's all this coming from?* "What happened?"

"Nothing happened, that's the problem. Where were the slaps and the scratches and the bites? I still have bruises from the park and now all I get is *soft kisses on my belly*." She spat the words out like they disgusted her.

"But I thought you lik—"

"Of course I *like* it. But I don't *want* to like it. I want you to hurt me."

"Sorry, I really don—"

"Hit me."

"Excuse me?"

"Hit me. Slap me. Tell me what a fucking bitch I am. Right now. You owe me, Kit. You got what you wanted, now I should get what I want. After everything I've done for you."

Nathalie stood up. She looked angrier than Kit had ever seen her. She was dressed in seconds and opened the door.

"Fuck you then, Kit. Fuck you."

She slammed the door on the way out as hard as she could.

* * *

Ash, Pinar, and Danny were ready to leave for the park and Danny was filling a water bottle from the kitchen tap.

"Do you ladies need to use the bathroom before we leave?" he asked. "It's a long walk."

Pinar shook her head and Ash declared simply: "I don't pee."

Danny gave her a quizzical look.

"I'm a trans woman dear," she explained. "I went decades without having public bathroom access. The women's was rarely an option.

The men's? God, no. For a while it was even illegal in some places for me to pee in public spaces at all. So I don't pee. Or at least not often."

"But where does it all...?" Danny began. "Actually, sorry, ignore me. Let's go?"

Ash smiled. "Let's."

They left the apartment building discreetly and taking a small road out of the centre, they began the journey to Dignity Park.

Pinar suggested taking the tunnels but Danny barely used them and wasn't good at navigating in the dark. Secretly, Ash was relieved.

I'd rather face State troopers in the street then be back down in that dark, concrete hell. Besides, I look masculine enough in my jeans and in this summer heat, Pinar's dark skin can almost pass for a tan. And Danny's protected...My God, how did we ever get to the point where we have to think about these things?

For Danny, who only ever cycled around town, it was a long walk. He could dance for five hours straight, but walking took different muscles and he just wasn't used to it. With that and the heat, his back was soon wet with sweat.

"Pff, I can barely keep up with you two!" he half-joked, breathlessly. "You're making me feel old."

"Well, back home we live a ways from each other so we've gotten used to walking long distances," said Pinar, looking at Ash who seemed quiet but much happier to be under the sky and moving again.

"Ah, I assumed you lived together. Aren't you, I mean, aren't you a couple?"

"You're not the first to make that mistake."

"Sorry..."

"No need to be, I take it as a compliment." Pinar smiled. "We're probably closer than most couples anyhow." She caught Ash's eye and she smiled back. "And you, Danny, anyone special in your life?"

"Who has time? My work keeps me super busy and after all that...erm...*meaningless sex* or whatever—I have no energy to meet anyone. Also, honestly, there's really just not many of us...*vergents*...left here." He whispered the word unconsciously although there was absolutely no one in the street. "Well, most of my clients probably are, but it's kind of an open secret."

They paused for a moment in the cool shade of an old lime tree to pass round some stale water from a bottle. Although it was late afternoon, the air was still hot and Danny gulped the water down.

"I used to turn tricks from time to time back in the day," Pinar said as she took the bottle from Danny and put it back in her pack.

They started walking again and, intrigued, Danny waited for her to continue.

I should probably be surprised to hear someone twice my age telling me she used to 'turn tricks' but these days basically everyone I know is a sex worker. I guess I've kind of come to expect it.

"It was useful for a while," Pinar continued finally. "At some point it got too much. Mostly the clients were just too much—and I needed to get out after a few years. Economically, things were already difficult back then so I didn't have too many options." She paused. "In the end it became difficult."

"I get that," Danny said, "It definitely can be."

"But somehow I miss it from time to time as well. I had some good fun."

Ash listened intently while Pinar talked. They rarely spoke about those days in the City from before they had met. Pinar had left sex work in a pretty bad way and when they met a few years afterwards, she still refused to talk about that time, or why she had left the industry. Ash was surprised to hear that she might miss it.

I guess there are some things sex workers can only share with other sex workers. Even after all these years, I still have so much to learn about her.

* * *

The air was warm and G dozed against a tree as the others busied themselves in the camp.

"Gus, are you feeling any better?" asked the grey haired woman.

After water and rest, he was actually feeling much better, but he didn't particularly feel like talking.

"A little..." he said, weakly. "Thank you for asking."

"My name's Sue by the way, I didn't get chance to introduce myself before."

"Nice to meet you, Sue."

"Likewise." She smiled and looked like she was going to bend over and give him cheek kisses as the norm always was after exchanging names, but she thought better of it and sat a few metres from him instead.

"Sorry," he said, looking down at his filthy clothes. "I kind of stink."

"No problem," she replied kindly. "Would you like to me to take your shirt down to the creek and rinse it for you?"

"That would be wonderful, Sue. Thank you!"

He stripped out of his disgusting trousers. He noticed that even after weeks in prison, his military trained body still looked great—if anything he thought he looked even better having lost a few pounds. He took off his shirt as seductively as he could and handed it to the old woman and he saw her eyes light up.

My abs have always been impressive. I can't blame her for taking a little look.

She smiled politely and left to clean Gus' shit-stained prison clothes in the creek.

One day, he thought to himself leaning back against the tree, *one day and I already have these idiots washing my clothes and eating out of my hand.*

* * *

A patrol passed by. At least a hundred uniformed men moved northwards on the other side of the street. Although the troopers were heading in the other direction to them, Ash and Pinar tensed as they continued walking. The troopers were armed to the teeth and Ash didn't want to think about where they were headed, which prison riot they had been ordered to suppress.

Pinar and Danny were chatting and signing very visibly about something inane.

All our disguises, Ash thought to herself. *If the troopers only knew who we really are, we'd be heading to a State lock up by now or facing a firing squad.*

Ash tried to join in the fake conversation but as usual, the masculine pronouns were clumsy and inauthentic in her hands. She gave up and focused on walking instead. After five minutes the troopers were gone, and they fell back into their usual rhythm—Pinar and Danny chatting like they'd known each other for years and Ash listening in, soothed by their voices.

* * *

Sue returned an hour later and brought Gus' clothes back to him. They were clean, dry and warm. *She must have hung them out in the sun for a while.*

As he put the shirt back on and she watched him expectantly, Gus managed to fake a smile for her.

Well, he thought to himself, *the smell of dried shit and prison has been replaced by the stink of stagnant river water which isn't a whole lot better. Good try anyway, Sue.*

"Thank you," he said. Sue smiled.

Gus joined the shoal, who were sitting in a circle as they often did, and helped himself to a bottle of well-water. He drank nearly a third of the bottle in one go.

It tastes like dirt. They must have carried these bottles from one of the resistance wells.

It was, what, two or three weeks ago that I was ordering the destruction of those very same wells? And punishing the grunts for their failure.

Today as he drank thirstily from the well water carried many miles by his new travel companions, Gus found himself strangely grateful for that failure.

* * *

Still walking, Ash, Pinar, and their new friend had left the city centre and were passing through abandoned suburban neighbourhoods.

Once in a while they passed signs of destruction—smashed windows, burned cars—and Ash noticed that it looked a lot like the post-apocalyptic movies she used to make fun of. But mostly the neighbourhood was clean and calm as if everyone had just gone on holiday for a while and any day now would be back to mow their lawns and walk their dogs. Ash knew that the truth was much more sinister than that.

These people are never coming home. We divergents ran this city, we were its greatest attraction. And this is what we left behind.

Pinar and Danny were still chatting about sex work as they walked through the surreal landscape.

"And how is it for you?" she asked him. "If you don't mind talking about work on your evening off, of course."

Danny smiled. "Honestly, it's nice to talk about it. I rarely get the chance. These days, I'm either working, in which case—obviously—I pretend I'm having the time of my life, or I'm in meetings representing the collective. Either way there's never time to talk about how it really is. Or whether I like it or not."

"And do you? Like it, I mean?"

"I'm not sure. It really depends. It's work, you know?" Danny had a distant look. "Obviously I get protection from having clients so high up—which is more important than ever these days. I probably wouldn't even be here without that." He took a Nutrition bar out of his backpack, took a bite and passed it on. "It also means that most of them are privileged sleazeballs, to be honest. And the constant lying is exhausting as I'm sure you remember—"

"Vividly."

"Yeah," Danny walked on thoughtfully for a moment. "I'm the king of compartmentalising my life, but I also hate that sometimes. I mostly hate my clients too. The worst are the ones who try to 'save' me from myself. Or from my job."

"In what way?"

"I don't know, it's stupid. It's like they find my job so *demeaning* and *dirty* that they need to save me from it, but you know, they're also employing me—They *are* my job so it makes no sense at all." He paused and fiddled with his fingers for a moment. "Sometimes the money just isn't enough to listen to all that bullshit."

"Totally."

"It's messed up. But not all the time. From time to time there's something like affection. Some of them are sweet to me."

"All work is complicated," said Pinar.

"Exactly. I love to dance though so all in all I'm doing okay."

"Good to hear it."

Danny held up the empty water bottle.

"Hey, we're all out of water. And we still have a way to go. If you like, we can stop off at one of the feminist squats in the neighbourhood. My friend told me about one that shouldn't be too far out of our way."

"Cool, let's do it," agreed Pinar. "I definitely wouldn't mind a short rest."

* * *

They arrived five minutes later at the squat. Danny had the address written down but it was very easy to spot—It was the only building in the block that *wasn't* covered in anti-State graffiti. The door was grand and oversized—it was probably a Post Office or something back in the day.

"This must be the place," said Ash. "If they really wanted to keep it a secret though, they should probably put up a few tags."

Danny knocked on the door. They heard someone arrive on the other side who whispered the first half of the pass-phrase and Danny completed it. The door opened and revealed a white woman dressed all in black standing just in the shadows.

"Hi, my name's Danny. I work with M, erm. Maria, I think her name is, at the State bar in town? She told me about this place. Could we come in for a drink? We've been walking a long way."

The woman at the door looked straight past Danny as if he wasn't there.

"You can come in," she said to Pinar. "But this is a women's-only space. You boys will have to wait outside."

"*Boys?*" said Pinar, her temper rising. She gestured towards Ash. "Can't you see my friend is a *woman?* What's wrong with you?"

Ash for her part, was surprisingly calm. She held Pinar's hand and said "It's okay, hon. It's fine."

"It's *not* fine!" shouted Danny. "This is A, Ash, from the frikking *Femme Riots.* If she isn't enough of a woman for your space, who the hell *is?*"

The squatter had nothing to say and retreated back into the building, closing the massive door and locking it loudly.

"What the *hell?*" Danny clenched his fists in frustration and looked like he might start punching the wall in front of him. He turned to Ash. "I'm so sorry about that. I mean, I don't mind waiting outside, but *you, Ash*? I'm so sorry. I didn't know that would happen."

"It's fine," repeated Ash with a tone of defeat. "Let's just go."

"Nothing about this is fine," said Danny. "Uff. We have another hour or so to walk. Will you be okay?"

"Let's go." Ash started walking.

Pinar was too angry to speak. But this wasn't the first time she and Ash had been torn apart by their bodies and she knew, as well as she knew anything in life, that it wouldn't be the last.

An hour later, the City seemed to stop suddenly at the horizon, dropping off into nothingness. Ash stared at the effect in confusion for a moment.

"The sea!" said Pinar. "We're here."

Chapter fifty-eight

Gus was strong enough to walk again, so the shoal broke camp and headed out in the direction of the City. He mumbled and swore to himself as he trailed along behind the others, tripping over branches and rocks.

I'm still weak and they're going too damn fast.

A while later, they arrived at a muddy river channel that blocked their path. In the winter it must have been a fast flowing river, but now it lay empty except for some puddles left behind at the bottom of the channel. Gus leaned against a tree on the river bank to rest.

Looking down into the channel, he saw that in one of the smallest puddles, barely two metres across, catfish gasped and flopped about, their whiskers and tails picked out in red by the light of the setting sun. Without rain, without the river, they were just waiting to die.

"We have to do something," said Sue. She looked over at Olly. "Are you with me?"

"Of course."

The river bank was mostly dried out and it didn't take long for everyone to climb down into the flat river bed. Gus watched on in amazement as Sue walked over to the puddle of gasping fish and using only her hands, started digging a trench in the mud to connect their small puddle with one of the larger ones. Olly joined her and eventually, the whole shoal—except Gus, who stood watching them with a look of total confusion—were working hard to connect the puddles.

After ten minutes, they stood back and watched as the water started to flow again and created one large pool that rose around the catfish. They soon stopped thrashing and disappeared below the surface.

Sue smiled, rinsed off her muddy hands and, without a word, climbed up the other side of the river channel and continued on her way. The group followed her and Gus came running after them.

He cast a glimpse back at the pool, amazed.

All that work for some lousy fish. They should have caught them for dinner!

Still despite himself, he was impressed by this love for nature. In his life, Gus had barely seen people express love for each *other*, much less for a catfish.

That's the way things work, he thought to himself. *Eat or be eaten. Survival of the fittest.*

And yet he couldn't deny it—what he had just seen had moved him.

He began to ask himself if, in fact, there might be other options; if maybe what he knew wasn't the only way of living. His head busy with questions, Gus silently picked up the pace and followed the resistance members through the forest. After walking for a while, he caught an unmistakable smell in the air. A scent he didn't know how much he'd missed until he smelt it again. It was the smell of the sea.

* * *

Ash and Pinar paused at the edge of the park. About four hundred metres ahead of them, the grass dropped suddenly away into rocky cliffs and they could hear the waves crashing beyond. Gulls flew above them, calling loudly.

"It's been so long, Pin. I wasn't sure we'd ever see the sea again."

"Admit it, Ash, you're just a little bit excited to be back here."

"Well..." she replied with a coy smile. "Maybe just a little."

* * *

As fast as they could, Gus and the rest of the shoal picked their way across the Ring and reached the City's walls without any sign of the State. Sue moved some brush and stones revealing an entrance to one of the tunnels.

As Gus climbed onto the ladder and began his descent, he realised that despite everything he had been through, everything he had survived, he was grinning.

This is it. I've made it.

And nothing on earth will stop me now.

5. Dignity

Chapter fifty-nine

D ignity Park was alive. More than a hundred people gathered amongst the tall grass and, above them, clouds of starlings darkened the reddening sky.

Danny went to find food but Ash and Pinar paused near the edge of the grass. It was a beautiful evening and Ash wasn't ready yet to be around crowds of people. Sitting down on a warm rock, they took in the spectacle as thousands of birds flew above them almost as a single organism. They pulsed and grew and split and re-joined in perfect, complex synchrony.

"I'd missed this," said Ash. "I remember going years without seeing even a single starling."

"Me too," Pinar replied. "I probably told you that a friend in my faculty was doing a study on their populations. She said that they went from being one of the most common birds in Europe to one of the rarest in a matter of decades. All because of industrial agriculture and pollution."

Above them, two clouds of birds joined into one and pulsed upwards.

"Yeah..." said Ash vaguely. "You know people always talk about the crash like it's the worst thing that ever happened, but I doubt the starlings see it that way."

"I guess not."

"After Chernobyl, wolves, deer, moose and boar populations rebounded in the human-free exclusion zone. Despite it being one of the worst nuclear accidents ever. I mean, the radiation was a total ecological disaster of course but farming, forestry and hunting were apparently worse."

"I remember you telling me," said Pinar, smiling. "Many times."

"Well...I still think it's a good story." Ash poked out her tongue. "Anyway, starlings, how do they fly in such big groups? How can they possibly coordinate themselves?"

Ash's question wasn't rhetorical. At the turn of the century, Pinar had worked and studied as a systems ecologist with a speciality in complexity and diversity. She was an expert on a lot of things and enjoyed sharing what she had learned.

"Well, interestingly their flocks have what's known as scale-free correlation. Basically, if one bird changes speed, then it affects all the others in the group, regardless of where they are. Normally that's the kind of thing that happens just at the edge of criticality—like snowflakes before an avalanche."

"—Okay—"

"In later studies, though, it was shown that when they change direction it only affects a starling's seven closest neighbours, then *their* neighbours and so on. Which is why we see ripples passing through the murmuration."

"Murmur what now?"

"A flock of starlings. It's called a murmuration."

"Oh. I just call it a 'flock of starlings'."

"Anyway..." Pinar laughed. "You know they're really musical as well. Each male can learn up to twenty different songs and they mimic just about anything—human speech, cats, technology. Apparently, Mozart had one as a pet and it learned his Piano Concerto in G major."

"I heard one do a really good car alarm once."

"They're amazing."

"They really are."

They sat and watched for a while and soon the starlings began to roost. They landed in small groups on the highest branches of the park trees and disappeared into shadows.

I wish they would just keep flying forever, thought Ash. *But they're tired. Like me.*

"Distraction over," she announced.

"Let's go in?"

Ash nodded and, holding hands with her best friend, she entered the park.

They arrived at the meeting circle, sat down and took some food and tea offered to them by other resistance members. The *mesa* was scheduled to start in twenty minutes.

Just enough time for a nap, thought Ash.

"Can I?" she asked, lying down with her head hovering above Pinar's lap.

"Of course, hon."

She lay her head down and fell immediately asleep.

* * *

Danny was poking a stick into the fire impatiently. Anxious to hear if his intel about Life Accounts had been verified, he stood up and walked around the park to distract himself. He came to an old gnarled tree and leaned against it to watch the whistling, squabbling birds in the branches above. Over by the edge of the park, he noticed someone was just arriving and was headed straight over to him.

I'd recognise those heels anywhere.

"Hi," said Kit quietly as she arrived and gave Danny a peck on the cheek. "How's things?"

"I'm great!" replied Danny enthusiastically. "Since you saved all our skins last night. Thank God for the sex workers, eh?

"Yeah."

Her voice was so quiet, she was almost whispering.

"Oh, and I have to tell you something. You won't believe who—"

He paused for a moment to really look at her. Her eyes were bloodshot, her hair was less perfect than usual.

By Kit's standards, she's a total wreck.

"Wait, are you okay?"

"Not very."

"Sit down. Tell me everything."

They sat together by the tree. Danny could see she was close to tears.

"It's Nathalie," she began. "We met up this afternoon and she was...weird and crappy."

"Weird how?"

"Well, she came over to my place. And we had sex. Soft, you know? Something different to normal and I dozed off for a while, and when I woke up she was totally angry. Stormed out, made a big drama."

"Wow, okay. Did she say anything? Like why she was angry?"

"She wanted me to hit her."

Danny was silent.

"She said I got what I wanted and she had to get what she wanted. What does that even mean? I— I *cried* with her, Danny. I opened up, you know? Then she throws all this shit at me."

Danny put his hand on her knee. He had never seen Kit so upset over a girl before.

"Is she coming tonight? Does she have clearance for the *mesa*?"

"Yeah, I think it came through last night. Clearance that *I* got her by the way. It's fucked up. I don't even want to see her."

She cried then, sobs pulsing through her body while Danny held her close to his chest. They sat like that for a few minutes, the noisy starlings slowly calming above them as they settled in for the night.

"Thanks." Kit pulled herself up and wiped her face. "*Well...*" she said loudly and tidied her hair with a false smile. "That's enough of all that."

Danny looked at his friend with admiration.

"Are you okay?"

"It's fine—What's done is done. Anyway, we should get over to the meeting." She pulled out a mirror and touched up her make up.

"By the way, who did you come here with?"

Danny pointed to where Pinar sat eating, Ash still dozing on her lap.

"You found yourself some sexy grannies?"

Danny grinned.

"Actually, it's Ash and Pinar from the forest."

"*The* Ash and Pinar?"

"Yep."

"Like the *mythological* A and P from before the Improvement?" Kit stood up. She started signing and speaking at the same time. "*From the riots? The women that started this whole damn movement?*"

"Stop waving your arms around—they'll read you!" laughed Danny. "But yes, one and the same."

"I thought they were *dead*! They must be a hundred years old!"

"Well...not quite."

"Wow. And they're still hot."

"I'll tell them you said so." He spoke seriously again. "Let's talk more about Nathalie later, okay?"

"I'm fine," Kit said with a smile that was altogether too bright. "Let's move on. It's meeting time now and I know how much you *love* being in meetings."

Danny smiled. "Well try not to check out my grannies too much. And if you're good, I'll introduce you to them later."

"You'd better!"

When everyone was gathered together in the tall, scratchy grass, the sky was already dark and the *mesa* finally began. First on the agenda was the eviction from the warehouse. Someone from the logistics collective, a black woman with short hair, was speaking.

"We can't stay here out in the open," she said in a worried tone. "Shoals are arriving every hour from the forest and the camp is already too visible as it is. We're sitting ducks out here."

Someone Danny vaguely recognised from the sex work collective responded.

"In all these years, the State has never stepped foot in this park. They seem to have forgotten about this neighbourhood entirely. Besides, it's only for two days and then we'll be out of here. The only other option is the tunnels which isn't really an option at all."

"It's way too dangerous, we need to think of something else—"

"It's fine. Stop worrying so much—"

After half an hour of arguments back and forth and plenty of strong facilitation, the group reached consensus. As there wasn't anywhere else in the City to move so many people to so late in the day, the camp would stay in the park for the time being and the logistics collective would keep looking for other options.

The meeting moved on to the most dramatic news. A resistance member in tight jeans stood up to deliver the report. They cleared their throat twice and began to speak.

"Hi everyone," they said, their voice carefully controlled. "According to sources, the Sett community was attacked by State troopers two nights ago."

The speaker paused for a moment to let the news settle in. They knew what they had to say next would come as a shock to everyone gathered. Taking a deep breath, they continued.

"Some of the community managed to escape into the mountains, but we're not sure yet how many made it out. The rest were taken prisoner and are being marched towards the City. They may have already arrived and we assume that they're being taken to prison. As you know, many of the community are *exiliadas* and a jail sentence would be very serious indeed."

Sitting at the edge of the group, Ash shuddered.

I hate to think what a State prison looks like these days.

Certainly the three times she had been arrested and put in the male prison hadn't been pretty. She reached out and took Pinar's hand. They both had dear friends in the Sett.

Ash wanted to ask about her friend Elias, but before she could put up her hand, the speaker answered her question for her.

"...According to a runner who was present for the event, but managed to get away unseen, one person was killed during the attack and the subsequent eviction."

The young speaker was still talking as unemotionally as they could. Ash saw that their hands were shaking.

Just deliver the news. Keep your distance.

"That person, I'm afraid, some of you probably know him...He was a mentor to so many of us. A resistance member for decades, a teacher and a fearless comrade—"

"Who, who was it?" someone asked.

The speaker blinked back tears and their voice broke a little. "It was...Elias. They fucking killed Elias."

Ash grabbed Pinar's hand tighter. She felt like she might throw up.

Elias is dead. Jason, imprisoned. The Sett, destroyed. This is so much bigger than we were prepared for.

Chapter sixty

After the tragic news, Ash just wanted to go hide in the tent. She went to the fire to pick up some soup and perched next to Pinar, eating as fast as she could. Danny came over with a friend.

"This is Kit," he said presenting her proudly. Her hair and face were immaculate again and she was smiling. Nathalie hadn't shown up for the *mesa*. Danny hoped she'd have the sensitivity to stay away tonight.

"Nice to meet you, Kit," Pinar stood up for the four kisses. Like Ash, she was sad about the news but she was an expert at maintaining her smile even in the hardest of times.

"Nice to meet you," said Kit, also smiling.

Ash ignored them all and poked at her soup.

"I told you about Kit," said Danny, "She was the one who warned us all about the raid last night."

"Well, thanks," Pinar sat back down, "For, you know, saving our asses. Did Danny mention that at the warehouse, he tried to strangle me and Ash nearly killed him?"

Kit gave her a curious look.

"Now *that's* a story I have to hear. I'll open us a beer and you can tell me all about it."

Kit dug around in her bag and pulled out a bottle. She opened it effortlessly on the edge of a rock. "We've heard a lot about you ladies." She passed the bottle to Pinar. "And Danny says you got to sleep in his bed. Not many can claim that privilege!"

"Well, it *was* a bit of squeeze but we all fit in the end," Pinar joked, taking a swig of warm beer.

"I would love to have seen that," said Kit and they both laughed.

Ash had checked out of the conversation completely. She knew she was being rude, but she was also in shock.

How can they all chat and smile like that? Elias was one of my oldest friends, and now he's gone and there's nothing I can do about it.

She wanted to leave. She wanted to curl up in the tent alone but she knew Pinar was in the mood to meet people.

And it's not a bad idea to be making friends.

One way or the other, Ash knew they'd be doing a major action together in the coming days and when that happened, these conversations, these social bonds, might mean the difference between life and death.

Ash stared at the sky and listened to the sea. *For tonight at least, Pin's charming enough for the both of us.*

"Looks like we finished this one," announced Kit ten minutes later, waving the empty beer bottle and reaching for her bag. "I'll get us another."

"How you ever fit so much into that tiny handbag is beyond me," joked Danny.

"Well, we all have our secrets, dear."

Danny turned to Pinar and looked serious for a moment.

The elephant in the room, he thought, and softly asked:

"Pinar, I was wondering...did you know anyone at the Sett? I haven't left the City in years, but as you live in the forest I thought you might..."

"Yeah," she said. "We did."

"I'm really sorry to hear about Elias," Kit said as she opened the beer. "I heard he was a great man."

Ash stood up abruptly and everyone felt silent.

"He was a grumpy old bugger who hated *everything* and *everyone!*" Pinar could see she was on the verge of tears. "But *yes*, he was unique. There was no one like him and there never will be again." Despite herself, she began to cry. "Sorry. Please excuse me."

Seeing Pinar's concerned look, she put her hand on her shoulder and gave a weak smile.

"Stay and be sociable. I'll see you at the tent."

And with that, Ash left the warmth of the fire.

* * *

It was night. The *mesa* had finished hours ago and those with homes in the City—including Danny and Kit—had gone back to them. The rest were spread out in a village of tents across the park.

Although nobody really expected any trouble out here, selected people took hourly shifts guarding the perimeter. After the warehouse and the news about the Sett, they couldn't be too safe.

Inside their little tent, Ash and Pinar were curled up together on their sleeping mats. Pinar snored lightly. But Ash was gone.

Her body was cold and she was somewhere else, far away. Not yet asleep, not yet dreaming, she was travelling back to another time and another place. To a distant continent she had once called home.

She stood in the doorway of a loud café, packed to the brim, every seat taken. She instantly recognised this place from photos, from legends. And here she was, instantly seduced by the unique smell of coffee brewing in the middle of the night mixed with perfume and fried food.

Compton Cafeteria, 101 Taylor Street, San Francisco.

It's just as I imagined.

The café was loud with the screams and giggles of trans people, sex workers, and others who gathered here every night for safety.

I'm here. I can't believe it.

Ash saw someone who reminded her of herself as a young adult—a woman of maybe eighteen—sitting in the cheap, cushioned booths of the café surrounded by friends. The young trans woman was dressed to the nines and had long hair cascading over a dark blue satin dress and wore long white gloves and killer heels.

She looks just like me. She even smiles like I used to.

Two loud couples got up to pay and Ash sat down in their booth and picked up a newspaper they'd left on the table.

August, 1966, just as I thought.

Although the precise date of the riot had been lost in history, Ash remembered it perfectly. It was a date that she could never forget because right now, on the other side of the city under bright hospital lights, Ash was being born.

As always, she was here in the past only as an observer and nobody seemed to notice her presence. Her clothes were completely wrong for the time, but here everybody's clothes were considered wrong most of the time, and nobody paid any attention to an old person sat alone at a booth. *Seconds ago I must have just appeared in the doorway like a vision—I wasn't there and then suddenly I was.*

But after a lifetime of travelling like this, Ash knew that people had a way of filtering out what they didn't expect.

And magically appearing and disappearing trans women are about as unexpected as anything can be.

A sullen waitress came by and served Ash some coffee without really making eye contact or particularly seeing her. Ash picked up the cup and gratefully sipped at the bitter liquid.

I'd almost forgotten what fresh, strong coffee could taste like.

And the feel of the cup, the sticky table, the smoke in her lungs brought a wave of nostalgia.

Although she'd been too young to see the café before it closed down, this place had been so important for the trans community she grew up in. It had been virtually their own safe space. She watched the young trans woman making her single cup of coffee last forever, gossiping with her friends.

At her age, I had friends like that too. Friends who took care of me as a young trans girl newly out in the big city. Friends who took me in when I had nothing. Friends who sometimes disappeared from one night to the next and were never heard from again.

Over by the front door there was a scuffle and raised voices. Ash could see flashing police lights through the shuttered windows.

Tonight's definitely the night.

The young woman and her friends were on their feet. A white cop was arresting someone they apparently knew—a tall, black trans woman in impossibly high platforms—and Ash heard the all-too-familiar words 'female impersonation' and 'public disturbance' as the cop pushed her up against the bar, tearing her long dress under his boots.

He reached down for the handcuffs in his belt, when, as if in slow motion, a delicate cup smashed against his head. Hot coffee splashed over his uniform. He dropped the handcuffs, turned and stared, but was too shocked to even react.

The young woman Ash had been watching stared at the cop looking almost as surprised as he was. Then she reached behind her, picked up another coffee cup and threw that one as well. The cop opened his mouth to shout when a greasy plate bounced off his chest. A piece of pie, a stiletto.

Suddenly, everyone in the room was on their feet shouting. More cops ran in. More plates were thrown. Waitresses screamed and dove behind the bar. And within minutes, the whole building was in chaos.

Ash wanted desperately to do something, but she held herself back. She watched the young woman grabbed by a cop from behind. She lifted off the ground but kicked another with her heels. She fought and screamed with all the rage she had inside her.

The arrests, the harassment, the sexual assaults.

She kicked and kicked, part of a wave of angry bodies pushing the cops towards the door.

The trumped-up charges, the poverty, the discrimination.

She pushed and they pushed back until finally the cops were back outside and for a few, brief seconds they had taken their space back.

Trans folk and hustlers filled the street with their screams and cries and curses. Tonight would belong to them and they weren't giving it back without a fight.

After tonight, trans rights, trans visibility, trans pride would be on everyone's lips—at least for a while.

It would take another six long decades of struggle, of being marginalised and betrayed by the gay community, of being demonised and illegalised by the mainstream before anything like equality would be achieved here.

And despite the expectations of those who told us to be patient, that things were always getting better, a few, short years and trans folks became the enemy again and we were driven back underground.

But this muggy summer's night was full of hope. It was the beginning of something unstoppable and Ash could feel it.

Another coffee cup flew through the air and suddenly she felt herself fading. The room began to lose its colour and depth and she realised that not only was she leaving, but she was sad to leave.

Yells and the sounds of smashing crockery faded away. An owl was calling. Ash was back in their small tent on the other side of the world.

"Pin?" she whispered. "Are you awake?"

Pinar grunted a little in her sleep, and rolled over. Ash snuggled against her and gave her a gentle kiss on the back.

She closed her eyes and blissfully slept.

Chapter sixty-one

Morning arrived suddenly and the park, so peaceful just a few hours before, was soon full of the clanking of pots and pans and the murmurs of camp. Ash tried to hide away by snuggling down under the sheets, but it was already hot and eventually she had to extricate herself. She unzipped the door and poked her head out.

It was even hotter outside, but the air was thick with the rich aromas of breakfast.

"Morning," said Pinar softly as she stirred the little pot of tea she was preparing over a small camp fire. She had been up for an hour already.

The smells of tea and flat breads were enough to entice Ash out of the tent and she sat down next to the fire and took a piece of bread that Pinar was offering to her.

"Hey," mumbled Ash sleepily. "Thanks for breakfast."

"You're welcome. Sorry there isn't any coffee."

Pinar poured the tea into the small, red cups that she always carried with her. "I can't stop thinking about Elias. "I barely even know him, apart from those first few weeks in the forest, but I know he was dear to you. This is all so messed up."

"I still don't really believe it..."

"Me neither."

They both fell silent for a minute as they drank their tea and listened to the sounds of the camp.

"I journeyed last night." Ash's voice was quiet.

"God, when to? Are you OK?"

"August '66. It was incredible."

"'66? Wait...your birthday?"

"Compton's."

"*Amazing.*"

"Yeah, it was cool." Ash sipped her tea. "That night was an important part of trans history, you know? It changed everything."

"Of course. It was important for *all* of us." Pinar looked thoughtful and put her cup down. "Ash I know you don't like to talk about evolutionary functions—"

"Yep, I still don't."

"—I get it. But can I?"

"Knock yourself out."

Pinar smiled. "I guess I've said it before, but I really think that your trait is adaptive somehow. That it's important to all of us. Maybe even as a species. It keeps our history alive and you help us remember. That's really massive."

"Yeah. Well, I've also said it before—I don't need science to explain who I am or why I have my 'trait,' as you call it. I'm not here to save the species, Pin. I'm here for myself, for my own intrinsic worth—"

"Of course, hon, I never meant to suggest—"

"And *besides*, most of my history—our history—has been hell. I'd really rather forget."

"I know..."

"Not everything comes down to biology."

"Okay, okay."

It wasn't the first time they'd had this argument. As soon as she had learned about Ash's capacity for moving through time, the biologist in Pinar had searched for some way to explain it, some evolutionary function that wasn't yet clear.

But sometimes things just are *and they don't need to be explained.*

There was nothing more to say so Pinar sat in silence for a few minutes carefully avoiding eye contact while Ash slurped her tea.

Finally, Pinar stood up.

"I should go soon," she announced. "My meeting's about to start." She pointed over to the circles of people forming over near the trees. "There's an open discussion on the prisoner situation then a practical meeting to start making some specific plans. Do you want to come?"

Ash was staring at her tea and didn't look up.

"There's also the logistics meeting just starting over there under the big lime..."

Ash made a grunting sound.

"It's too early for any of that. I think I'll take a walk around and clear my head and then decide what to do."

"Okay. Danny and Kit are going to be around in a few hours too. I know Kit was very keen to meet you. She called you the mythological A!"

Ash grunted again and went back to staring at her tea.

* * *

After breakfast, Ash took a walk to stretch her legs. The park looked entirely different in the morning light. For one, it was much bigger than she'd thought last night and much more wooded. Giant limes, oaks and plane trees, some at least a century old, cast welcome shade across the overgrown paths and long, dry grass.

She passed through an abandoned play park with rusted swings and broken roundabouts that were being consumed by buddleia bushes. In places, the concrete itself had been broken through and covered by brambles and nettles. Amidst such beautiful rebirth, Ash noticed something colourful amongst the thorns. As she walked closer she saw it was a stroller with a small plastic doll inside. Ash felt a shudder go through her and she continued her walk.

Overlooking the park and the sea was a derelict five-star hotel and Ash went over to take a look. Once a world-renowned gem with rooms costing several thousand a night and chandeliers in every dining room, it stood forgotten and burned out, a monument to a decadence that belonged to another time.

Much of the outside wall had already disintegrated or been swallowed up by ivy and Ash could see trees pushing themselves out of broken windows. Curious, she stepped inside the main entrance and saw the entire building was blackened and burned inside.

Must have been one hell of a fire.

She went deeper inside, passing by what might have once been a kitchen. The hotel was dark. The smell of burned carpets and curtains and beds was overwhelming.

I should be freaked out, this place is creepy as hell, but there's something about it...

She soon came to a massive, solid door at least twice her height. On the other side was something important. She knew it; she felt it.

She tried the door, but it was too heavy or too stuck, she couldn't tell which. She pulled again, bracing herself against the wall with one foot, but it only budged ever so slightly. Ash was already out of breath.

I'll come back later and I'll bring Danny. All that muscle must be good for something.

She touched the door one last time and turned to leave.

I don't know how I know, but whatever is behind that door is crucial to us. It could mean the difference between life and death.

Chapter sixty-two

Kit arrived back at the park dressed in an elegant grey top, short black skirt, and her last pair of good tights. She carried a plastic bag full of Nutrition snacks. She marched over to Pinar who sat in the grass taking a break from a long meeting.

"Pinar! I come baring gifts!"

"Ah great. Well, thanks." Pinar took the bag. "Good to see you again, Kit. Maybe we could share them out in the next meeting?"

"No way. I got them all for you and Ash! You're my heroines. You changed my life. At least let me feed you."

"Oh, well...thanks. That's sweet of you." Pinar looked dubiously inside the bag at the little wrapped food bars. "I should actually get back to the meeting soon—"

"No problem. I'll join you soon, I just want to say hi to Ash. I didn't really get to talk to her last night. Where is she actually?"

"Over by the hotel I think."

"Awesome! See you later, *heroine*." Kit signed the word simultaneously for extra effect.

"Err. Yeah. See you later, Kit."

Ash was just emerging from the hotel and she squinted in the bright light as Kit ran over to her.

"Ash!"

"Oh hey...erm—"

"Kit. My name's Kit."

"Yeah, sorry. Names were always difficult and well, I'm very old you know."

"No way, you don't look a day over fifty."

"I find that a little hard to believe."

"I brought a tonne of Nutrition snacks for you and Pinar. I have a trick who works for Nutrition and he always brings me a bag."

"Great." Ash tried to smile politely.

More rat bars, she thought to herself. *I would kill for a fresh tomato right now.*

"God, I can't believe I'm talking to you, you know? We used to tell stories about you two. We called you the mythological A and P!"

Ash squirmed, but Kit continued unabated.

"All the resistance knows the stories of the Femme Riots, how you took on the entire State and fought for the right to dress how you wanted. You were a big inspiration to me you know? Especially when I came out and *transitioned.*"

"You're trans?"

"I am. Not so many of us around these days."

"No...I guess not."

"Actually, I gathered from Pinar last night that I have you and her to thank for the meds and herbs we've been receiving for the last couple of years."

"Ah yeah, that was us."

"Thank you!"

"No problem."

"Oh, and Pinar also told me that you have something of a coffee addiction..."

Ash flashed on her journey last night, cups flying across the cafeteria and splashing over neatly pressed uniforms.

"I love coffee," she said simply.

"Me too. And actually, my girlfriend—or my ex-girlfriend or something—stole me some beans from her office. Can I make you a cup?"

"Well..." said Ash, finally relaxing a little. "I've never been able to say no to a cup of coffee."

* * *

Pinar came over to the fire the second her meeting ended.

"Looks like you found your fix!"

"The greatest herbal medicine on earth." Ash sipped her coffee and smiled. "How was your meeting?"

"Actually, pretty good. We have a plan. And I have quite an important part in it. I'm not sure how that happened really..."

"Tell us."

"Coffee first, then I'll tell you everything!"

Pouring herself a cup, Pinar began to explain the plan. The next morning before dawn, she would lead a shoal through the tunnels to the Life Accounts building. Scouts had been sent and confirmed Danny's intel—the system was as vulnerable now as it would ever be.

Decades back, Pinar had worked a couple of summers for a small company installing solar panels on roofs. As the Life Accounts servers were run almost entirely on solar energy these days, Pinar hoped she'd be able to use her knowledge of the system to cause another overload and shut down the last of the servers.

"It'll look like an accident which will be safer than simply cutting the wires. And in the time it takes them to set up a generator, the system should go down across the City." She grinned. "All those little transactions that keep the State's economy working will grind to a halt and there'll be absolute chaos."

"Meanwhile on the other side of the City, another shoal will take advantage of the diversion and hopefully break the resistance prisoners out of jail."

I don't like the sound of any of this, thought Ash.

"So, let me get this right—" she said. "You're going to clamber around on the roof of a State building in the middle of the night and what? Do some rewiring?"

"I think I can do it." Pinar replied. "And if not I can explain it to the others. Apparently, the system's virtually the same as the ones I know. They never replaced them in all this time."

"Maybe we should just wait for the technology to die by itself? It can't have much time left."

"It's now or never, hon. Almost the entire resistance is back in the City and the last shoals are arriving tonight. The prisons are bursting and the State isn't keeping up. It's the perfect time."

"*Yes, yes.* I know all that. But I'm worried."

"I'll be fine, Ash. It'll work.

Kit joined in the conversation.

"And do you know where we're all meeting, Pinar—after the actions, I mean?"

"After we shut down the Life Accounts system, we'll hit the tunnels and come meet the second shoal—and the prisoners—at the halfway point, which will be the Mall."

"Cool. That's what I figured."

"And then?" asked Ash.

"We'll head back here, pick up the shoals who stayed in the park—which I guess will include you, Ash—and head out the tunnels back to the forest."

"Just like that..." said Ash cynically.

"Just like that. I know it sounds too simple, but each working group is taking responsibility for their part. I'm confident that if we can coordinate well, it'll work."

'If being the operative word.

Ash gave her a doubtful look. Pinar ignored it.

"We need to try," she continued. "Even if the best we can do is give the State a kick in the ass, it'll give us something to work with. So, as for your role Ash..."

Kit's face ached from smiling so much. She was in an action meeting with two of her greatest heroines and she couldn't stop grinning.

I'll be telling this story for years! she thought to herself. *Ash and*

Pinar! It doesn't get any better than th—

Her heart dropped as she saw Nathalie marching towards her from the other side of the park.

* * *

Arriving at the fire with a determined look on her face, Nathalie walked straight over to Kit.

"Hi," she said to her, ignoring the others completely. "Can we talk?"

Kit's face made it clear that leaving the intimate coffee meeting was the last thing she wanted to do.

"Erm. OK. I guess. Sorry ladies," she said to Ash and Pinar. "I'll be back soon."

"Let's go somewhere private," said Nathalie and they walked together to a bench close to the edge of the park, where the cliffs dropped dramatically down to the sea. Kit realised it was the very same bench they'd sat on after their long evening together in the bushes. It felt like months ago.

"So wha—" Kit began.

"Let me start, please, Kit," Nathalie's voice was forceful. "I want you to know that I'm really sorry. I apologise for the argument yesterday. I don't know what happened and I'm sorry."

"OK, bu—"

"I'm sure it wasn't completely my fault, but I don't want it to come between us. I still have feelings for you and I want things to be like they were before we fought."

Kit was confused.

We didn't fight. You freaked out, threw all your toys out of the pram and stormed off. I was barely involved at all.

"OK. But I want to know what happened. Of course you can leave the room any time you want to when we're...being intimate, but I really didn't understand. Didn't you like the sex? Was I too emotional?"

"I don't want to talk about it. Let's just let it go, OK?"

"I guess..."

"Good. I only have an hour or so before my evening shift, but—" Nathalie glanced coyly over to the bushes where they had first met. There was no-one around, everyone was either in a meeting or working on the camp.

"—Maybe we could go and have a make up fuck first? I'm in the mood for some violence."

Kit looked at the ground. She almost whispered her reply. "Okay."

Deep down, Kit knew that she was being manipulated.

She only wants the pro-Domme version of me, not the real me. She's objectifying me for my work, forcing me into a position I don't want to be in. Why don't I just walk away? Why don't I just say no?

But as they kissed and stripped under the sun, hidden among toxic rhododendrons and the sharp thorns of brambles, Kit knew she had no choice.

How did this even happen?

* * *

Nathalie couldn't stop smiling. She lay, hidden amongst the bushes, her head resting on Kit's chest while Kit gently stroked her hair. Nathalie's ass and face still stung from the slaps she'd been given.

It's better again, she thought to herself. *Kit loves me. I know that.*

She closed her eyes and enjoyed the sensation of Kit's gentle fingers on her hair.

We were stupid to fight. She makes me feel complete and that's enough.

Kit stared up at the bright sky. She watched gulls flying above calling to each other.

I wish I could join them, she thought. *I wish I could escape this.*

Absently her hand stroked Nathalie's hair, but she was far away; her body, a distant sensation.

This is domination from the bottom up. I know that. And I hate it. And I hate myself for letting it happen. I'm strong; I'm fierce. I can leave any time I want. What the hell is wrong with me?

She wanted to cry again but she knew she wasn't allowed.

"That was great, hon," said Nathalie after a few minutes, sitting up and tidying her hair.

"Yeah." Kit's voice was cold.

"I need to get to work soon. I can't be late."

"Shall I bring you some lunch before you go?"

"Good idea," said Nathalie. "And Kit?"

"Yes?"

"Be quick."

* * *

Ash sat in a meeting suffering. She figured she should probably go to at least one that day, but as she watched the young people gathered in circles, rehashing the same arguments she had heard over five decades ago, it only confirmed for her that she no longer belonged in these spaces.

"Ok, so can we move on to food now...?" asked the facilitator, already exhausted after 'security,' the first agenda item had overstretched by twenty minutes.

In theory, this kind of meeting should have been perfect for Ash. The logistics group were discussing how to keep the camp supplied with food for the next two days, how to maintain twenty-four-hour security at the park and how to set up an emergency area to receive people injured or traumatised in the actions. This 'background' work—which she preferred to think of as 'maintenance"—was what

Ash knew best.

"Look," said a young activist. "I don't think we can even start talking about food until we know the camp is secure."

"But how will it be secure," asked another. "If we don't decide if it's a vegan space or not? Not all of us feel safe being around animal products, remember?"

"Not all of us are able to live without them, *remember?*"

Ash sighed. *Even here away from the heroics, these young people just don't think the same way as me or understand the connections of the world. There are bigger things at stake here. Of course we need to feel safe and heard and included. But there's more to it than that. We're more than individuals looking out for ourselves while ignoring the needs of our friends. We're more than consumers making decisions about which awful thing we should buy next from Capitalism. Resistance was never meant to be an aesthetic, or a way to feel better than other people.*

Ash looked up.

We should be like the starlings. Something bigger.

"People are arriving every hour," said the facilitator. "I think all of these points are important, but we really need to make some decisions about—"

"This whole meeting is a joke! I won't stand by while you turn this space into an animal slaughterhouse."

"We just discussed having non-vegan options on the side for those who need them. I think you might be overstat—"

"This is speciesism!"

"And a vegan space is ableist!"

Ash could feel herself descending into a bad mood.

We have no grounding in history. No connection to our environment. And we spend all our time fighting each other instead of the real enemy.

She sat for a while, watching the group, observing their manipulations, superiority complexes, and insecurities.

Some things just never change.

She stood up and walked away.

Ten minutes later, clambering up a rocky outcrop and overlooking the park and the cliffs, Ash was still angry. Angry at this political scene with all its squabbles and power plays and angry at herself.

What good am I here? Tomorrow we're going to face all kinds of danger and here I am, a grumpy old woman who can't even be in a meeting for more than ten minutes.

I should be miles away in my comfortable little boat. I should be working in the garden, or helping the forest. I should be anywhere on Earth but in this toxic city.

She kicked a stone over the edge of the cliff and allowed the tears to come again.

As she sat, gusts of wind washed over her and brought salty, fresh air and the sounds of waves and seabirds. She took a deep lungful and took in the world around her.

Every nook and niche of the steep cliffs was filled with the nests of guillemots, fulmers, and puffins. The granite resonated with their calls and flocks filled the skies, casting great, moving shadows.

She looked over the park and watched the starlings roaming in gangs across the open grass, whistling and squeaking to each other, their iridescent plumage shining violet and green in the sunlight. At the far end of the park, a young deer appeared and disappeared between the trees.

Everywhere there was a pulse moving through this place. Ash felt calmer now. She was grateful again to be in the presence of so much life.

She had hardly ever come to Dignity Park—Independence Park as it was back then—in all her long years of living, and fighting, in the City. She had always been too busy, too consumed by her work, by the mobilisations, the in-fighting and the endless, endless meetings.

Besides, she reminded herself, *it hadn't looked like this back then.*

This park, like all green urban spaces, had been barren and polluted, virtually cleared of all life except grass and manicured flower beds. Every weekend it had swarmed with humans with their phones and cameras trying to capture every last special, precious moment before it was gone.

The Crash had been terrible, the change to human life, total and devastating. But as Ash watched the young deer and another dense cloud of starlings passing overhead, she remembered that for the rest of life here it had been the best thing that possibly could have happened.

Chapter sixty-three

Barely centimetres from the edge of the cliff lay Ash's body. Her eyes were open. Her skin was cold. Despite her best efforts to stop it, she was journeying again.

She stood on a balcony looking down over a park. Sweat prickling her bald head, she felt sick looking far below her.

Dignity Park, I guess. The trees, the beach all seem the same—

—But what had been their encampment had been replaced by total chaos. Tear gas filled the air and she could hear screams and bullets and the terrifying sounds of horses and dogs.

She blinked away tears and gripped the rail of the balcony. It was covered in soot.

The hotel, she realised. *And I must be near the top floor, but how did I get up here? And this must be the future, I'd certainly remember all* this *happening. But how far in the future? It's almost dark. Is this tonight? Tomorrow?*

Another tear gas canister was launched with a loud bang.

God...What can I do?

I need to find out what happened here. Maybe I can find my future self and—

Wait! Down there—

At the centre of the park, staying just ahead of a wall of gas, Ash saw herself running towards the hotel. Hundreds of people were following her and behind them, gaining fast, were lines of troopers on horseback.

Her future self was shouting as she ran and high above, wearing identical clothes and leaning over the balcony to hear, Ash could just make out the words.

"To the Hotel! To the tunnels!"

They made eye contact for the briefest of moments and then they were separated by the cloud of gas and black smoke. Turning back towards the hotel, Ash began to run towards the stairs.

I need to get down there. I need to find out what happened.

Just then the world took a fast spin. The charred room in front of her was moving, bleaching of its colour. She reached out to steady herself, taking one last look at her hands, totally covered in soot—

—And she was back on the cliff side. One arm was sticking out into space and she looked down at the waves crashing below her. She yelled and pulled herself quickly back from the edge. Her heart was racing and she could hardly breathe.

I have to get back there. I need more information.

But she knew it was out of her control. She stood up and brushed herself off. Her hands were clean again.

I have to tell Pinar. We have to warn the others.

Chapter sixty-four

Nathalie arrived at work for the afternoon shift. As usual, she was five minutes late. She ran up the stairs and into the office. She was sweating and her hair was a tangled mess, but her sleep-deprived colleagues paid no attention to her as she sat down at her desk and looked through the pile of handwritten notes she had already accumulated. She looked around her at the other cubicles. No-one had even looked up.

As she always did at the beginning of a shift, Nathalie walked over to the coffee pot in the corner of the room. She was always glad for this little office privilege. *Who cares where it comes from?*

She poured herself a generous mug full.

"Does anyone want a cup?" she asked, turning to face her colleagues. No-one stirred. In fact, no-one reacted at all.

That's odd.

Although people usually ignored her late, flustered arrivals and rarely spoke amongst themselves during a shift, coffee—and the weather—were the two easy subjects that always broke the ice.

She tried again.

"Is it me or is it just getting hotter every day?"

Nothing. Silence. *It's like everyone in the room is avoiding making eye contact with me.*

The guy who worked in the next cubicle got up and nervously shuffled some papers in the other corner of the room.

Confused, Nathalie sat back down at her untidy cubicle and nursed her coffee.

This is so weird. What's going on with everyone today?

* * *

"Pin, I need to talk to you."

Pinar took in Ash's panicked expression and strained voice.

"Is everything ok? Come, let's talk in private."

Pinar got up from the fireside where she'd been eating dinner with Kit and went over with Ash to their little tent. They sat on the ground together and Pinar held Ash's hands as she described her vision.

"It was horrible. The screams. I can't get them out of my head."

"It's ok, it's ok. You're back now."

"They're coming every day now, more and more often. I can't control it, Pin. I can't stop them."

Ash was talking manically, tears pouring down her wrinkled cheeks. "It could be any minute now, what I saw. I didn't have time to find my...future self. I was just there—" Ash pointed up to the abandoned hotel that loomed over the park. "I couldn't do anything. I felt so helpless—"

She collapsed into tears and Pinar held her close until she could speak again.

"We should tell the others—"

"Tell them what? That your friend, the time-travelling trans woman just had a vision of an uncertain future in which we all get our asses handed to us by the State and the park gets burned to the ground? Who's going to listen to that?"

"But we should do *something*. We have to prepare somehow."

"I agree, but what?

"There's a general meeting soon, I'll present what you saw on your behalf if you like? It would mean outing you though, about your journeying."

"I'm too old to care about that anymore," said Ash sadly, staring off into space. "Go ahead, if you want to."

"—Okay—"

"But I doubt they'll listen."

Twenty minutes later, Pinar stood surrounded by the concentric meeting circles. She had to shout to be heard over the gulls and waves.

"Hi everyone, thanks for letting me speak. I have something important to let you know and it affects the whole camp. As you know, I'm here with my friend Ash and, well, this isn't easy to explain, but she had—let's call it a vision of our future here in the park. And it was bad."

"A vision?" said a young white guy with a ponytail, jumping the queue of people waiting to speak. "What kind of vision?"

"My friend has the ability to erm...move through time. I know that sounds a little hard to believe, but—"

"Sounds like fucking science fiction to me," said the guy. "Seriously, don't we have better things to talk about?"

"I can assure you that it's quite real. There have many cases in which—"

"*Bullshit*," said the guy and signed the word simultaneously. "Let's move on."

"But her vision was very serious. We could all be in dange—"

"Next!"

Pinar realised it was hopeless. She threw an angry glance at the facilitator, who was chatting to someone next to him and paying no attention at all to the proceedings, and stormed over to where Ash sat on the very edge of the outer circle.

"Told you," said Ash as her friend sat down next to her. "We're old and poor and women, dear. Really what did you expect?"

"I was never that disrespectful! Even when I was this guy's age."

"Well, even if someone listened to us, there's nowhere to move all these people to tonight. We're leaving Dignity tomorrow anyway. Let's get some sleep and see how things are in the morning."

"Okay, hon. The best thing right now is to take care of ourselves and keep our eyes open."

"Let's escape this meeting?"

"Let's go."

* * *

It all happened so fast, Nathalie didn't even have time to react.

She had finished most of her paperwork from the morning and was getting up to go to the bathroom when five heavily armed troopers—all massive, uniformed men—burst into the office.

"Miss N?" one of them demanded, coming towards her. He was a massive guy, his face completely emotionless.

"Err...yes, yes, that's me." She looked around at her colleagues who stared carefully at their desks and coffee cups, one fiddling hopelessly with a stapler.

What the hell is happening here?

"Come with us please. Leave your things behind."

Before she knew it, Nathalie was outside and standing in the street in front of the building. She could see her colleagues watching her from the window of the office. The troopers surrounded her menacingly and the one in charge stepped towards her, he was nearly two metres tall.

"So you're a *dyke* are you?" He spat the words out loud enough to get the attention of some passers-by who stopped to watch. "A fucking *lesbo.*"

"I...excuse me? I don't..."

"Don't even try, girl. Your *friends* at the office reported you. We know you've been fraternising with some foreign whore from downtown—"

"My colleagues...God..." It suddenly all fit into place.

I knew there was something wrong from the moment I arrived. Of course! That's why no-one would look at me. I'm already dead to them.

"They earned themselves a nice little bonus there, I dare say." He stepped forward and poked the butt of his rifle into her chest. "Now

273

this can go two ways. You give us this whore's name and the bar she works at or we show all the good people in the street what a dirty slut you really are."

Nathalie was frozen.

I have to think fast.

"There is a girl, okay. I admit it. But she's...*protected*. You can't get her."

"Protected, eh?" The trooper looked thoughtful. "So she's probably resistance too, no doubt."

There wasn't really a connection between being protected and being resistance, but he was fishing for information. Nathalie waited just a second too long to answer.

"I see," he gloated. "And if she is, then you are too."

Nathalie couldn't keep eye contact. She'd always been horrible at lying. She looked at the ground.

She felt a searing pain as the butt of the trooper's rifle cracked against her skull. She was flat out on the ground before she could even scream. The troopers stood over her. The leader lifted his foot and looked like he would kick her in the face.

"Stop! Wait! Please!" She shielded her bleeding face with both arms.

It came to her then. *A way out of this. There'll be a big sacrifice to be made, but it'll be worth it. As long as me and Kit can be together.*

"I have an idea," she said desperately. "Another option...please...wait."

The trooper put his boot back down on the ground.

"The dyke has an idea!" He laughed, looking at his subordinates who laughed along obediently. "Well, go on then, girl. We're all ears..."

Chapter sixty-five

Ash and Pinar were sleeping soundly, curled up together in their little tent. The camp was quiet except for a pair of owls calling to each other and the quiet murmur of waves.

Suddenly Ash was woken up by loud voices on all sides of the tent. Her vision of the future still vivid in her memory, she sat upright and strained to hear what the unfamiliar voices were saying. It was completely dark and her heart was pounding in her chest.

"Thank God, we made it. I forgot how far the tunnels are from here," said one of the voices.

"Look," said another, "the fire's still burning. There's probably some food left over as well."

"I can't walk on this bloody ankle anymore. Sue, find me a log to sit on will you?"

Ash relaxed a little.

It's just another shoal arriving from the forest. They must have come through the tunnels and walked the few blocks from the nearest exit. They sound exhausted.

Pinar was still snoring lightly. She had to get up in a few hours so Ash left her to sleep and, still wearing her nightdress, she unzipped the tent and climbed out. The night was warm and almost completely dark except for a small fire about a hundred metres away where the new arrivals were standing around and talking. Ash slipped on her boots and walked over to them.

"Welcome," she said formally as she arrived. Switching to USL she said "*Sign please, it's late and people are sleeping.*"

Several of the group smiled at her politely and looked like they were about to start a round of formal introductions. Ash was feeling exposed in her nightdress and wanted to avoid all the kisses so she distracted them as elegantly as she could—

"—*There's some food left in the pot,*" she signed, pointing over to the little kitchen space. "*I'm a physical therapist—did I hear something about a sprained ankle?*"

"*That was Gus here,*" signed an older woman with long, silver hair. "*He hurt himself on one of the escalators.*"

Gus hobbled out from the darkness. As she usually did, Ash assessed him quickly.

He looks to be in his mid-fifties. White. Tall. Face is a little gaunt but his body looks well built, which these days also means well fed. His hair is messy and short—maybe an outgrown crew cut of some kind. His clothes are filthy.

Without a word, the older woman helped him sit down on a log and rested his injured foot on a crate.

"Relax here and I'll bring you something to eat," she whispered, and bustled off towards the kitchen space.

Ash could sense that the others liked this Gus person. She could see from their expressions that they were worried about him and looked at him with genuine affection.

But her intuition was prickling. She had always been good at reading people. It was the plus side to being so sensitive to everything around her. She knew there was something wrong with this person, that he didn't belong there. She could feel it in her very bones.

As she got closer to him to look at his twisted ankle, her knowing grew even stronger.

He even smells wrong, she realised. *He smells like danger.*

Ash tried to keep calm as she worked on Gus' ankle.

"*My name's Ash,*" she signed.

"Gus."

Even that sounds like a lie. Who is this guy?

"*I'm just going to take a look at your ankle.*"

She mobilised it a little, palpitated around the swelling, checked for any kind of break. She tried to focus on his injury, but she caught him giving her nightdress a strange look, a look that bordered on disgust. Subconsciously, she pulled away from him.

She knew his ankle would be fine. It was nothing too serious. She guessed just a stretched ligament or two.

It probably isn't even very painful, although you'd never know from all the fuss he's making.

"Akh, it *hurts*. Can't you do that a little softer?" he said angrily as Ash carefully pushed and held a pressure point.

She took a deep breath and reminded herself to stay calm. He was her patient. She had work to do. And she could get away from him soon enough.

"Just a little while longer," she whispered as much to herself as to him. She took a handful of chopped comfrey from her handbag. Dipping the leaves in a little hot water from the kettle, she wrapped the resulting green mass in a small cloth.

"You'll need to keep this tied against your ankle for a couple of days." she said, softly, fixing the poultice into position with another strip of cloth she produced from her bag. "Rest it for a week or so and you'll be fine."

She felt herself becoming anxious to get away from him and started packing up her things.

"A *week?*" her patient complained loudly.

Ash, with all the dignity she could muster, turned her back on him and walked away.

The older woman came over to her as she was walking back to her tent.

"I'm Sue by the way."

Ash looked at her tent longingly, she wanted to be back in bed.

"Ash, nice to meet you."

They exchanged kisses.

"Will he be okay?" Sue asked.

"He'll be fine. Where did you pick him up from anyway?"

"What do you mean?"

"He's clearly not resistance."

"Oh, Gus is an *exiliado*," Sue explained. "We found him on his way back to the City. He's trying to find his boyfriend here. He was in a bad way when we found him."

"I see," said Ash. "Let's speak more tomorrow, okay?"

"Sure. Good night."

Ash stood for a while and wandered off into her thoughts.

There's something wrong with this story. Just because someone is an exiliado—or queer for that matter—doesn't make them a good person.

She stared out into the dark night and listened to the waves far below them.

Somehow in the west there's still this idea of gay guys being feminine or wearing skirts or something. But those people just haven't been paying attention. If this Gus is gay, then I know his type. Hyper-masculine, hyper-femmephobic, hyper-misogynist. The kind who, back in the day of internet cruising, used 'masculine' as a compliment when chatting to hook ups and probably had 'no fats, no femmes' or something equally hideous written all over his online profiles.

There was nothing more to do tonight. Pinar would be getting up for her action soon so there was no point going back to bed. Ash was overwhelmed. She went to the kitchen tent and, as she always did when she felt like this, she ate.

* * *

An hour before sunrise, Pinar woke up and came over to the fire. The group she'd be doing the action with were already gathered there, eating a massive breakfast prepared for them with the best things Ash could find in the kitchen. But Ash herself was nowhere to be seen.

278

Listening to her shoal chat around her, Pinar ate quietly. She was worried about her friend. She looked around the park, but away from the fire it was still too dark to see.

Ten minutes later, as the rest of the camp was just beginning to wake up, the shoal prepared to leave Dignity. The closest tunnel entrance was a few blocks away and the sky would soon be getting light.

Pinar walked with the shoal to the edge of the park as they chatted amongst themselves and discussed the plans. She looked around again for her friend.

It was time to go.

Then suddenly she heard her name being called. She saw Ash running over to her through the thick grass and in the faint light, Pinar could see she had been crying.

"You're not going," Ash declared breathlessly as she arrived.

"What?" said Pinar, confused. "Of course I'm going."

"I forbid it. I won't let you go." Ash's voice was angry and loud. "It's too dangerous, you're too damn *old*."

"Ash, what are you talki—"

"You can't *leave* me here." Ash crossed her arms and looked around at the shoal. "This weird Gus guy arrived tonight and it made me realise, Pin, we barely *know* these people. The plan's too dangerous, there's no way that you can pull it off. You're not going."

"Honey, I need to do this. We all do, it's important. I'm sorry, bu—"

"Fine then!" Ash raised her hands in the air and Pinar flinched. "Go, do whatever the hell you want to!" She turned and stormed away back into the park.

"Ash—come back!" Pinar shouted after her.

But Ash kept walking.

One of the shoal came over to Pinar.

"Sorry," she said, "But if we're doing this, we need to go now. The sky's getting lighter already."

Pinar nodded and took one final look over the park. *Damn it all Ash. Don't leave it like this.*

"Let's go," she said finally and they walked out into the street.

Swallowing her angry tears, Ash stormed back into the park where the rest of the camp were already awake and bustling around. *Why did I shout at her? Why have I still not learned to control my anger after all this time?*

Ash tried to push the argument out of her mind.

All these people need feeding in the next hour. Their tents need packing and they need to be ready to fight. I have work to do.

Gritting her teeth, she walked over to the kitchen and began to cook. Slowly, the sad realisation came to her that this was the first time in weeks that she was truly alone.

* * *

In the first light of the morning, accompanied by a loud techno track, Danny was so hot he thought he might actually pass out on the stage.

It was his last dance of the night and he was having trouble concentrating. As soon as he finished, he was going to rush down to the tunnels and join the main shoal for the action at the prison complex. He was excited and apprehensive in equal parts and couldn't tell if he was sweating so much from the heat, nerves, or both.

Dancing's good for me on days like this.

When he was on the pole he had to focus, to stay in the moment. If he lost himself in a daydream, he invariably slipped and sometimes hurt himself. It wasn't always easy to concentrate though. There was so much to think about, so much to plan. The prison break was the biggest thing he'd been involved with in his many years with the resistance. And because of the careful way that they kept information segmented, he didn't even know what else was planned, just that they'd have to wait for some kind of signal—apparently Kit would know what it was—before they came above ground.

He slipped again.

I'm going to ruin this dance completely if I don't stay focused. He redoubled his efforts. *Not that anyone really cares.*

He looked over to the handful of officers still at the bar since last night, smoking and drinking.

They're too drunk to even stand up, much less much pay attention to my art. It's fine, whatever. On a day like this, work is just a distraction anyway.

* * *

Ash managed to distract herself from her anxiety by preparing flat breads in the kitchen. The rhythm was familiar as she flipped them from hand to hand, flattening them out and tossing them in the pan. She thought about the last time she had done the same thing in her boat house.

Just before Pin came for dinner.

Ash missed her already and despite her best attempts not to think about it, she knew she was worried. *If only I could have stopped her somehow. If only I could have found a way.*

Angry again, she threw another flat bread on the pan.

It was then that Ash heard the screaming.

Chapter sixty-six

With her heart pounding in her chest, Ash ran out of the kitchen tent. She saw someone lying on the grass, her face, beaten and bruised, her hair covered in blood. Others from the park were running over.

Shit. Is this how it begins?

As Ash came closer, she realised that she recognised the person. *Kit's friend—or girlfriend or something—Nathalie was it? God, she's covered in blood. I wish Pin was here.*

Switching into emergency mode, Ash barked orders at the nearest person as she knelt down by Nathalie's side.

"Bring me water, towels, the first aid kit from the kitchen!"

"OK, you're going to be OK," she said softly to Nathalie. "Please try to stop screaming, tell me where you're injured."

"My head...They hit me with a gun. And they pulled my hair so hard...I can't see out of my left eye. It hurts!"

The first aid kit arrived and Ash pulled on a pair of latex gloves and began to inspect Nathalie's wounds. *There's a lot of blood but the cuts don't look too deep.*

She began cleaning the wounds with alcohol from the kit.

"How did this happen?" she asked.

"At work. My colleagues reported me. They saw me with Kit and... when I got to work, troopers came and dragged me out of the office and...and..."

"It's OK, you're safe now."

"No! You don't understand!" Nathalie grabbed Ash's wrist, her eyes wide with fear. "They told me that the sex work protection has been withdrawn. None of us are safe anymore...I have to tell Kit! She has to get out of work, out of the City...We *all* do! There's no time!"

"OK, just sit back, let me look at your eye." Ash turned to the small group standing near them. "I need more water please."

"There's no time!" screamed Nathalie again. "We have to send a runner through the tunnels and bring Kit here. We have to bring them *all* here!"

"I'll go!" said a young woman. "I'll take two of the other runners. Almost all the protected workers work at the same four bars. We can have everyone here within an hour. We'll bring the rest of the sex work collective too. This affects all of us."

Ash tried to stay focused on her work but she didn't like the idea of having even more people gathered here.

We're supposed to be leaving Dignity Park, not bringing more people. This is all happening way too fast. She continued cleaning the cut on Nathalie's scalp. *The prison groups are leaving the park soon for probably the most ambitious action the resistance has ever attempted. My best friend in the world is already out there somewhere committing sabotage and putting herself in great danger and here's this girl lying in my arms bleeding and babbling about the protection.*

Down in her gut, Ash knew something was very wrong here.

This is all happening too fast.

Chapter sixty-seven

With a loud slam of the door, Kit came running into the bar. She wore very, very high heels but looked like she'd been running for a while. The five drunk officers turned to stare at her. Women never came into this bar and they looked at her like she'd just arrived from another planet. She ignored them and marched up to the stage where Danny was in the middle of a complicated upside down manoeuvre on the pole, his sneakers squeaking against the polished metal.

"L, come down from there! I need to talk to you."

Danny stayed where he was, hanging from the pole, the blood rushing to his head.

"Shh...go away! I'm dancing!"

Kit pointed at the officers by the bar.

"For these drunk *vergers*? Forget it. It's an emergency. Come down from there."

Danny climbed down. He was covered in sweat.

"Come out back, we'll talk there," he said, opening the door to the little back room for her.

She was signing before he'd even closed the door.

"*They hurt Nathalie. I don't know how. I just got a message that we need to get to Dignity as soon as possible. Something about the protection.*"

"*Nathalie? Protection? What are you talking about?*"

"Here." She handed him the note.

"*I can't be bothered to decode it, anyway I forgot the key as usual. Just tell me?*"

"I already did. Nathalie got hurt—beaten up—at work I guess. She's at the park now—"

"And the protection?"

"—It just says 'Protection in danger,' whatever that means. Either way, that includes you. Let's go."

"I haven't finished my shift yet!"

"Make an excuse, anything! No-one cares. I'll meet you outside in two minutes. *We'll take the tunnels just in case.*"

"And the...action?"

"Please stop asking me questions I can't answer. We have to go now."

* * *

"Go a little slower, could you?" complained Danny. "I can't see a thing and the candle's just blinding me. It's really frikking dark down here."

"If I can run in eight inch heels, I'm sure you can keep up in those sweaty sneakers of yours," said Kit without slowing down. "Keep moving."

Following as fast as he could, Danny turned a corner and their tunnel suddenly opened onto a concourse with lots of other tunnels. A faded sign hung on the wall that said simply 'Independence Park'.

In front of them stood a dead escalator leading up to the exit sign and the street beyond.

"Look, we're here already. You can quit your whining," said Kit. "I see lights ahead..."

* * *

The park was full again. Within two hours of Nathalie arriving, almost the entire sex work collective—in particular those who lived under protection—had arrived. Combined with all the resistance who were already there preparing to head out to the action, there were more than three hundred people gathered.

An emergency plenary was called and people sat down together in seven, concentric circles in the centre of the park. Everyone was gathered except Ash who was over by the empty fireplace taking care of Nathalie's wounds and Kit who came running over to them through the dry grass.

"Nathalie, are you OK?" She knelt down at her side. All of their tension from the last two days—the manipulation and control and pressure was suddenly forgotten. Nathalie was still crying uncontrollably and Ash stood up to let them hold each other.

"Is she okay? How did this happen?" Kit demanded.

"She'll be fine. Her wounds are superficial, although she got a pretty bad hit on the head." Ash took a step back. "I can leave you two alone if you like."

"Yeah, thanks," said Kit and pulled Nathalie close to her.

"It's okay, my love, I'm here now..."

"I'll come check on her in a bit," said Ash as she began to walk to the plenary. Suddenly she stopped dead still. Above the usual sounds of voices and waves and seagulls, she heard a sound. A sound she hoped she'd never hear again.

It was the sound of her nightmares and her visions and her memories of too many violent demonstrations and it was getting closer and louder every second.

The sound of horses.

Chapter sixty-eight

The pounding of hooves was all around them. Ash turned to face Nathalie who stopped crying for a moment, her face racked with guilt.

Like fog lifting, Ash suddenly saw it all so clearly. *The convenient timing. The desperation to bring the others to the park.*

"Oh Nathalie," she said, her voice cold. "You did this, didn't you?"

"I didn't mean...I...I'm sorry," Nathalie whined, curling up into Kit's arms. She looked up at her lovingly through bleary eyes. "I did it for us, Kit. Don't worry, you and me will be saved..."

"Did what, Nathalie? What are you talking about? What's going on?"

But Ash already knew. She could hear the horses coming closer—*there must be hundreds of them*—and though she couldn't yet see the troopers, she guessed the park was already surrounded. *We're stuck firmly between the full power of the State and a steep, rocky cliff to nowhere.*

"She set you up. She set us *all* up."

Chapter sixty-nine

Ash could already see the first of the troopers arriving at the far end of the park as she ran towards the plenary. Everyone was standing, looking around, confused and scared.

People were panicking. Some looked like they were going to bolt towards the street. A few people she saw were backing up towards the cliff. A hundred voices cried out in confusion.

I've seen this before. And it can't go like this. They need to be guided.

"We need to get to the tunnels right now!" Ash shouted at the top of her lungs.

Suddenly hers was the only voice in the park, it rang out clear and loud even above the thundering hooves. *But the nearest tunnel entrance is blocks away. There's no way we'll get past the troopers.*

The first tear gas grenades flew over the trees and Ash felt herself panicking.

Breathe. Just breathe. Find a solution. Get your people out of here.

Suddenly a memory flashed across her mind's eye. In her vision of the future she was leading the resistance across the park to the hotel and shouting something about the tunnels. *But there are no tunnels in the hotel. And the hotel is abandoned, destroyed.*

Understanding slowly enveloped her. The door. The massive door in the hotel that she couldn't open.

I knew there was something important behind it. It all makes sense now. She was as certain as she'd ever been in her life.

"Follow me!" she shouted as she turned and ran towards the hotel.

For a brief moment, Ash forgot how old she was. She forgot how tired her bones were from living a long, hard life. She forgot all her worries, her insecurities. There was just running.

Her earrings sparkled in the morning sunlight as she pushed each footstep into the grass and pushed off again. She let herself look back for just a brief second. More than three hundred people ran after her, their panic turned into determination to reach the hotel. To escape their fate. To write their own destiny.

Behind them a wall of troopers, their enslaved animals, and their weapons, followed close behind.

She turned back and kept running. She heard a scream.

The troopers must have caught up with those at the back. But there's nothing I can do to help. If we're cut off from the tunnels, we'll be stuck here with nowhere to go.

Ash's eyes bleared with gas and smoke as she pushed on with all the strength she could find.

She saw the hotel growing closer, a blackened wall of balconies and luxury suites. And on one of those balconies, Ash saw her own face looking out over the chaos. She blinked her eyes against the tear gas. It was herself, her journeying self from just a day before. This was her vision. This is how it happened.

Time was inescapable. She knew what she had to do. What she had already done. With all the force in her lungs she shouted up to the balcony.

"To the Hotel! To the tunnels!"

Chapter seventy

Ash's lungs burned but she couldn't stop running. She could already see the grand entrance and foyer to the hotel and she knew that inside, behind the heavy door, were the tunnels and their only chance of escape.

She was barely a hundred metres away. She heard running footsteps behind her. The others were catching her up.

Just a little farther.

But as the gas cloud cleared for a moment, Ash's breath caught in her throat—Ahead, standing directly between them and the hotel, a line of troopers was moving into position to stop them.

"You have nowhere to go. We have you surrounded."

Silence fell over the park and for a moment, the whole world seemed to hold its breath.

And then Ash and three hundred fighters were running towards the hotel. Ash and three hundred fighters against a world of weaponry and power.

She curled her arms up in front of her face as the troopers ahead of them lifted their truncheons. She ran and she ran. And there was nothing else.

Ash was gone.

6. Home

Chapter seventy-one

Pinar was completely absorbed in writing. She was halfway through her dissertation and had been sat at her desk for what seemed like days, staring at her laptop screen, daylight coming and going. Dawn was just breaking, the early sun shining through the blinds into her tiny student apartment and she was exhausted.

She was in a slow hour. Some hours flew by as inspiration took over her fingers and seemed to type the words for her. Others, like this one, dragged painfully. She lost herself in internet searches and digging through her research and some out-of-date science journals. *They all seemed so promising at the library, but they're just another distraction. I should sleep. I should already be sleeping.*

Espresso and the hope for more inspiration were keeping her awake and at her desk but her eyelids were heavier by the second. Pinar's head was cradled in her hands, her elbows nestled in a pile of print-outs and redrafts.

One more article and I'll call it a day.

Pinar's eyelids were definitely drooping. Her thoughts were getting confused. *Maybe, actually, I'm already asleep. I must be dreaming.*

Across the room, someone who looked a lot like an elderly version of her dear friend, Ash had just appeared and was sitting on her bed. She was balding, dressed like a guy and saying something to her.

It has to be a dream, I'm already sleeping. I should go to bed.

"Pinar?...Pinar? Can you hear me? Are you asleep? Wake up already!"

"Whassat musbedreamin..."

"You're not dreaming. I'm here. Hello?"

Ash leaned forward and waved her hands in front of Pinar's half-shut eyes.

"I'm here. From the future. My God, you look so young. What year is it?"

Pinar sat up straight and shook her head.

"Ash? Is it you? What...what are you doing here?" She rubbed her eyes. "Sorry, I've been up all night."

She stood up and immediately knocked a pile of papers and files onto the floor. Ignoring the mess, she sat down next to her friend on the bed.

"It's 2017 here, I mean, now. You told me last year about your...special ability, but wow. This is amazing!"

"It's so good to see you, Pinar. I'm from 2040. And am I here actually, I mean, the younger me?"

"No, my Ash is away at the moment. You're in Quito, taking an organising break. You've been having a hard time lately."

"Ah ok, I remember that. It's so weird. Have you ever met a future me before? Is this something that starts happening?"

"No, never. And it's strange; it's like I see you, but it feels a bit dreamy, like you're here, but not really." Pinar gave Ash's arm a friendly squeeze. "No. You're definitely real."

"Hang on a sec..."

Ash stood up and went over to the sink. She poured herself a glass of water, gulped it down without stopping and poured herself another. She drank that too and came back to the bed.

"Are you okay?" asked Pinar. "I mean, where you were before you came here?"

"Not really, it's a mess. I guess I'll be back there soon though—I only ever travel for a short while."

"So let's get you fed and cleaned up so you're ready for whatever's going on. I'll fix us some breakfast. Coffee and eggs?"

Ash nodded gratefully.

"Have a rest and don't go anywhere until I've finished."

Ash lay back on the bed. Everything about it was familiar: the squeaky springs, the smell of her friend on the soft pillows, the noise of Pinar rattling around in the kitchen. Despite her best attempts to stay awake, she soon felt herself dozing off.

* * *

Gus was no longer in Dignity Park.

At the first sound of horse hooves, he'd slipped out through the bushes and into the street, staying as close to the buildings as he could. His ankle was slowing him down but the light was fading and it wouldn't be hard to get away if he kept quiet.

The others will be much slower than me. They can't do anything alone, not even escape. They're fucking sheep.

Gus climbed over a small, brick wall and looked back for just a second.

I wouldn't have made it out of the forest without them—I would have died out there. Maybe I should...

He pushed the unfamiliar feelings deep down.

No. Better to be a lone wolf. A fighter. A survivor.

He looked around. He was on the lawn of a grand manor house that was slowly being consumed by brambles. With no-one to tend them, rose bushes had spread all across the walls and up the ornamental trees and the air was thick with their heavy scent.

It's beautiful, Gus noticed vaguely. *But I'm too exposed. I need a place to hunker down, wait until the troopers have passed by. The last thing I need is to get mistaken for resistance.*

He felt another unfamiliar feeling pass through his chest.

Even if I am like them. Just one more fucking vergent.

From a few streets away he could hear dogs barking.

No fuck that. I'm nothing like them. Always complaining and protesting about the way things are. You have to be practical in this world if you want to survive. Once I'm away, I'll call on old friends, pull some strings to get back into the State or find some other placement. I'll get a nice place to live, work my way back up. I'll be fine. I always am. I just need to keep moving.

Walking carefully over broken patio slabs, Gus looked around the outside of the house for a way in. The French windows were locked and breaking in would make too much noise.

No good. I can't stay here.

The other wall of the garden was much higher than the first. Gus knew there was no way he'd be able to climb over with his twisted ankle.

He looked around for something to climb on.

There. A trash can.

Panting from the effort, he dragged the metal bin over as quietly as he could, put one foot on the lid and began to pull himself up.

Seconds too late he realised his mistake.

My bad leg.

With all his will he tried to push past the pain but his ankle collapsed and Gus crashed to the ground. The trash can followed him and made a deafening noise as it hit the floor.

Shit.

Gus lay flat on the ground, surrounded by stinking garbage, the wind knocked completely out of him. He stared at the wall in disbelief.

I'm dirty again, he realised, his thoughts slow and disconnected. *And I only just got clean.* He saw stars and, within seconds, he was surrounded.

Chapter seventy-two

The delicious smell of coffee woke Ash up.

"Well, you're still here, hon. Eat up quickly before you go. You were asleep for ten minutes or so."

Pinar put the heavy tray of food in front of her and, without a word, Ash dug in, downing the coffee in one gulp and eating the toast and fried eggs almost without chewing.

"You *are* hungry. Let me get you some juice to go with that. Has it been so long since you ate?" She filled a glass and brought it over. "Wait. I guess you probably shouldn't tell me, time paradoxes and all that."

"I have no clue," said Ash between gulps of juice. "This never happened before. Maybe don't tell my present self about it. It's weird."

"No problem, I can keep a secret. You're probably leaving soon. Do you need anything else?"

"It's already been longer than usual. I won't be here much longer."

"Have a rest and if you're still here when you wake up, let's talk, okay?"

Ash didn't even have the energy to disagree. Pinar put the tray on the floor on a pile of other plates and journals. Covering them both with a blanket, she curled up next to her friend and within seconds they were both fast asleep.

Ash woke up a while later.

Sleepily she rolled over and looked at the clock on the desk.

Two P.M.—and I'm still here!

She quietly got out of bed without disturbing Pinar and went into the bathroom to take a shower.

Nothing about this is normal. First, I'm in a time and place where I'm not even present, which is unusual enough. And now it seems like I'm stuck here.

But in the present—my present—I'm in danger; we all are. I'm probably still lying there in the park, useless—and for all intents and purposes, asleep—surrounded by the State, or already in prison. I have to get back, to help the others.

Ash sighed loudly as she took off her clothes.

Nothing I can do for now. Just have to wait and see what happens.

"I'll be quick," she told herself as she pulled the cord and climbed into the tiny, cramped shower cubicle she knew so well.

* * *

Gus was trapped. Six troopers and a massive Rottweiler that growled and pulled on its leash, stood above him. He still lay on his back, surrounded by trash, his ankle sending wave after wave of sharp pain through his body.

There's no way it ends like this, he decided. *I'll die before I got back to the factory. I have to find a way out.*

"Stop, you don't understand!" he shouted as the soldiers lifted their weapons. "*I'm undercover.*"

The troopers paused.

"I've been following the resistance for months," Gus continued without skipping a beat. "I've been collecting information for the State."

"Undercover, eh?" said one of the troopers, a corporal barely out of his teens. "Sounds fucking unlikely to me."

Think, think.

"Lieutenant Green. 40793 Alpha Romeo."

I should win a fucking medal.

From memory, Gus had just quoted the identity of one of his subordinates from back at the base: Lieutenant Green who had disappeared from one day to the next—with a sex worker according to the rumours.

And if they check, it'll be easy enough to fabricate a service record for the last year. It's the perfect cover.

"I report to Admiral Mako of the Thirty Second," he continued. "And I doubt he'll be happy to hear about this. And you call me *Sir*, Sergeant."

"But...erm...*Sir*..." the Sergeant stuttered, already looking less certain of himself. "Why were you running?"

"I got caught out. They figured out who I was and I had to get away. Then you guys came."

"Kind of convenient timing..."

"Kind of convenient timing, *Sir!*" shouted Gus, pulling himself painfully up onto his ankle and leaning against the wall for support. He puffed out his chest. "Don't *question* me, soldier. I'm injured and unless you want Admiral Mako asking whose fault it was, I suggest you take me back to base so I can make my report."

"I...well..." the Sergeant looked at his inferiors who looked back at him doubtfully. He realised there was only one way for him to save face. "Yes, Sir. Of course, Sir." He turned to one of his inferiors and barked at him "Corporal! Get the Lieutenant a ride back to base."

"Yes, Sir!" said the Corporal obediently before crossing the garden and disappearing back over the wall.

"Sorry about all this."

"Forget about it," Gus said hobbling over to the short wall and carefully climbing back over. He paused on the other side and called back. "Good luck with the raid, and Sergeant...?"

"Yes, Sir?"

"Give those resistance bastards everything they've got coming to them."

Chapter seventy-three

Y our toothbrush is in the usual place," called Pinar from outside the bathroom. "And I left you some clean clothes outside the door."

"Great, thanks," Ash called back over the sound of running water.

Pinar was already back at her desk, surrounded by files on top of files. She had never been the tidiest student and with something as interdisciplinary as her latest paper she was forever jumping from subject to subject—biochemistry one second, physics and chaos theory the next—which meant even more files, books—and mess—than usual.

She knew she was obsessed with her paper. She had barely thought about anything else for months.

Pinar couldn't imagine when she might finish it. For a woman in science to get published—even in 2017—was still an uphill struggle. But she was enraptured, enthralled. Every page she wrote was making love. Her thesis was elegant in its simplicity.

After nearly a year of research, she aimed to show how behavioural diversity—including sexual and gender diversity—formed an integral part of the biodiversity of life.

As such, she argued, it was essential to the adaptability of species, communities and ecosystems and to their long-term survival. All of which was precisely the opposite of what religious conservatives had been telling her her whole life.

Her paper was ambitious and courageous but in a way, it was also a statement of the obvious: diversity is everywhere, and it's good for us.

Neuro-diversity, linguistics, culture, gender, sexuality: the more she looked, the more diversity and complexity she found. And—Pinar was beginning to realise—there were other new traits appearing which made the world even richer. She listened to Ash singing happily in the shower. The ability to move through time for example.

Five minutes later, Ash emerged from the shower in a cloud of steam wearing a satin, teal dress of Pinar's. It was a tight fit, but after a week of wearing pants, boots and a t-shirt she felt relieved to be wearing something that she actually liked again. Pinar was lost in her journals.

"Good shower?" she asked distantly.

"It was perfect. It's been a long time. And God, I didn't even know how much I missed toothpaste!"

Pinar gave her a curious look. "Maybe I should stockpile some in a bunker somewhere?" she suggested.

"Maybe you already have," Ash replied with a mysterious smile as she cleared plates and papers off a chair and sat down. She picked up a journal titled "Animal Behaviour" with a photo on the front of two female squirrel monkeys mating. "So how's your paper going?"

"It's slow. I have good days and bad days. My research has been pretty conclusive—behavioural plasticity, queer animal behaviour, heterogeneous causes of complex traits—I just need to bring it all together. It's getting kind of exciting!"

"Sounds fun," said Ash vaguely.

"Yeah, well the current you isn't so happy about it either. But in a way you took me on this path. I mean I can't exactly mention your...*unique behavioural trait* in my paper but I'm more and more sure that moving through time is just a new piece of our behaviour, just one more part of our adaptive biodiversity."

"And we're still having this conversation twenty-three years later..."

"I imagine! The current you is always arguing with me over it: she thinks that I'm trying to justify and explain queerness when no one ever tries to justify breeding or straightness or sexual reproduction in general. She calls it a double standard—one thing is marked and needs explanation, the other doesn't."

"I remember that argument." Ash smiled and poured herself some coffee from the pot on the table. "I had a point, you know, but I also know that that wasn't what you were trying to do with your paper. I was pretty defensive those days."

"And now you're all grown up?"

"Something like that!" laughed Ash.

It was early afternoon and the spring sun was streaming in through Pinar's open skylight. Ash stood and put her head out the window. She heard wood pigeons calling in the poplar trees outside. The air was sweet and cool.

"Well, as I don't seem to be going anywhere any time soon..." she said. "Shall we take a walk?"

Pinar smiled.

"You never did like to be cooped up inside." She stretched, yawned and looked around her at the mess. "Sure thing. Let's get out of here. I need to get some groceries anyway."

Ash looked down at the dress she was wearing.

"Do I need to change?" she asked with an edge to her voice that Pinar knew only too well.

Ash had rarely felt safe wearing feminine clothing in the street. It saddened her every time she self-censored at the front door and put on something more conforming to society's expectations, but she had resolved long ago to do what she had to to avoid the violence of standing out.

Maybe the world just isn't ready for stubble surrounding lipstick, a balding head with long earrings or silk dresses flowing over a muscled chest.

"We can both get changed if it's more comfortable for you?" Pinar suggested.

She knew how painful it was for her friend to constantly monitor her femininity and had soon got into the habit of matching her style. If Ash didn't feel safe in a dress, then Pinar would slip out of hers too and wear jeans that day. Pinar refused to talk about it—for her it was just basic solidarity.

"I think I'm too old to care," said Ash. "Besides I'm kind of invisible, right?"

"Kind of. And things are a little better these days. Since Sense8 and the Wachowskis and Laverne Cox and Julia Serano and Chelsea Manning. And with all the celebrities coming out recently, trans has suddenly become hot news. They're calling it a tipping point. Nothing really changed obviously, but suddenly everyone's talking about trans women like you just didn't exist five years ago. It's something like the gay movement but forty years late."

"I remember vividly. It's 2017?"

"Yeah."

"Then it's as good as it's ever going to get," said Ash in an ominous tone. "Let's go."

Pinar wanted to ask more, but thought better of it. She opened the front door and held it open.

"You look gorgeous."

Ash stepped out of the door, her head high. "I know."

Chapter seventy-four

I t was a perfect afternoon. The sun was warm and the streets of the City were quiet in the short lull between rush hours. Pinar and Ash walked hand in hand and Ash was enjoying the feeling of the breeze over her legs and bare shoulders. She studiously avoided eye contact with people in the street and they in turn seemed to not notice her at all.

Anonymity, she remembered, *was the best I could ever hope for living here.*

Pinar stopped suddenly and turned to her friend, her eyes bright with excitement.

"Ash, I forgot to tell you! There's a femme pride march planned today. It should be starting soon downtown. Shall we go?"

Ash looked into the distance thoughtfully for a moment.

"Is it April by any chance?" she asked.

"Yes..."

"Then let's go!"

Pinar gave her an intrigued look and they turned left at the next junction. They could hear the police sirens before they even reached the square. Lights flashed off skyscrapers and they could hear—and feel—the familiar rhythm of a crowd chanting. Pinar was also pretty sure she heard someone screaming.

"My god, it sounds big."

"It is," said Ash with a knowing smile. "It really is."

They turned another corner and Pinar's eyes opened wide in surprise. The square was a mess of people, police cars and flames. Her eyes watered instantly from tear gas.

"Ash. What the h—" Pinar stopped mid-sentence.

Next to her, lay the satin dress in a pile on the pavement. She sighed sadly and bent down to pick it up.

"Good luck hon..." she whispered. She picked up the dress, put it into her handbag and headed for the square.

Chapter seventy-five

Ash was lying somewhere cold and hard. And she was blind. She moved her hands in front of her face. Nothing. She sat up and looked around her. The world was completely dark. She reached out with her arms. She was somewhere open; there were no walls. No light. Nothing to give her a clue where she might be. She'd been in the past too long—had the State caught up with them? Was she in a prison cell? Had something happened to her eyes?

Her heart was racing. She didn't know if she should call out. Maybe it was better to just stay quiet until she knew where she was.

The floor was cold and damp and her old bones ached. Her arthritis had come back and was slowly reclaiming her joints, waves of dull pain moving through her body. She stood up to get away from the cold, carefully shielding her head in case there was a low ceiling of some kind. There was only air above. She stood in silence, surrounded by nothing except a faint breeze blowing over her cold body.

Just a moment ago I was at a turning point of history, the beginning. And now this.

Ash was overcome with a desperate desire to journey again.

Past or future, I don't care. Anything has to be better than this.

She strained and hoped and willed herself to go, but nothing.

Ash had never felt more alone.

* * *

Her hands held out in front of her, Ash tentatively stepped forward. Another step. One more. Still she touched nothing. She turned slowly around, her hands still waving in open air. She took a step in another direction and immediately banged into something large and hard.

As she stepped back in surprise, whoever, whatever it was, followed her and fell onto her. Ash screamed and struggled to get away but the new thing seemed to hold on somehow. She struggled, hitting at it until finally, it crashed to the floor.

Standing still for a moment, Ash waited to hear if the creature moved. She poked at it with her foot, but nothing.

Bending down, she moved her hands over its surface. It was cold and large, maybe the size of a person, maybe bigger. Her hands came to one end of it where there was some kind of sphere. Curiosity took over from her fear. She felt indentations, a lump sticking out, something cold like glass. And then softness, something long that lifted off the object. Something like...she yelled and jumped back.

Hair! It's hair!

She tried to steady her breathing.

What kind of hell is this?

Suddenly, blinding white light washed over her.

Instinctively Ash stepped back and shielded her eyes.

"What? Who...?" she stuttered, her eyes screwed up against the sudden sensory overload.

She braced herself then and prepared to fight.

Chapter seventy-six

"**A**sh, it's me," said a familiar voice. "Are you okay?"

"I...I was blind..." said Ash, the words sticking in her throat.

"Oh my god, I'm so sorry," said the voice. Ash noticed that the light became less extreme. "I left you with a couple of candles, but they must have burned out already. Look, it's me, Kit. It's okay; don't be scared."

"Where am I?" Ash demanded. She was too shocked to be polite. Her eyes began to adjust and she could see Kit's form, her familiar straight, dark hair. She was holding a candle in a jar, slightly shielded by her hand.

"We're in the mall. You've been erm...*gone*...for a few hours and we brought you in here to be safe while everything was happening. Are you okay? You look terrified..."

"I thought I was...I didn't know where..."

Ash shook herself off.

I'm fine. I'm safe.

She looked down at the thing that had fallen on her. At her feet was a naked mannequin lying face up, its arms straight out and its plastic hair splayed over the floor. She looked around her—several other naked mannequins were lined up staring out of a window. There was a broken till on a desk and piles of coat hangers on the floor. *I'm in a clothes stores, just an ordinary clothes store. I was, at most, barely ten metres from the door.*

Ash felt suddenly exposed and embarrassed by her panic.

"I'm okay, I'm fine. Thank you for taking care of me." Shivers ran through her body. "Can we get somewhere warmer though? I'm half frozen."

"Of course. Let's go downstairs. The others are just arriving. They're gathering in the main hall—"

Suddenly, Ash remembered where she'd been before she'd journeyed.

"—And Pinar? And the break-out?"

"She's here too. I just saw her arriving. The break out was a complete success," said Kit, smiling broadly.

"Please take me to her. I need her."

"Right this way."

* * *

Gus arrived at a guarded gate and following the single soldier who had been assigned to him, he entered the gardens of the City.

After the dry grass and weeds of Dignity Park, the gardens were impressive, immaculately maintained and full of colour. Everywhere, flowers bloomed in complex patterned beds and stone pathways cut across extensive, lush green lawns. Gus saw sprinklers everywhere keeping the lawns watered—so many that water splashed onto the pathways and into the little fish ponds. The rest of the State might be in severe drought, but here in the gardens, there was always water to waste.

Gus began to walk over a delicate bridge that crossed a small stream. He saw well-fed koi swimming in the clear water and, for a moment, flashed on the catfish back in the forest.

The way those resistance idiots wasted valuable time saving a bunch of slimy catfish. The way they...

Gus paused for a moment, watching the fish.

...also saved my life. But then, the park...the troopers...

Gus shook his head and continued through the gardens.

As he and the other soldier arrived at the edge of the gardens, Gus felt a water droplet land on his head.

It must be a sprinkler, he reasoned, but as he felt another drop, he looked up and saw the sky was darkening, thick black clouds were pulling in from the east.

"Looks like rain," he said to the soldier.

"Yes, Sir. Let's get you to the office."

Another gate opened in front of them and Gus left the gardens. He glanced back before the gate closed and realised he felt a little sad to leave.

It really is beautiful here.

An hour later, Gus was leaning back in a reclining office chair, sipping from a glass of cool water. His ankle was throbbing again from the walk through the gardens but for now he was glad just to be safe and inside. He could hear what sounded like a month's worth of rain thundering down on the roof of the State building.

So far, no-one had questioned his story. The State always had so many operations going on at once that few people knew about them all. Besides, everyone seemed too busy today to pay much attention to him.

Gus overheard two women talking to each other in the corridor.

"What do you mean the Life Accounts is down? How can it be down?"

"I tell you, I tried to go the bathroom about an hour ago and nothing was working. I couldn't even get past the turnstile."

"Could it be the rain?"

"I heard a rumour it might be the—" she lowered her voice, "—*resistance.*"

"Don't even say it. Let's get back to the office."

So that's it! thought Gus. *I knew those resistance scum were planning something big. Well, good. That combined with the rain and the raid on the park will mean more distractions to cover me. I might even get out of this without ever seeing the inside of a prison again.*

He leaned back in the chair, his hands locked behind his head, and smiled.

Chapter seventy-seven

Ash walked with Kit down a corridor lit only by their small candle. Shivers ran down her spine. She was still nervous from waking up in the dark.

After a hundred metres, the walls of the corridor opened up and Ash could see they were on a gallery of some kind overlooking a concourse.

The old Mall. How I hate this place.

"How did I get here?" she asked.

"Danny carried you after you, erm, *left* us at the park. And we found the tunnels in the hotel, just as you said. How did you know by the way?"

"It's a long story."

"I imagined it might be."

They paused at the top of the escalators that lead down to the central concourse. Below them, hundreds of people were gathering in flickering candlelight, at least half still wore prison clothes and many were spread out on the floor, sleeping.

Out of all those people, Ash's eyes instantly found a deeply familiar face and, forgetting her arthritis for a moment, she ran down the escalator taking two steps at a time. Pinar saw her too and they met at the bottom in a fierce hug. Pinar was already in tears.

"I'm so sorry..."

"I'm sorry too. Why do we always argue when we're leaving each other?"

With relief, with exhaustion, Ash began to cry. She felt an undefinable rush of emotion that shook her and erased the rest of the world. As she held Pinar, there was only here and now, the smell of her best friend's sweat, her hair and the salt of her tears. She wanted to hold her in this moment forever. She never wanted to be further from her than right now, their faces inches apart. From the bottom of her heart, she wished for time to stop.

But time, as Ash knew better than anyone, was wild and untameable. She let the moment, and her friend, go and wiped her eyes.

"Are you okay?" she asked finally. "And Jason?"

"He's over there." Pinar smiled and pointed to the other side of the mall where he was helping move bags and make space for people who were just arriving. "We made it. All because of you, Ash."

"But I was gone, I was back with you—back on the day of the first riots...do you remember?"

"Of course!" Pinar smiled broadly at the memory. "So *now* I understand why you looked like such a wreck that day. I never really knew if I should tell you or not, I decided it was safer to keep the secret—and I did. For a very long time!"

"For me, it was literally an hour ago."

Her journey was still with her: the smells of coffee and Pinar's fancy shampoo, the warmth of her kitchen, even the coolness of the street.

And here I am deep under the ground breathing this musty, dirty air again.

She would never admit it, but she was suddenly torn apart with nostalgia. She swallowed it all down, snapped back to the present and asked:

"But wait, I still don't understand. What happened at Life Accounts? And the break out? I need to know everything!"

"Don't worry," said Pinar gently, holding her hand. "There's time."

* * *

After half an hour, a high-brass Admiral walked into the office. He was immaculately dressed but Gus noticed he looked a little flustered. He thought he might be vaguely familiar from some meeting or other but he knew he himself would be unrecognisable today.

His filthy clothes, matted hair, and long beard screamed resistance, or—he hoped—convincing undercover officer. No-one would connect him to the proud General who had been caught trying to rape his subordinate in the shower and later dumped unceremoniously in the forest.

They probably left me to die out there rather than face a public execution precisely to keep the whole shameful story quiet. No-one, except the people I worked with and a few prisoners even knew. I just have to keep spinning my lies and I'll be fine.

The Admiral sat down opposite Gus and lit up a cigarette.

"Crazy fucking day out there."

Gus nodded politely.

"Let's get started then, Lieutenant. What do you know?"

* * *

"Ash! I'm so glad to see you!" Jason ran over and hugged her. He looked gaunt and had a large bruise across his right cheek. His prison overalls were filthy and smelt awful. He was smiling though and Ash saw a familiar twinkle in his eyes.

"I heard you're quite the heroine!" he said, stepping back. "Leading everyone into the tunnels, escaping the State—"

"—Well, I shouted a bit and ran a bit and then I don't even know what else happened. I woke up here just a few minutes ago. I was—"

" —Journeying?"

"Yeah." Ash turned to Pinar. "I think you need to catch me up, hon."

"Of course." Pinar gestured to the low wall surrounding what used to be a fountain. "Let's sit. We have quite the story to tell you!"

* * *

"And after the servers were fried, we hit the tunnels and made our way here," Pinar was explaining, sitting next to the fountain, hand in hand with Jason. "Evidently we made a real mess out there because the second shoal broke the prisoners out with almost no problem at all."

"Yeah," said Jason. "Your friend Kit was just telling me that there was barely a guard to be seen. And the few that were there, ran or hid when they saw a hundred people running towards them."

"How did the shoal get past all the doors and gates?" asked Ash. "And they didn't call for backup?"

"I don't know the technicalities," said Pinar. "I stayed focused on my part of the whole thing and well, apparently it worked."

"Apparently."

"To be honest," said Jason, "We heard that there might be some kind of action this week but I never thought it would happen. I was down in the factory, like every day, and then before I knew it, I was in the tunnels and back with Pinar."

She smiled and gave his hand a squeeze.

"I'm so sorry you were in there for so long," said Ash, avoiding eye contact and staring at the floor. "We came as fast as we could."

"I know. Thank you. I was okay, really. But some of the trans folk from the Sett. Well, not all of us made it, I guess..." His voice trailed off and Ash didn't push the point. There's only so many horrific things a human brain can take in at a time.

"And Nathalie?" she asked, suddenly remembering.

"Kit says she disappeared after the State arrived at the park," Pinar replied. "We haven't seen her down here and, honestly, I think they arrested her. They would have taken Kit too if she hadn't followed you out of there."

"Poor Kit," said Ash, sadly. "She must be heartbroken."

"She's keeping herself busy, I guess." Pinar nodded across the mall where Kit and Danny were carrying cups of water to late-comers. "Oh and that Gus guy you disliked so much disappeared as well. Good riddance to them both, I say."

"Yeah," said Ash with a tone of finality. "Good riddance."

* * *

Gus told the Admiral everything he knew about the resistance. Every name and description, every vague plan he'd overheard. Truth be told, he didn't have much to tell. As an unknown, he'd been kept out of all but the most basic and logistical meetings both during his time with the forest shoal and later at the park. What he didn't know, he seamlessly fabricated and speculated to make his report more convincing.

The Admiral noted down every word, without looking up once.

* * *

"Why didn't the troopers follow us into the tunnels?" Ash asked, still filling in the story.

"Apparently, the shoal managed to trigger some kind of collapse," said Pinar. "The hotel was so old and burned out, a few hundred people running through it brought half the lobby down. That gave them enough time to get in and lock the hatch behind them."

"Was anyone hurt?"

"Some people got pretty beaten up during the raid but nothing compared to what would have happened if we hadn't gotten away. Everyone made it inside the tunnels – thanks to you and your journeying."

They sat quietly together for a while and looked out over the busy concourse. People sat everywhere they could find a space including the escalators and the dry fountains. At least half of the people gathered, including Kit and Danny, had effectively become refugees and were about to be torn away from their lives in the City. But the atmosphere in the mall was electric. This day, they had delivered a great blow to the State. They had freed their *compañeras* from jail and soon they would be building a new future in the forest.

"Two shoals have been sent out. They're checking the tunnels are safe to take us back to the forest," explained Pinar. "Once they're back, we'll be ready to head out."

"Not a moment too soon," said Ash. "I'll be glad to never set foot in this place again."

* * *

"I see," said the Admiral, still making notes. "And what are the plans of the resistance now after the *little incident* at Life Accounts?"

"They're going to make a break for it. They'll head to the tunnels and out of the City."

The Admiral looked up for the first time.

"The tunnels?"

* * *

Someone Ash didn't recognise climbed up onto a wobbly café table to address the crowd. He clapped his hands until he had everyone's attention and began an announcement.

"Today we have escaped the State and we will soon escape the City," he announced grandly. "Some of us leave behind our homes here, but together we–"

"*Emergency!*"

The shout came from the other end of the concourse as a young man pushed through the crowds shouting at the top of his lungs.

"*Socorro!* Emergency!"

"What is it?" the speaker asked as he reached the table. "Climb up, climb up."

Pinar, Ash, and Jason looked on in surprise as the young man climbed up onto the table and nearly fell off. He looked terrified.

"*The rain has come!*" he shouted and signed simultaneously. "*And it's flooding the tunnels.*" There were gasps all around the concourse.

This is it, thought Ash. *Nothing ever goes smoothly for very long.*

"*It's been dry for too long, the sewerage system is totally overwhelmed,*" the person still balanced on the table continued. "*We only just made it here—the mall is almost cut off. We need to get above ground quickly—*"

"But we can't leave the City above ground," the speaker interrupted him. "We'd never get past the gate."

"No choice!" shouted the young man. The water will be here soon. We need to leave, right now!"

* * *

"Which tunnels?" The Admiral looked confused.

"Erm...the under-city connecting to the mall—" Gus began tentatively.

"Ah yes. Of course. *Those* tunnels. We've suspected for a while that the resistance might be using them. Ahem."

As an expert liar, Gus always knew when he wasn't hearing the truth.

"Of course, Sir. Well those that escape the raid, if any do, will be heading that way—making a run for the forest."

The Admiral had already received a report from a State runner that the entire resistance had escaped Dignity Park a few hours before. The runner had told him that—impossible as it seemed—an elderly person had led them into the hotel and, apparently, they'd simply disappeared into the ground bringing half the hotel down around them. Now he understood—they must have gone down into the tunnels.

The Admiral looked thoughtful for a moment and listened to the rain pounding heavily on the roof.

"And if the tunnels flood?"

* * *

At the edge of the concourse, people were already yelling and pushing into the crowd. Water was gushing in and within seconds the entire concourse floor was wet. The water level was rising fast and there was no way they'd be able to hold it back.

The crowd begin to panic and pulse towards the escalators and Ash was pushed along with them.

Chapter seventy-eight

They become a herd, a swarm; a perfectly aligned mass of bodies moving upwards through escalators and staircases and corridors and ladders. The weak and the slow were helped by the fast and the strong. Collective panic was pushed down by the will to survive.

They moved quickly, efficiently, staying just above the fetid water rising all around them. They were a crowd of nervous systems bound together by eye contact, by voice and by hands that grabbed and guided.

We're like the starlings, thought Ash. *This is our murmuration.*

The crowd rose through the building quickly. But the water was faster.

Someone slipped on the rungs of a ladder and suddenly four people were in the murky water. A dozen hands helped them back out and in less than a minute they had rejoined the upwards surge to safety.

The last of the candles puffed out and the resistance was instantly swallowed by darkness. Ash and Pinar stood dead still on an escalator, their hands sweating against the rubber rail. Above them, others hung in the air, clinging breathlessly.

Ash could feel her heart beating and her panicked breath tight in her chest.

One. Two. Thr—

Up ahead someone snapped on a precious glowstick and there was light again. Not much, but just enough for the exodus to continue. The crowd surged forward and they entered a steep stairwell. Ash followed the person ahead of her and Pinar followed Ash, everyone hoping that up above them, someone knew the way.

We have no other choice; we can't stop now.

Floor after floor they rose through the narrow stairwell, surrounded by yells of confusion and terror. Up and up until the staircase ended abruptly.

A door. A fire exit.

Suddenly Ash and Pinar were pushed out into the world. They covered their eyes to prepare for an onslaught of daylight as, with the crowd behind them, they left the Mall for the last time.

Chapter seventy-nine

Ash stood in amazement.

It's night—how can it be night?

The City was dark. And cold. But it wasn't night. Thick black clouds had covered the sky and blocked out the morning sun. Rain pounded down against the concrete. Lightning tore the sky and a deep rumble of thunder soon followed. The streets had become rivers.

I've never seen rain like it.

Her clothes were wet through in an instant.

"Pin," she said grabbing her friend's hand. "We can't stay out here."

Pinar looked stunned. After months of drought, so much water was hard to take in. Hard to believe.

"Pinar! We're too exposed here. We have to find shelter."

* * *

Gus listened to the hammering of water on the roof and thought for a moment.

The Admiral sat impatiently waiting for "Lieutenant Green" to come up with something. Some idea of what the resistance would do next.

The Admiral has a point, thought Gus. *No-one could have planned for the rain. After months of drought, the tunnels will flood for sure.*

The tunnels or the gates were the only real ways out of the City and the East Gate was too heavily guarded to even attempt an escape. *They'll think of something, though. The resistance always comes up with something.*

* * *

Standing outside the mall, the perfectly coordinated shoal was falling apart. Stressed by the rain and the lightning, the thunder and the cold, in shock from suddenly being out in the open, the crowd had fractured. Everyone shouted at once.

"—We should wait it out, it can't rain forever—"

"—*Not so bad? We'll die out here! We have to find somewhere to hide*—"

"The gate! We just need to get to the gate! It's now or never—"

"As long as we stay together, we—"

"Who cares? We just need to get out of the damn rain!"

Pinar turned to Ash, a wise, knowing look on her face.

"They need you."

"What?"

"They need a leader."

"No," she shouted back. "Not again! I'm an old woman for heaven's sake! People can sort themselves out. We just need to form into smaller groups, feed our decisions into a central hub then we can—"

"Ash, we don't have time for any of that and you know it. We need to get out of the City and we have to stay together. If we split now, the State will hunt us down group by group, one by one. They need you."

Maybe she's right. Ash had seen the nods of respect in the mall. *They followed me before, and they'd do it again.*

"No Pin," she said defiantly. "They need *us*."

Holding hands, they climbed up a pile of rubble that put them slightly above the rest of the crowd. They waved their arms to get people's attention and when people saw them, they hushed down quickly.

Pinar braced herself against her friend and, lifting her arms up, she began to sign as wide and clear as she could, her hands shining bright as more lightning raced across the dark sky above her.

"*We have to stay together,*" she signed above her head and shouted at the same time. "*But we can't stay in the City any longer. We have to leave.*"

"But how?" someone shouted from the crowd.

Pinar paused for a second to think.

It's a valid question. The main gate is heavily guarded at the best of times. The tunnels are hopeless. The walls are unbreachable. We need another way out...

Then it came to her—*of course! The solar trains!* There was a train track running from the Central terminal—just a few blocks away from the Mall—to the North Gate station. From there it went through a narrow tunnel in the wall and out to the wasteland beyond.

"*We'll follow the train tracks out from Central terminal to the North Exit.*"

Pinar knew the exit was never heavily guarded. That section of the tracks was lined with razor wire and the trains running through such a tight tunnel had proven to be enough of a disincentive to anyone trying to get in—or out—of the City.

"*The trains won't be running in this weather,*" she signed with more confidence than she felt. "*If we stay together, we'll be okay. We can do this.*"

She looked at Ash who smiled back at her with admiration.

* * *

322

"The North Gate, Admiral," said Gus confidently. "They'll make a dash for the North Gate and try to get out the train tunnel. It's the only other way out. We should send troops there immediately."

* * *

Ash and Pinar gazed out at the crowd of wet, exhausted people looking to them desperately for hope. Pinar was full of doubt.

I'm making this up as I go along. I'm probably taking them all to disaster. What chance do we have really?

To her surprise, Ash suddenly cried out as loud as she could —

"To the forest!"

Her voice was immediately joined by countless others. Hundreds of voices shouting out together against the rain.

"To the forest! To the forest!"

Ash and Pinar carefully climbed down from the rubble pile. "Job done," said Ash. "You were awesome."

"I kind of *was,* wasn't I...?"

* * *

The Admiral looked pleased.

"Very good Lieutenant. We'll send a battalion immediately."

Gus couldn't help but smile.

This is working perfectly. If they catch the resistance trying to escape, I'll probably get a promotion—if not a medal. I'm already back en route to getting my life back.

"Care to join us?"

"I'd love to, Sir."

"I thought you might."

The Admiral stood, walked over to the window and pulled the

blinds closed. "But there's something I want from you first, *Lieutenant.*"

"Yes, Sir?"

The Admiral walked over and stood in front of Gus's chair. He began to unfasten his belt and Gus's mouth went dry.

"Yes, soldier," said the Admiral. "Now, on your knees."

Chapter eighty

The train tracks lay at the bottom of a steep concrete valley that bisected the City from North to South. On any given day, they were busy with the constant back and forth of solar trains carrying soldiers, food, and building materials.

As Ash and Pinar arrived at the Central terminal, they expected to see the tracks empty, the trains shut down because of the bad weather. What they saw made them gasp in horror. The tracks *were* empty of trains, but they were also covered by metres of dark, frothing water. The concrete valley of the tracks had become a river.

And that, Ash realised, *means our only way out of the City is blocked.*

Pinar was shouting something at her but the pounding of the rain and the water flowing into the river made it impossible to hear.

"*Sign! I can't hear you.*"

"*I said 'Fuck'!*" replied Pinar. "*It's completely flooded.*"

"*Yeah I noticed that.*"

"*What do we do now?*"

"*I have no clue.*"

"*We have to think of something.*"

"*Still no clue.*"

They stood for a moment watching tree branches and other debris rushing downstream. Waterfalls cascaded down to the tracks from the streets on either side.

It's impossible to get down there, much less walk—or swim—the two kilometres to the gate. And the streets running parallel to the tracks are flooded and dangerous.

Kit appeared from the crowd and came to stand next to them. She was soaking wet like everyone else.

But, Pinar noticed, *her hair still looks really good.*

"*What about over there?*" Kit signed and pointed.

Following her finger, Ash and Pinar saw a narrow sidewalk running along the river between the flooded street and the concrete that sloped down dramatically to the tracks. It was barely a metre wide but raised just enough to keep them out of the water.

"*It looks dangerous,*" signed Pinar.

Ash nodded.

"*But it's as good as we're going to get.*"

"*How do we get across?*"

"*There should be a footbridge, a bit further along,*" signed Kit. "*I use it to get to work sometimes.*"

"*Let's go.*"

Still holding hands, Ash and Pinar waded into the street. The water was knee deep but they were already as wet as they could possibly be. Dragging their tired legs through the water, they climbed out onto the raised path and turned back to check the others were following. The massive crowd followed them, holding their bags above their heads as they pushed against the current.

"We're leaders again, Pin," shouted Ash. "How did that even happen?"

"Honestly, I have no idea."

Soon everyone was up on the narrow, slippery path, a long line of three hundred and something people standing soaked and tired, deafened by the downpour and the roaring river. Without another word, Ash and Pinar turned and began the walk north. The resistance followed closely behind.

* * *

Water was everywhere. The sun, already high in the sky, was hidden by clouds and the City was as dark as early morning.

Ash had to stay completely focussed on the ground in front of her just to avoid slipping and tumbling into the deluge below her. After a while when she could take no more, she stopped and turned around.

"*Let's pause for a moment!*" she signed above her head, as large as she could. The crowd came to a halt.

"*Pinar, we're completely exposed here and it's dangerous. How long before one of us falls in?*" Ash looked down at the river below them, her fingers trembling as she signed.

"*I know.*"

"*And if the tracks are as flooded there as they are here, there's no way we'll make it out through the train tunnel.*"

"I know. But let's just get there and cross that bridge when we come to it," Pinar shouted back. "You never know, the rain might stop."

Ash said something under her breath that Pinar didn't hear.

"We don't have much choice," Pinar continued. "And besides, the City's flooded and the Life Accounts system is in total crisis. The State probably has better things to do."

Ash rolled her eyes. Pinar's eternal optimism could be a bit much sometimes.

"*I hope you're right.*" She turned back to the north. "Let's keep going."

* * *

Gus was on his knees, his eyes watering.
I hate this. Who does this upstart think he is?
Gus held his breath and kept sucking.

* * *

Another slip and Ash was on her knees, barely centimetres from the edge of the sidewalk. The pain flashing through her joints was almost more than she could take. She grabbed Pinar's offered hand and pulled herself back up. They both unconsciously looked down at the water cascading onto the flooded tracks.

That was way too close.

"Are you okay?" someone shouted to her.

It was Danny. He had seen her stumble and had come running up.

"You must be exhausted," he yelled.

"*I'm old is what I am,*" replied Ash curtly.

And it's true, she thought. *I've already lived a long, long life. I'm far too old to be here. Every part of me is crying out for rest. I just want to lie down, curl up and never move again.*

"*I could carry you.*" Danny suggested carefully.

"*I can walk myself thank you very much.*" Ash crossed her arms.

"*Sorry, I didn't mean to suggest...I just—*"

Pinar joined in the conversation.

"Stop being so damn proud, Ash. Falling off this path and drowning won't make you a better feminist."

Ash didn't reply. They walked in an awkward silence for a few minutes listening to the unrelenting water all around them.

"*Fine. But I'm not light, you know.*"

"*No problem—hold on tight!*" He bent his knees and crouched over slightly while she jumped onto his back and threw her arms around his chest. His balance was perfect.

All those years of working the pole came in useful, he thought to himself as he hoisted Ash up a little higher and continued walking.

* * *

Ash soon got used to being carried. She felt safer and although she had to hold on tight and didn't dare look down at the river below them, she could feel her tired legs recovering, the pain in her knees lessening.

She also had a taste for the dramatic and after a while of being carried high up, supported by Danny's strong body, bolts of lightning racing above them, she looked down as almost the entire resistance followed her and realised that she actually was starting to enjoy herself.

Through the blur of rain, the North terminal finally appeared up ahead and beyond it, the City walls filled the horizon as far as Ash could see.

And still no sign of the State.

Within minutes, the mass of people, soaked and exhausted, arrived in front of the station. The line spread out around an old, lifeless clock tower and although the pavement was slightly higher here, several inches of water still splashed around their heels.

Ash patted Danny on the head.

"Get me down from here," she shouted in a voice that was more commanding than she intended.

Danny obediently crouched down and let her slide off.

"Okay?" he asked.

"Thank you." She was relieved to be back on her own two feet. "Much better."

"Glad to be of service." He smiled back. "So what's the plan now?"

Ash looked over at the tracks beyond the terminal that disappeared into a dark tunnel through the wall. The water was a little lower here, but there was still at least a metre flowing over the tracks.

I can't imagine how we'll ever get through there in the dark. The State isn't going to just let us walk out of the City, not after everything we've done.

She looked around at the hundreds of people gathering around the clock tower, at the faces she knew—Jason and Pinar hugging each other, trying to stay warm in the rain, Vicki, the runner from the forest, Kit still in her improbable heels helping someone with their bags, and a few others that she'd met and chatted to over the last week. Then she scanned over the hundreds of people that she hadn't had chance to speak to.

She might never know their names but she knew they would follow her and Pinar to the end of the world if she asked them to.

Turning to Danny and looking him straight in the eye, she said:

"Honestly? I have no fucking clue."

Chapter eighty-one

The State's army arrived like a vision in a nightmare. Lines and lines of soldiers and their dogs appeared from the east along the wall and troopers on horseback galloped in from the west. By the time the resistance could see or hear them through the rain, they were already there, armed and completely impassable. They stood barely thirty metres ahead, blocking their only way out of the City. Ash held Pinar's hand and Pinar held Jason's.

We're already too late.

Pinar felt a shudder go through her body or maybe through Ash's body. She couldn't be sure. She didn't need to look at her friend's face to know she was crying. She wanted to comfort her but there was nothing she could think of to say. She saw only the hell that lay before them.

After everything we've been through, Pinar thought, *it comes down to this. We'll live out the end of our lives enslaved in a factory, our hard work powering the State's economy. Gender oppression will split us apart as surely and unquestionably as death. And Ash will be locked away with men until the day her brave life ends. We'll probably never even see each other again.*

The only blessing, Pinar realised, blinking back tears of her own, *is that at least that day won't be too far off.*

Chapter eighty-two

Using a loudspeaker, an Admiral on horseback was shouting at the crowd, but the rain was so loud that they could barely make out what he was saying.

"—End of the line. Stay where you are and you—harmed. We—" the loudspeaker crackled as lightning tore across the sky. "—Factories. You can't escape."

As the Admiral's horse came closer, Ash could see that there was someone sitting behind him. Another flash of lightning lit up the sky and she recognised who it was. She felt suddenly so sick she thought she might throw up. It was Gus and he was grinning at her. *I knew from the beginning that he was bad news, that he couldn't be trusted. I always knew.*

"*What next?*" Jason signed to Pinar and Ash. Ash looked around for a way out, but already the State lines were moving closer. *If we had more time, we could have escaped the way we came—back along the walkway—but where would we go? The City is a trap and we're as good as dead here anyway.*

She looked at Pinar and could see that she was losing hope. Hundreds of people stood near her, wet and exhausted. Before she realised that she'd made up her mind, Ash was already walking towards the troops.

Chapter eighty-three

The crowd opened up and allowed Ash to pass. Too shocked to even speak, much less do anything to stop her, Pinar stood frozen and watched her friend go.

Ash waded across the concourse and towards the station, stopping barely ten metres in front of the first line of troopers. She could smell the horses. She could hear the dogs growling. She had no idea what she was doing but she also knew that there was nothing else to do. She had only her soaked, exhausted body left to fight with and she wanted to go home. She thought desperately of the forest, her forest, and the happiness that she'd found there.

I wish I could see it just once more. I wish I could die out there, not here surrounded by concrete.

And as fast as she wished it, she was there.

Chapter eighty-four

Ash stood on the deck of her boat.

She faced upstream in a warm, dry breeze as the boat moved along a stretch of river she had never seen before. This is a dream. I'm dreaming.

Behind her, Pinar stepped out onto the deck, her hair shining in the bright sunlight.

"I thought I might see you here," she said standing next to her friend, holding the rail and looking out at the river.

"Are we...okay?" asked Ash.

Pinar turned.

"Most of us. Just look."

Ash turned downstream then and she saw. On the river, following them was a fleet of boats. She could see Kit and Danny on the closest one and at least another thirty behind them. Beyond, far behind them, stood the mountains and the trees of the forest, black and smoking.

"Where are we going?" asked Ash, but she already knew the answer.

"We're going to find a new home."

Chapter eighty-five

There was concrete beneath Ash's feet again and she lifted her hands and prepared to fight. She took a deep breath in and got ready to shout over the noise of the rain.

But there *was* no noise.

There *was* no rain.

The City had fallen silent.

Sunlight flooded the streets as dark clouds tore themselves apart. The only sound came from the gurgling drains as the rainwater flowed away and the street cleared. Ash stood, her arms still lifted, unable to speak.

The rain had stopped.

And the State was terrified.

The Admiral stepped his horse towards Ash and she could see Gus sitting behind him holding on tight. He looked as stunned as the Admiral.

Looking over her head at the approaching crowd the Admiral lifted the loudspeaker to his mouth.

"Witches!" he shouted. "*Vergers!*" But Ash could see the fear on his face, she could practically smell it. "Prison is too good," the Admiral shouted. "We'll make an example of the lot of you today and stamp out the resistance for good."

His horse stepped closer. "And here—" He turned and with a sinister grin, gave his passenger a hard shove. Gus fell to the ground hard enough Ash could hear him thump as he hit the ground.

"—Take this traitorous scum to hell with you!"

Gus looked back up at the Admiral, confused and terrified.

"But I—"

"What?" the Admiral shouted down at him. "You thought I didn't know who you were? The General who turned faggot? The proud officer who got caught with his pants down? Go join your fellow *vergents* where you belong!"

The Admiral had his horse step back in line and Gus lay stunned where he fell, sprawled out on the wet concrete. He tried to stand up but his ankle hurt too much.

It's broken for sure this time, he thought as he collapsed back down onto the concrete.

And so am I.

Ash stood, frozen, still half lost in the future and shocked silent by the present until, like a cold wind descending upon her, she had sudden clarity.

Her whole life, she had struggled to find her place, to know who she was in a society that hated difference and hated her. But it was all for this moment. For this precise second in time. Ash wasn't pushing forward with hope any longer but with certainty. The certainty that they would never give up until balance was restored. That resistance could never be killed. That—

A flock of crows flew across the sun, sending shadows across the ground, for a moment darkening the resistance and the State and Ash standing alone in between them. The flock passed by and disappeared beyond the walls of the City.

It's now or never.

Locking eyes with the Admiral, Ash's voice came back to her.

"We're leaving!" she shouted, her powerful voice echoing off the high walls ahead. "You will not stop us—and you never have. We will fight you to the death if you get in our way."

She turned to the mass of people behind her.

"*Now!*" she shouted and the crowd surged towards her, heels and crutches raised to fight.

* * *

The horses attacked as a single, terrifying being. Desensitised to screams and fear, their masters drove them forward to crush and kill as many of the people in front of them as they could.

The resistance, with nothing left to lose, threw their own bodies forward toward the flooded tunnel, towards the forest and towards freedom.

Ash was enveloped by the crowd as it pulsed forward. To the left, she saw the first people running, older and less able folk were carried into the tunnel and disappeared. To the right, she heard the first screams as the horses and soldiers attacked her family.

Amongst the hundreds of bodies, Ash found Pinar's hand and grabbed it. *This is it,* she knew. And they ran.

If you enjoyed this novel, please consider helping the author to write more transfeminist speculative fiction by supporting her through Patreon, spreading the word on social media or leaving reviews online.

Margins and Murmurations has been recorded as a full-length audiobook by the author herself and will be available soon to Patreon supporters.

www.patreon.com/otterlieffe